# Loving
# Dallas

# *Loving Dallas*

## A NEON DREAMS NOVEL

## CAISEY QUINN

*wm*

WILLIAM MORROW

*An Imprint of* HarperCollins*Publishers*

LOVING DALLAS. Copyright © 2015 by Caisey Quinn. Excerpt from *Missing Dixie* copyright © 2015 by Caisey Quinn. All rights reserved. Printed in the United States of America. No part of this book may be used or reproduced in any manner whatsoever without written permission except in the case of brief quotations embodied in critical articles and reviews. For information address HarperCollins Publishers, 195 Broadway, New York, NY 10007.

HarperCollins books may be purchased for educational, business, or sales promotional use. For information please e-mail the Special Markets Department at SPsales@harpercollins.com.

FIRST EDITION

*Designed by Diahann Sturge*

Library of Congress Cataloging-in-Publication Data has been applied for.

ISBN 978-0-06-236683-2

15 16 17 18 19   OV/RRD   10 9 8 7 6 5 4 3 2 1

*For country music fans far and wide—*
*you're my favorite kind of folks.*

# Loving Dallas

*You don't love someone for their looks, or their clothes, or their fancy car, but because they sing a song only you can hear.*
—Oscar Wilde

# Prologue | Dallas

THE AIRPORT IS ABOUT AS CROWDED AS I EXPECT HELL TO BE WHEN I get there. Everyone's either on their phone or eating or staring up at the electronic flight schedules. A few moms scream at their kids to stay the fuck where they are and not move. Even one who has hers on a leash attached to a teddy bear backpack. Christ. Why would anyone travel with these tiny gremlins?

My phone buzzes with a text from my manager.

*See you in Omaha! Safe travels, Superstar!*

I stare at it for a full minute. This is it. I'm joining an actual tour paid for by someone other than myself. And if all goes well, a record deal will follow.

"We're now boarding passengers in groups one and two; that includes all first-class passengers and those of you in our Elite and Platinum Traveler Rewards programs."

The overhead announcement is at my gate so I take my place in line toward the back with the other folks in coach. An attractive brunette with a microphone to her mouth makes eye contact as she rattles off more of the flight information. I tip my cowboy hat at her.

My pulse amps up with each step closer to the sky bridge that connects the building to the plane. Just as my turn to hand over my ticket comes, I step out of line in a moment of panic. Groups three and four come and go. I watch as everyone else says their goodbyes and boards the plane.

My granddad used to say that there are times in a man's life when he has to make hard decisions. Might be choosing between two good things, or picking the lesser of two evils, he'd say. When the time comes, it isn't always the choice itself that matters so much as the ability to make it and more important, to stand behind it and commit to it. For better or worse your choices are yours and you have to own them. It's what makes you a man, he'd say.

"Sir? Will you be flying with us today?" The brunette reaches for my boarding pass.

I check my phone again. The last text message from my sister says that yes, she is fine, stop worrying and go live my dream already. But I can still hear my father's voice in my head, reminding me that I'm supposed to take care of her. I should be home, looking out for her, making sure she's safe and sound and has everything she needs.

My mind and heart engage in an all-out war. Turn tail and head home to my sister and my best friend—to the band I abandoned—or get on this plane and leave them behind.

"Sir?" The flight attendant looks less interested and more irritated than before.

Handing over my boarding pass, I adjust the guitar on my back and take the first step toward a neon dream I've been chasing for as long as I can remember.

I knew I'd get here one day—I just didn't expect to be alone.

# 1 | Dallas

THIRTY-SIX CITIES BLURRED BY ME SO QUICKLY I FELT LIKE I'D BEEN on a six-week drinking binge. I'd busted my ass on stage after stage and it had been worth it. Or at least I hope it was. Technically I'm still waiting to hear if I've been officially signed by Capitol Records.

After the final show in Atlanta, I grab a beer with Afton Tate, another artist on the tour who's become a pretty good buddy. He settles onto the stool beside me in the Porter Beer Bar—a place in Little Five Points that he suggested because it supposedly has fantastic beer. The sleek steel and exposed brick combined with the relaxed vibe is welcoming and I make a note to remember this place. Mumford & Sons can barely be heard over the din of first dates and groups of twenty-somethings surrounding us.

"To finishing one hell of a tour," I say, lifting my amber-filled glass in Tate's direction.

"To whatever the hell comes next," he says with a grin.

I take a long pull of the lager I ordered and am thankful that he was right about the beer. Tate laughs lightly as an attractive brunette wedging her way to the bar to order a drink bumps my elbow accidentally. Or maybe accidentally on purpose.

I smile and tip my chin at her and she smiles back with interest gleaming in whiskey-colored eyes. Her rectangular framed glasses are cute and her face is pretty, but she's a little vanilla for me. Her blazer and lack of cleavage shout "looking for something long term." Not my style. Probably my drinking buddy's type, though.

Taking another drink, I glance over at Tate, then subtly tilt my head to the girl to see if he's interested.

He regards her for a full minute before he shakes his head and shrugs. "I'm tired, man. I'm going to turn in early. You're not?"

"Never too tired for that," I say, shifting my eyes toward one of the brunette's friends—a blonde who has that good-time girl look about her.

"You will be," he mutters under his breath before tipping his bottle back.

Before I can respond my phone buzzes in my pocket. I motion to the bartender for another beer while retrieving my phone.

Mandy Lantram, the screen informs me.

"It's my manager," I tell Tate before plugging my open ear and accepting the call.

"They chose you, Dallas," she says in place of a greeting. It's the call I've been waiting for. The one I feared wouldn't come. "You're the new opener on Jase Wade's Kickin' Up Crazy tour. Barry has the paperwork ready to sign, and the tour kicks off in a few weeks. I know you mentioned maybe heading home, but I think your down-time would be better spent recording in the studio."

She goes on to detail a schedule that includes every moment I'm permitted to sleep and breathe. But this is everything I ever wanted, so I'm not complaining.

When I finally end the call, Afton claps me on the back and offers to buy the next round to celebrate. I'm still trying to wrap my head around the fact that this is actually happening. It's everything I ever wanted . . . well, mostly. I wanted my *band* to make it big, but some dreams don't come made to order.

The bartender sets our new drinks in front of us and I excuse myself to make a phone call. I'm pulling her name up as I make my way out of the boisterous crowd filling the bar.

I hold the door open on my way and a group of attractive women comes in thanking me for being a gentleman.

Stepping outside, I place the phone to my ear and hear it still ringing. I feel the grin spread across my face when she finally picks up.

"Hey. Where are you?"

"Well hello to you, too." She laughs lightly. "I'm on the Blue Ridge Parkway. You wouldn't believe how beautiful it is. I think fall is my new favorite season."

My sister is on some epic road trip that gives me heartburn and panic attacks on a regular basis. But she seems to be enjoying herself, so I try to tamp down my brotherly instincts. She's twenty years old now so I can't exactly order her to go home where she's safe like I could when we were kids.

"No truck stops after dark, okay? And be sure you're—"

"Locking the doors, keeping the gas tank filled, checking the air in the tires, and carrying my Mace with me at all times." She finishes my much-repeated spiel for me. "I know, big brother. I got this. I've only got a few more stops, then I'll head home and you can rest easy."

"I'm glad you're having a good time," I say, meaning it. "I just worry about you is all."

"I know, *Dad*," she teases. "And I appreciate your concern."

It's not the first time she's called me that and in some ways, I suppose I do treat her more like a daughter than a sister. Our actual dad was from a low-income section of Amarillo, Texas. He grew up working from the time he could ride a bike. Paper route. Lawn boy. Window, car, whatever washer. Dog walker. You name it, he did it. He ran errands for the elderly, started painting houses by the time he was sixteen, and pretty much did anything and everything he could to earn a buck. Over the years he saved his pennies and by the time he was eighteen, he was able to afford to send himself to college. He'd met my mom there. She was a cello player studying music education. My grandparents helped as much as they could, of course, but for the most part, my dad was a self-made man. He was proud of that, it was part of who he was, and his work ethic was ingrained in my DNA. As were his protective tendencies. Even though he's been dead ten years now, the beliefs he instilled in me live on.

"Take care of each other," he'd said to my sister and me before he and my mother were killed in a car accident involving a drunk driver. But he'd given me this look before he left and I knew what he really meant. *Take care of your sister, Dallas,* he'd conveyed silently.

I've done my best to honor his final request, which is why being away from her feels so strange. When we'd moved from our two-story house in a suburb of Austin to a tiny two-bedroom shack with our grandparents in Amarillo, I'd done everything I could to make sure my sister didn't suffer more than necessary. I'd taken the converted closet as a bedroom so she could have the bigger one. I'd mowed the same lawns my father had as a kid to make sure she had extra spending money for ice cream or earrings or whatever her little heart desired. I'd even been careful not to be too rough on my clothes because I knew she'd likely have to wear them as hand-me-downs.

"So you're okay then? Having a good time still?" I'm glad she's enjoying herself, I am. But I won't be too upset when she's done traipsing across the countryside, either.

"I am having a *great* time," my sister tells me. "Somehow it's like . . . never mind."

"Tell me."

"It's like they're here with me." She sighs, the heavy losses we've experienced over the years weighing down her breath. "That sounds dumb, right? I mean, I'm not hallucinating or anything. I just . . . *feel* them."

She means our grandparents. Because she's on the road trip they'd planned to spend their life savings on but never got the chance to. And I know exactly how she feels. Between the memories of my parents and my granddad's voice in my head, I feel them, too.

"I know exactly what you mean, Dixie Leigh. Not a day goes by that I don't think about the guitar lessons Papa gave me. And I could sure go for some of Nana's cooking right now. Man can only eat so much diner food."

She laughs and I use the moment to tell her about joining Jase Wade's tour.

"Dallas!" she practically squeals at me. "And here I thought you were calling just to check in. Congratulations! I'm so happy for you, big brother."

"Thanks."

Some siblings might be jealous of each other's success or resentful, especially since this was our dream once upon a time. But Dixie has always been one of the most selfless people I know.

"I can talk to the label again. They loved your song, Dix. I can convince them that you need to—"

"I need to be right where I am, Dallas." She pauses a moment and I can picture her expression as she chooses her words carefully. "After this, I'm going to New Mexico. Then I'm going home for a while, so you can rest easy. I love you, and I'm happy for you. I miss you and I miss . . ." For a second I'm sure she's going to say Gavin and that's going to turn this into an entirely different conversation. But she doesn't. "The band," she says instead.

"Me, too."

"But the label wanted you, Dallas. And I needed this trip even more than I realized. I needed to make peace with all that we've lost before I could appreciate what I have. So you do what you need to and stop worrying about me so much. I can take care of myself. Promise."

I know that she can. Despite our dad's last words, Dixie always made it fairly easy on me. She rarely asked for anything. When I tried to give her the money I'd saved over the years so that she could go to college, she informed me that she'd applied for a scholarship and that she'd only go if she got it. Which she did, because she's one of the most talented musicians I've ever known.

Dixie has the same passion for music that our mother did and the talent that flowed from our father's fingertips. Our dad wasn't as interested in music professionally, maybe because he grew up with a musician father who'd never managed to make a successful career from it—but like our mom used to say, Dad had music in his soul whether he wanted it there or not. He was one of those people who could find a beat anywhere. And according to my granddad, he never met an instrument he couldn't tame.

My sister plays with this superhuman ease, almost as if playing is effortless for her, something that just occurs when she touches an instrument. But I'm more like my mom. I had to practice my ass off. Playing the guitar began as something I did for fun, just fooling around. But when people started paying me fifty bucks to play at their parties, I realized I could earn money doing something I thought was fun instead of schlepping a push mower all around town.

Fifty bucks bought my sister new blue jeans of her very own. And all the ice cream she could eat.

I'd saved and sacrificed and given everything I had to give. I'd even tried to give up my shot at making it when a label executive didn't want my sister as part of the deal. But Dixie had shoved me out the door, telling me that I'd given up enough and it was my turn to live my dream now.

Part of me is here for selfish reasons. Because I love the thrill of performing, and because it feels like I'm proving something to my late father. I like to think he'd be proud of me. But mostly, my hope is that I can make the kind of living with music that will ensure my sister doesn't have to do anything she doesn't want to. Like spend her life in an orchestra pit. Or work as a waitress in Amarillo for the rest of her life.

"It's your turn now," she's told me several times. "This is your dream. Stop worrying about me and go get it already."

"Dallas," my sister says slightly louder, breaking into my thoughts. "This is still what you want, right? The tour? The music?"

It takes me too long to answer. So I make sure to add plenty of gusto to my voice when I do.

"Yeah. Yeah, of course it is."

"You sure everything's okay? Is Gavin okay? He told me about the whole probation thing, but maybe now you can get the label to talk to someone and explain—"

"Everything's fine. I should go, Dixie. Afton Tate says hello, by the way. I'm grabbing a few drinks with him now. Call and check in when you get to New Mexico, okay?"

"Okay," she says, so low I have to strain to hear over the sounds of cars passing by. "I'll call you soon. Love you."

"Love you, too," I say before disconnecting the call.

For a second I thought she was about to say something else, but I wait a beat and she doesn't text or dial me back.

My skin prickles at my lie of omission as I make my way back inside the bar. Gavin Garrison isn't with me and he hasn't been since he left after the audition in Nashville. I thought he would've gotten in touch with her by now and as much as I want to tell her, it doesn't feel like my truth to tell.

Then there's the fact that I feel like I'm faking it until I make it out on the road alone. I haven't written a full song in over a year. Not one that was any good, anyway. If it weren't for my sister's lyrics, I probably wouldn't even be here. But I have to push aside my writer's block or inspiration block or whatever the hell it is that's blocking me. Because I'm here now, right where I always dreamed of being.

# 2 | Robyn

IT IS DAYS LIKE THIS THAT MAKE ME THANKFUL PEOPLE ASSUME I am a bitch. Something about my red hair, I guess. Usually I'm pretty chill, actually. But incompetence irritates the ever-loving shit out of me. And I've been dealing with it all morning. There isn't enough coffee in the world to make this day run smoothly.

Ignoring the pinch of pain my Louboutins cause and the dull ache in my calves, I stomp over to where two muscle-covered men are setting up the Midnight Bay blue line display.

"What part of 'forward facing' is unclear?" Reaching toward the LED-lit shelf, I turn the bottles so that the labels can be seen. Both men give me their what-do-you-want-from-us-lady face. Once I have the bottles positioned correctly, I force a smile at them. "There. See? Now it actually makes sense to spend several thousand dollars on this display."

The younger of the two rolls his eyes so I narrow mine.

My blood pressure skyrockets as he hops down from the ladder and smirks at me. "Think you can do it better, Red? Knock yourself out."

He's cocky in a way that reminds me of a southern boy who made me a woman. Taking a deep breath, I glance at the older gentleman still arranging the display. With the labels turned every which way.

"You know what? Why don't you fellas take a break?"

"Gladly," the one glaring at me says before walking away in a huff.

"Don't worry about me. I got this," I call out after him, causing several people in the Midnight Bay Bourbon Distillery to turn and look at me.

"My apologies, ma'am," the older man tells me, scratching his beard as he climbs down from the ladder himself. His gray T-shirt has "Sanderson & Sons Convention Services" stamped on the pocket. "This is the family business, and believe me, not his first choice." There's heavy regret in his voice and I can see the resemblance. Junior is his son, apparently, and I just made an already tense situation worse.

Well now I feel like an asshole.

Sighing, I give him a genuine smile instead of my usual resting bitch face. "It's okay. I'm just really particular. Y'all did great on this setup. I can handle arranging the bottles from here."

He nods, but tense lines of worry are etched into his aging face. "We need this job, ma'am. The last thing we need is to lose Midnight Bay's business because of an attitude problem. Please—"

"It's Robyn," I say, reaching out a hand and realizing I never introduced myself. I greeted them when they arrived by giving orders. Maybe bitchy has become my default setting. Damn fiery hair. "And no worries, Mr. Sanderson. It looks great." I glance up at the nine-foot tower of bourbon bottles. It does look pretty fantastic, minus some hidden labels that can easily be fixed.

"I'll just go, um, deal with—" He gestures toward the direction where his son stalked off.

"Good idea. Sorry if I was a little snappy. I've only recently been promoted to the head of this huge campaign and the stress must be getting to me."

"Just doing your job, ma'am. Can't fault you for that." He winks, giving me a tired grin before following after his son.

The real reason I'm stretched within centimeters of my breaking point is the meeting I had with my boss this morning.

*"This is huge for Midnight Bay. There is no safety net, no acceptable margin of error where this tour is concerned. Is that clear, Miss Breeland?"*

I'd "yes, sir'd" my way through the half-hour meeting that detailed just how high the stakes were. It was made abundantly clear that my career would either rise or fall based on my performance heading up this campaign. For nine months I'd planned the pre-release, launch luncheons, and post-party events down to every last infinitesimal detail.

I got this. I fought for this opportunity and I'm not going to screw it up just because this particular client makes me a little twitchy. The promotion to public relations specialist is as good as mine.

But every other week it seems the king of country music wants a change. Two of his opening acts have been replaced within weeks of each other for undisclosed reasons, so that meant all new print materials. He didn't like his picture on the life-size cutout for the display so it had to be reshot several times. He also didn't care for the original placement of Midnight Bay's logo on the art for the entourage of eighteen-wheelers that hauls his tour equipment, and I'm pretty sure he's here today to discuss the shirts and hats he's supposed to wear on the tour to promote the company.

I get heartburn just thinking about his next request.

I used to have plants in my apartment. They all died. Because I was never home to water them.

But that's okay. It will all be worth it eventually. And if you want something done your way, you have to do it yourself, as my dad was fond of reminding me. Which reminds me of the display towering beside me.

The ladder dares me to climb up and gift everyone in the reception area a flash of my lace panties. My OCD brain tells me to get over myself and get my ass up there and fix those labels. Slipping out of my stilettos and tugging my skirt down, I grip the metal rails and make my way up several rungs. No one seems to be paying much attention to me, so I continue my ascent.

My equilibrium dances out of my reach for a split second, but I compose myself and angle the top two rows as they should be before taking a step down. Once I've completed the top four rows, I breathe a little easier.

There. The hard part is over.

I step down a rung, but I must've misjudged the distance because my foot slips and I see myself fall through the air before it happens.

As every muscle in my body tenses, the air whooshes out of my lungs and I flail hopelessly in an attempt to grab something solid.

Surprisingly, I don't hear the crack of my skull on the slate floor. What I do hear is a man grunt out a noise on impact when I land in his arms.

"Whoa there, darlin'," my knight in shining denim drawls. "Not that I wasn't enjoying the view, but I'd leave the stunts to the professionals."

From underneath a black Stetson, crystal-clear green eyes gleam with a twinkle of mischief and flirtation.

I close my eyes and attempt to make myself disappear like that chick did in *Bewitched*.

No such luck.

When I open them, I'm still in the arms of Jase Wade, last year's Country Music Artist of the Year and Midnight Bay's biggest client. We're sponsoring his upcoming tour and I'm in charge of the promotional campaign. He's walking temptation in tight jeans and I've vowed to keep it professional where he's concerned.

Professional as in not swooning in his arms. Like I am right this very second.

Awesome.

My face probably matches my crimson lip stain right about now.

"Um, Mr. Wade, now would probably be an excellent time to put me down." I chuckle nervously.

"You got it, Red." He complies just in time for my boss to round the corner.

"Mr. Martin," I say breathlessly. "I was just going to show Mr. Wade the new display. We'll have a scaled version at each show in the VIP meet-and-greet area and I thought it would be a good idea to—"

"Sure. Great," Alexander Martin cuts me off, as he tends to do. His uncle Bennett is the original founder of Midnight Bay, but Alex took over around the time I was hired for my internship. He's barely thirty years old, but he's a "time is money" type of guy and I can count on one hand the number of sentences I've actually finished in his presence. Jase Wade's hand still resting on the small of my back is not something I ever intended to happen in my boss's presence, however. "There's been a few adjustments to the tour and I want to be sure that we're prepared. New print materials will be sent to your office this week, Miss Breeland. I just spoke with . . ."

Mr. Martin is still talking. His squared, clean-shaven jaw is still moving, as is his mouth. But I have no idea what he's saying because despite the fact that I've taken an entire step to my left, I'm still within Wade's reach. I know this because his fingertips are still lightly brushing my lower back. Feels like he's turned my spine into a lightning rod, so that's a tad distracting. Glancing over at his chiseled face, I see that he's showing no signs of being nearly as affected as I am by the contact. Clearly I need to get laid. It's been . . . a while.

I take a deep breath and press my lips together, nodding so that Mr. Martin doesn't realize I've completely lost my grip on reality.

" . . . Walker has a solid social media presence and is fairly well-known here in Texas. So you'll need to plan meet-and-greets for him as well. Nothing as extensive as Mr. Wade's, of course." Mr. Martin finishes and winks at Jase.

"You got it. I'm on it."

I have no idea what I'm on.

"Great." My boss grins at me with approval, then turns to Jase Wade. "Come on, Jase. I'll introduce you to my uncle; he's retired but he's visiting the distillery today, and we'll get my assistant to organize that fishing trip."

Oh, the good ol' boys network. How nice it must be to have a penis working in your favor. I can't remember the last time one did *me* any favors. My gaze dips involuntarily to the bulge in Wade's Wranglers.

*Dear God. Stop yourself, Breeland.*

But I stop myself a split second too late because when I look up, Jase's eyes are on mine. He quirks his mouth and raises a brow. I can practically hear him asking if I see something I like.

"I'll see you in Denver next week," I say quickly, hoping to dispel the awkwardness of my flushed cheeks.

"Yes, ma'am," he says with a tip of his hat. "And by the way, I really enjoyed the display." He nods to the tower of liquor bottles behind me but I'm pretty sure that's not all he's referring to.

He walks away leaving me speechless in his wake. Sweet mother he's doing those damn jeans a favor. If my boss ever catches me losing my composure like this around such a high-profile person we're partnering with, I have been told in no uncertain terms, I will be fired before I can wipe the drool from my chin. Since my dad passed when I was in high school, my mom and I have been on our own. She took out a second mortgage to help me get through college, and I am not going to screw up a chance at my dream career for sex in tight jeans.

I repeat: I am not going to throw away my amazing job for orgasms. No matter how long it's been since I've had one that involved another person being in the vicinity.

So I take a deep breath and ignore the fact that Jase Wade just had his arms around me, that he smelled like expensive sins and whiskey, and that I haven't been held by anyone in over a year. Paying no attention to my still-racing pulse and sweaty palms, I return my attention to the display and use my phone to snap a few shots of it for the company website.

I've got this. I'm cool, calm, collected. Totally together. The picture of professionalism.

That is, until Jase Wade gives me a lingering look full of dark promises before winking at me on his way out. I force a completely awkward smile and give him two thumbs up.

I just gave Jase freaking Wade two thumbs up. Once he's out of sight, I cover my face with my hands, including my two humiliating thumbs, and groan.

I have so got to get laid. Preferably by someone who won't cost me my job.

# 3 | Dallas

"HEY, SUPERSTAR," MY MANAGER GREETS ME AT THE FAIRMONT hotel. She lowers the phone she was texting on when the car I was in pulled up. "Just got the official word from your agent. He heard back from Midnight Bay. We're all set for a meet-and-greet in Denver. You ready for this, baby? You're about to be the next big thing."

I still bristle a little at her overly familiar terms of endearment, but I've heard her on the phone with her other clients and I know I'm not the only one she uses them on.

"Sounds great."

The Kickin' Up Crazy tour is kicking off in Denver, but we're doing some press first in Nashville. From there we'll zigzag across the country—Wade on his luxury bus and the rest of us on something a little more modest. Some of the guys in the band grumbled about it, but I couldn't care less. It's sure the hell a step up from EmmyLou, the Chevy Express van that me, my sister, Dixie, and my best friend, Gavin, hauled our equipment and ourselves in.

My chest constricts just thinking about Leaving Amarillo. Not the physical act of actually leaving it—that part I was ready for. I just didn't expect to leave without the other two members of my band.

"You seem a little off, Dallas," Mandy says as we head to the hotel restaurant where we're having a quick meeting before I get to crash in my room. "You need to focus on why you're here. This is about you and *your* dream. Whatever else is on your mind, you need to have it handled before tomorrow morning."

"Got it. I'm good. Just a little tired. Nothing a good night's sleep won't fix." *And a good thorough fucking would help,* I think but don't say out loud. It feels like it's been a lifetime since I've gotten laid. In reality it's only been a few weeks since my wild night with Deidre or maybe it was Debra, a waitress I hooked up with in Atlanta. I'm kind of pissed that I was drunk at the time and can't exactly remember if I was worth a shit or not. Ah well. One-offs are kind of like cold pizza. Not spectacular or worth writing home about, but still enjoyable so not a total waste of time.

While we eat, Mandy says something else about the meeting with the tour sponsors tomorrow and staying focused, but I keep checking my phone to see if Dixie has texted an update on her location and I'm so exhausted my vision is blurring. My manager has a consistent habit of reminding me to keep my eyes on the prize and stop stressing out over what my little sister is up to.

The check comes and Mandy slips a shiny black credit card inside the padfolio before handing it back to the waiter. Before I can thank her, or her management company, I suppose, for dinner, my phone buzzes in my pocket. Retrieving it, I see a photo my sister sent from some cheese monument in God knows where. After that comes one of her grinning like a maniac beside a giant ball of twine. The fuck?

I'm mildly concerned that she's having some sort of weird grief-induced breakdown, but every time I talk to her she assures me that she's fine.

I start to text her a message to call me and let me know her exact coordinates—yes, I'm serious—when Mandy reaches out and places her perfectly manicured nails over the screen of my phone.

Glancing up, I can see that I've offended her by texting during out meeting. Pretty ironic since she probably texts in her sleep.

"My sister is on a road trip. She's alone and I can't help but—"

"Dallas. Please, *please* do not make me remind you once again how huge this opportunity is. Wade's album is number one on every outlet right now. The tour is sold out. And you are on it. Do you even have any idea how hard Neil and I have worked for this? For you?"

I nod, being careful to keep my mouth shut. I know that she and my agent have both worked hard. I've worked pretty fucking hard, too, but that rarely gets mentioned or even acknowledged.

"It's been a long day. I'm good. Tired. But good. Promise." Basically a bus and then a tiny hotel room in Nashville have been home for the past few weeks. And I'm about to hop my ass right back on the road tomorrow night. Thank fuck my sister is ending her little excursion just as this tour is beginning. I really don't think I could handle this and worrying about her, too.

"Well, get some sleep then. The car will be waiting out front at nine A.M. sharp to take you to the airport."

I nod while standing up from the table. "Got it. See you in the morning."

"You're not walking me to my room?" Mandy pouts. "And here I thought you were a gentleman."

I swallow the uneasy feeling that rises in my throat. It's not the first time she's hinted at crossing the professional line with me and I can't ever tell just how serious she is.

"I am a gentleman, Miss Lantram. That's why it's better if I don't.

Have a good night now." I grin and make my way quickly out of the room.

There. Maybe she'll feel flattered.

For as much as Mandy Lantram keeps reminding me to stay focused and keep my eyes on the prize, I've noticed her focus and her eyes wandering a bit. To my mouth, across the expanse of my chest, and down to my cock.

More than once.

E ither my alarm is going off or the building is on fire.

I roll over and groan, throwing an arm over my face when sunlight hits me square in the face. Stretching as far as my back will allow, I yawn before my hand drops to my morning wood.

*Sorry, buddy.*

My schedule is so fucking tight I don't even have time to jerk off these days. A cold shower and a cold breakfast and then I'm dressed and sliding into a black Lincoln beside my manager.

"Good morning, Superstar," Mandy purrs while lowering the cell phone that seems permanently attached to her palm. A thick curtain of black hair sweeps over her left shoulder.

How she manages to look this hot at nine in the morning is beyond me, but I'm trying damn hard not to notice. She smells like expensive shampoo and flowers—it's almost overwhelming but my dick has no sense of smell so he twitches to inquire about whether or not she's available.

*Not to us, big guy.*

If there is one thing I don't want to fuck up, literally, it's my relationship with anyone who has power over my career. So there's a line, whether Mandy's wandering eyes realize it or not, and it's one I won't cross. No matter how interested my dick is when she stretches her mile-long legs.

Thankfully the airport isn't far from the hotel and I'm free from the suffocating confines of the backseat.

As we make our way through security checkpoints, Mandy hands out tips as if I haven't just finished one tour.

"Be sure you're tweeting and posting on Facebook about how excited and honored you are to be on this tour. Tag Jase and Midnight Bay Bourbon when you do. Hashtag KickinUpCrazy."

I grumble a little under my breath. Dixie typically handled the social media bullshit for Leaving Amarillo. Pulling out my phone, I try to fire off a quick text to my sister to see if she's heard from Gavin yet, but I have no service.

Mandy scoffs at me. "I didn't mean right this second. I just meant later tonight. You need to put your phone on airplane mode anyway."

I don't bother informing her of what I was actually up to.

Mandy stops walking down the aisle. "Oh. This is me," she says halfway through the first-class cabin.

I glance down at my ticket. I'm in coach. I chuckle under my breath. Of course she wouldn't lower her standards even though Capitol has yet to consider me worthy of a first-class upgrade.

"See ya in Denver," I call out as I pass. I'm actually relieved to have a break from her.

A few drinks in and the exclusive mile-high club might become a little too accessible.

# 4 | Robyn

"YOU READY TO CALL IT A DAY?" MY ROOMMATE, ANOTHER MAR-
keting assistant at Midnight Bay named Katie O'Rourke and whom
I call Katie-O for fun, laughs when she opens the door to the office
we share and finds me sitting on the floor already half into a bottle
of bourbon. It's the single-barrel blue line and it's my favorite, but
despite my favorite coffee mug that proclaims "this is probably bourbon," I don't usually imbibe at work. "Damn, girl. It's not even the
weekend yet. Why you no invite me to the party?"

I start to answer but I gesture a little too wildly with my arm and
knock over the bottle. Thankfully it's mostly empty so not much
spills before she sets it upright.

"Oh, it's a party all right. A what-did-I-do-to-the-universe-to-
make-it-hate-me-so-much party."

"Okay," Katie says, lowering herself onto the floor beside me. I'm
far too honest to have a horde of female friends, but Katie is pretty
fantastic. And she has a thick skin so she puts up with me just fine. "I
give. What did you do?"

I shrug and glance listlessly down at the mock-up of the poster in
front of me.

"I don't know, Katie-O, but it must've been something bad. Like shove orphans in front of a speeding train for kicks bad." I tip my empty highball glass back in hopes of a few merciful drops landing on my tongue. They don't. Not even when I tap the bottom of the glass, causing it to clink against my teeth.

"Wade still flirting with you? Is that what's got you all worked up?" Katie's tone is empathetic and even in my stupor I appreciate that she isn't being condescending about it. Some of the other girls we work with would jump at the chance to hook up with Wade. And most all of them wouldn't pity me for being on the receiving end of his flirting.

"No. I mean, yeah, he kind of is. But that's not why I'm swilling liquor like a sailor."

"Do sailors drink a lot of bourbon? I feel like they're more into rum."

I huff out a laugh on a breath. "You know what I mean."

She sighs and lifts the Kickin' Up Crazy tour poster from the floor beside me. "You have to admit, he's a good-looking son of a bitch."

I nod. "He is."

"So . . . sailor, you gonna fess up or what? Did you hook up with him? I promise I won't tell Mr. Martin. You work your ass off for this company and Wade hasn't exactly been discreet about his interest in you. I'd say you could probably—"

"It's not Wade. And no, we didn't hook up or anything. It's, um, this guy." I point to the name at the bottom of poster, the recently added one that I just googled.

"The Baker Street Boys?"

"The other one."

"Who's Dallas Walker?"

Now there's a million-dollar question.

Who *is* Dallas Walker?

Taking a deep breath, I turn my laptop to face her. Katie scrolls down the page and whistles when she presses play on the YouTube video on his website.

"Well. Hello, handsome."

Bile rises in my throat. I'd prayed it was a coincidence. It wasn't. It was him.

"Robyn? You okay? You look like you're going to be sick."

I just shake my head. No, I'm not okay. And no, I'm not going to be sick. But yes, I am having a panic attack because the only man I've ever loved, the one who's made it so completely clear he's no longer interested in me that a diamond mining company would envy his clarity, is on the tour I'm heading up the promotional campaign for.

"You know this guy?" Katie hits play on the song again, the damn song that is so full of shit it makes me want to chuck my computer out the window. "Better to Burn," it's called and it's about risking it all for love, which I'm not sure Dallas Walker would ever actually do.

I struggle to find my voice and the words to accurately describe how I know this man, this man I haven't spoken more than a few words to in years, the man who at a funeral not that long ago basically told me he couldn't care less if he ever saw me again.

"I do. I do know him."

She whistles again. "Lucky you." When I don't say anything else, she reaches out and touches me on the arm. "Robyn? You mean you like *know* him know him? Oh God. Oh no. He's *the one,* isn't he?"

Oxygen is suddenly a scarce commodity.

"Yeah," I say slowly. "He's the one."

# 5 | Dallas

DENVER IS SLIGHTLY COLDER THAN I EXPECTED AND MORE MOUN-
tainous than anywhere I've ever been.

Mandy and I arrive at the amphitheater for sound check just as
the sun slips below the giant peaks. I slide off my sunglasses and out
of the backseat.

Holy fuck. The entire amphitheater has just been carved out of
the red rock and it's unlike anything I've ever seen.

My manager seems amused at my wide-eyed gaping as I stand
there awestruck by the sight of it.

"See what I mean? This is where you belong. Not in those Podunk
back-alley bars." Mandy presses her full lips together in a self-
congratulatory smirk. "Come on. I'll introduce you to a few people.
The reviewer for *Country Music Weekly* is here and some local radio
people are, too. Oh and the tour sponsor is here. They've set up a
meet-and-greet for you tonight."

I'm still processing the fact that I'm about to play in front of at
least ten thousand people when she links her arm with mine and tugs
me toward the stage.

Half a dozen eighteen-wheelers are parked beside where we pulled in. A giant Jase Wade is giving everyone "come suck my cock" face from beneath his cowboy hat. Neon blue letters scream about Midnight Bay Bourbon sponsoring the Kickin' Up Crazy tour.

About a million shirts and hats and can coozies with the sponsor's name were delivered to me via Mandy this morning.

"That'll be your face on those trailers one day," Mandy says, noticing where my attention has drifted.

"Remind me not to make some stupid-ass pouty face when it is."

She laughs but her grip on me tightens. "Behave, Dallas. He's the headliner this time so be humble. Even if you have to fake it."

"Fake it till I make it. Got it." I nod as we make our way up the metal stairs, and try not to acknowledge just how true that statement currently is.

A roar of laughter goes up from where a group of guys are gathered.

"So I told her, darlin', I'll give you a ride wherever you want to go. Just let me get my pants on first." More laughter rolls outward. The guy in the center pulls his hat off when he sees us approaching. "My bad, Miss Lantram. Didn't know there was a lady present."

"There isn't," she says evenly. "Jase, this is Dallas Walker. He's Capitol's newest artist and your new opening act."

She's already filled me in on how this spot came open at the last minute. Some other new guy rightfully had it. But he snaked one of Wade's groupies and Wade had him kicked off.

Wade eyes me up and down before giving that same expression that irked me on the tour trailers. "Nice to meet you, Dallas."

He extends his hand and so do I. We shake hands briefly and I can feel the entire group sizing me up.

"Same here." I keep my shoulders straight and maintain eye contact. Not because I have something to prove but because I want him to know I belong here. And that the last thing I care about is competing with him when it comes to women. He can have all the groupies to himself.

Wade smirks. "Guess we'll have to watch our language around here, fellas. Seein' as Dallas here is going to have his babysitter with him."

The urge rises in my throat to laugh—and not with him. At his juvenile bullshit. Wade has some chart-topping hits. Several successful albums.

Guess how many of the songs he wrote himself?

Zero. None. Zip. Zilch. Not a single fucking lyric.

Not that I have much room to talk at the moment, but typically I do write my own music.

Dude probably knows all of three chords. I may not have his sales numbers, but at the end of the day, I can look myself in the mirror and be proud of working my ass off for music I believe in instead of shit that was forced on me by someone else.

So if he wants to put me down to establish his alpha male dominance? No sweat off my balls. I'm just here to play my music.

"She spank you if you act up?" Wade nods to Mandy, who stiffens beside me.

"Only if he asks real nice," she snaps back.

I toss both of my hands up in a gesture to let them know I'm bowing out of this little scuffle. I didn't know they had history but it's clear now that they do. Even some of the members of Wade's crew are backing away.

"You two enjoy your foreplay. I'm going to go introduce myself to the tour sponsor."

"Tell Red hi for me," Wade says without taking his eyes off Mandy.

"I'll do that," I say, even though I have no idea who Red is. Don't know, don't care.

It's the number-one rule Mandy has reiterated since the moment we found out I was being added to this tour. Hands off Wade's women. I highly doubt he and I have the same taste anyway. Wade likes the drunk ones with the biggest tits from the front rows, from what I hear. I'll pass on those walking sex tapes and TMZ exposés waiting to happen, thank you very fucking much.

Stepping offstage, I glance at the empty seats once more.

According to the sign posted by the stage, maximum capacity is 9,450 people. The largest audience I played for on the unsigned artists tour was a little under five thousand folks.

This is it. I made it.

There's a lyric here somewhere. The quiet before the storm. I know it's in there somewhere, but I can't find it with both hands.

Despite my writer's block, I can feel the enormity of this moment in my bones. The building buzz in my veins. Adrenaline and anticipation fortifying me in their purest forms.

This is only the beginning.

And no amount of adolescent fuckery from Wade or Mandy or anyone else is going to get in my way.

# 6 | Robyn

"HEY, DIXIE. THANKS FOR GETTING BACK TO ME."

I'm half out of breath from running across the amphitheater. I've left half a dozen voice mails for her but I didn't know how to ask what I needed to on a recording.

"Sure. Sorry I crashed early last night. But I got your messages. What's up?"

I move behind a concession booth for a modicum of privacy. The VIP fans are already in line and Dallas and Jase will be down here any minute for the meet-and-greet.

"It's about Dallas. Well, me and Dallas. We're on the same tour."

"Oh God, Robyn. I meant to call you. I completely forgot you told me you were heading up the promo for Wade's tour. Dallas was so excited about getting added to it and I was on the road when he called me. The pieces didn't snap together until last weekend and I—"

"It's fine. Really. I just, um, I just wanted to know . . . Does *he* know? That he'll be working with me?"

The other end of the line is quiet. Then I hear her exhale audibly.

"No. I was trying to recall if I'd mentioned your job to him. But I haven't. Our conversations have been pretty short, actually. I think he's keeping something from me, something about Gavin, which I can't really complain about because I'm keeping some information on our favorite broody drummer from him, too. But I know for a fact I haven't said anything about your job or you working on Wade's tour."

Relief spreads through my chest, clearing it of the intricate webs of tension that had formed when I'd been researching Jase's new opening act.

I want to ask her what she thinks is going on with Gavin, if she's okay, and what she thinks I should do about Dallas. But before I can, he appears in my line of sight and I have to go. Jase Wade follows not far behind and a curvy brunette is hot on his heels and looks mad as hell. Probably a woman scorned. He seems to leave a trail of them in his wake.

"Hey, thanks. I have to go. I'm actually at work right now. But I'll call you later, okay?"

"Sounds good. And I am so sorry, Robyn. Seriously. I suck. I should've—"

"It's fine. Promise. I'm a big girl. I can handle it."

Him, I mean. I can handle him.

At least I hope I can. Because he's walking directly toward me.

The brunette stops Dallas and pulls him aside so Jase reaches me first. He gestures to the pyramid of bottles behind me.

"Lookin' good."

I smile and smooth the lace dress I'm wearing under my denim blazer. "I'm glad you like it."

"The display looks great, too," he adds with a sly smile.

I shake my head and turn just in time to see the brunette glaring at Jase. I'm distracted by the outrage glowing in her eyes so I notice a second too late that Dallas is close enough to recognize me.

Our eyes meet and I wonder for a full minute if this is the movie of my life being shot without my permission.

He looks different than when I saw him at his grandfather's funeral a couple of months ago. There's just enough dark scruff on his chin and jaw to make me wonder what it would feel like in the palms of my hands, in the valley between my breasts, and Heaven help me, on the sensitive skin of my inner thighs. I would slap some sense into myself if I were alone right now.

Dallas stills completely, the questions clear in his gaze. He has no idea what the hell I'm doing here. Tension ripples tight on both sides of his jaw. He probably thinks he's having some kind of nightmare.

"Drew here will get a few shots of both of you with the display." I smile at the freelance photographer that works for Midnight Bay from time to time. "Then he'll take the VIP shots separately. Just smile and act natural."

That's what I'll be trying to do.

Drew's been doing this a lot longer than I have. He already has his camera up and is snapping candids. I can only imagine what the shots of Dallas's face are going to look like.

*You're prepared, Robyn. Dallas isn't. Brace yourself for him to possibly behave like an ass in five . . . four . . . three. . .*

"Robyn? What are you doing here?"

He doesn't look at all happy to see me. Not that I can blame him.

"Hi, Dallas. It's nice to see you, too. Now if you'll just step over to where Jase is standing we can get a few shots of both of you with the—"

"Is this some kind of joke?" he asks low so that only I can hear. I watch helplessly as he looks around as if he expects a film crew to pop out and tell him he's been Punk'd.

The entire group has turned its attention to us since he hasn't stepped over to where he should be standing. I take a deep breath and school my features so they remain professionally polite. "No joke. I am here working. Same as you." I force a tight smile while making deliberate eye contact. I telepathically send him a harsh *"We have a job to do, suck it up, you big baby"* message but he narrows his eyes and sends one right back. *"We will discuss this later."*

He has questions. I'll probably have to answer them. Honestly.

I am so screwed.

But for now, my career is more important than explaining myself. And our exchange is garnering entirely too much attention. So I usher the guys over to where I need them and Drew takes several pictures. Two different women and one man from local radio stations come up and interview each of them briefly before the fans get to come in. Dallas has a few young girls in his line but Jase's is never-ending.

Once the dozen or so young women are satisfied with Dallas's photo and autographs, he walks purposefully over to where I'm hanging back off to the side. His broad shoulders have remained stiff and slightly bowed since the moment he laid eyes on me.

Every inch of my body is alert and aware of just how close he's standing. I can smell the scent of his sharp, clean cologne and beneath that, masculine soap. There's always the hint of wood in the air around him, as if that guitar he's permanently attached to has somehow seeped into his skin.

My mouth waters at the intoxicating aroma that is Dallas so I swallow hard and keep my eyes trained on where Jase is standing smiling with fans, some of whom are crying and others practically groping him. What a strange life these guys lead. I couldn't imagine part of my job being letting people fall all over me.

"Well, I can honestly say you're the last person I expected to see here." His voice is low in my ear, causing a shiver to roll down my spine. "Want to tell me what the hell is going on?"

I answer without looking at him. "I'm not stalking you, if that's what you're thinking. I told you. I'm working. I'm an assistant marketing coordinator and promotional relations specialist for Midnight Bay Bourbon. I was on this tour before you were."

"You just caught me off guard is all." He clears his throat harshly. His hand falls to a spot that used to be familiar to him—the small of my back—and I feel it like fireworks.

It isn't quite as startling as it was when Jase placed his unwelcome hand there. Dallas places his hand on my lower back like it *belongs* there, and my traitorous body welcomes his touch as if it agrees.

This is ridiculous. I'm twenty-three years old—a grown woman. And when a man who hasn't touched me in years places his hand on my lower back, my bones become blobs of jelly. Damn him. Damn bones.

I fist my fingers in an attempt to return my body to a solid mass. "So you're not gonna call my boss and request they remove me from this tour?"

"Jesus, Robyn. No." As I breathe a sigh of relief, he huffs out a breath that tickles my ear. "I know I wasn't exactly friendly at my grandfather's funeral. And seeing you here certainly is a surprise. But I won't interfere with your job. I'm not a complete asshole. Even if I behave like one from time to time."

My shoulders relax and my body betrays me. It eases backward almost into his arms. His chest brushes my back and I flinch at the contact. This cannot happen.

"You can't help your true nature."

Dallas chuckles and it warms my blood to a dangerously high temperature. I have to get away from him. Now.

"Look, I know it's not ideal, having to see someone from your past intruding on your shiny new future."

*Believe me,* I almost add. I'm speaking from experience now because every ounce of confidence I'd mustered about my ability to do my job, to handle this tour, dissipated into thin air the moment I learned that Dallas Walker was the Dallas Lark who had taken my virginity in a pickup truck. Kind of hard to hold on to your sophisticated big-girl dignity around a guy who once helped you search for your underwear on a Chevy floorboard. Okay, more than once.

Dallas gives me a boyish half grin. "We're both adults here. We can handle this, right?"

I turn and let his ice-blue eyes burn into me. My head says, "Yeah, Robyn, we got this. No worries." My heart says, "Run. Quit your job and get as far away from him as you possibly can. Immediately."

I'm so busy listening to my heart and head battle it out that I miss what Dallas says.

"I'm sorry. What?"

I tilt my head and he smiles his sexy half smile that I have no doubt has dropped panties across the nation in epidemic proportions. If it hasn't already, it will. And I'll get to watch from the sidelines.

Fantastic.

"I asked if you wanted to get dinner after the show. You know, food, conversation, maybe a discussion about how we go about dealing with this situation."

My brows lift because I'm confused. This man I've kept buried in the back of my past has risen and is standing in front of me asking me to dinner.

I check my internal decision-making faculties.

Head: Sure. Dinner sounds great. Making peace will be good for you. Yay, closure!

Heart: Run. I said run. Why aren't you running? For fuck's sakes, run already!

"As nice as that sounds, um, I think the show will probably run late so . . ."

"So I was thinking pancakes," he says, using his secret weapon against me. "There's a diner we passed between here and the hotel."

I despise breakfast. In the mornings. Try to show me food before noon and I will gag. Literally. But breakfast for dinner, or even better, in the middle of the night? My one true weakness.

"Wow. Pulling out the big guns, huh? You must really feel bad."

His voice drops even lower, the cadence rolling through me like perfectly aged bourbon. "It's been a while since you've seen the big gun, darlin'. I'll only pull it out if you ask me to."

My eyes widen with shock and my mouth falls open. I feel my face heating so I angle it away from him. I turn just in time to see the angry woman from before striding over to us in heels that put my Ariat boots to shame.

"Dallas," she barks his name like a command. "You're needed on-stage."

He nods at her but his eyes flicker back to mine. "Pancakes?" he mouths without sound.

I roll mine, because what the hell? Our past is one big fat mess, and our future is even more complicated now that we'll be working together. But yeah, pancakes should definitely straighten all of that out.

I shake my head and mouth "no" back at him.

His lips press together and then his tongue snakes out and licks them. Ever felt your ovaries quiver? No? It's an alarming feeling.

"The diner is open all night. I'll be there. Waiting for you to change your mind."

With that, he lets his lady friend link her arm into his and they walk away leaving me standing there.

"Come on, Superstar," the woman says, making my stomach turn. Superstar? Really? *Ugh*.

I'm trying really hard not to gape at his retreating figure. Returning my attention to where Jase is wrapping up his meet-and-greets, I give him the biggest smile I can manage. This is what I'm here for— not to rehash a high school romance gone to hell.

Everything in my life is finally coming together. Dallas Lark isn't going to waltz in and tear it all apart.

Besides, he's apparently Dallas Walker now, and who the hell that is I haven't a clue.

# 7 | Dallas

THE UNIVERSE MUST HATE ME. NO, IT MUST DOWNRIGHT FUCKING despise me.

Of all the concerts in all the world, she has to be at mine. In fucking Denver of all places. Literally the last place in the universe I would expect to see her.

My mind can't stop replaying our exchange. Or how lovingly that dress clung to her mouthwatering curves. Seeing her conjured up memories I keep firmly locked in the box of Robyn that I never open. Ever.

Seeing her unexpectedly reminded me of the first time I ever laid eyes on her and practically transported me back in time.

"God, I love this song," she'd announced the night we met. "Come dance with me."

She'd grabbed my hand with surprising strength for a petite redhead who couldn't have weighed a hundred pounds soaking wet. She had the kind of raspy voice that instantly made you think of dirty talk. Or maybe that was just me. I had just turned sixteen and was basically a hard-on with a pulse.

Gavin had raised his eyebrows and smirked as she dragged me

closer to the truck blaring the music. She shook her sexy ass and sang at the top of her lungs, off key, but proudly off key. I couldn't take my eyes or my hands off her. For several years.

That damn song was on some bootleg CD someone had from a random folk concert they'd gone to. Just to torture me, the same damn song hit it big, spending a fuck-ton of weeks at number one on the mainstream *Billboard* charts around the time Robyn and I ended things. That was some weird poetic full-circle bullshit I still couldn't wrap my head around.

Fucking Lumineers.

I can't let myself get distracted right now, can't afford a pointless trip down messed-up memory lane trying to figure out what happened with the one that got away. I need to focus.

The biggest break of my career is right around the corner—literally—and I have to leave everything I have out on the stage. I don't have time to get caught up in memories that don't matter. No matter how damn beautiful they are.

I have no idea what's gotten into me. Except the overwhelming desire to be alone with her, to feed her pancakes and then . . . I really can't go there right now. And yet, here I am.

"So the redhead from Midnight Bay. You're acquainted with her?" Mandy's words snap my attention back to the present. Her question is innocent enough—but the images it conjures aren't.

I have been buried deep inside Robyn Breeland's body while she came around my cock. I've felt the pulsating waves of ecstasy radiating from the writhing figure that fit perfectly in my arms. I was her first. And her second and third and we lost count after a year.

"Yeah. She's from Amarillo. You could say we're acquainted." To put it mildly.

"Well, relax on mooning around after the liquor girl when fans are around. We're promoting you as a single guy looking for the right girl. Fans don't want to see you tripping over yourself for some scrawny nobody."

There is venom in her voice. I frown at her as I tune my guitar. "She's not nobody. She's a girl I dated in high school. She's a friend." She's a C-cup, too, so I'd hardly call her scrawny, but whatever.

Mandy's eyes practically bug out of her head. "Are you kidding me?" Before I answer she mumbles something under her breath about "the fucking odds."

"No. I'm not. It's not that big of a deal. So she works for the tour sponsor." I shrug to convince her I believe this. Or maybe to convince myself. At this point I'm not sure.

"Well, that's just great, Dallas. Go enjoy your show." She throws a hand out toward the stage. "It'll probably be your last one on this tour."

Wait. *What?* I tell myself I must've misunderstood her.

"Why? Is there some rule about fraternization among sponsors and artists?"

She glares at me like I'm the biggest moron on the planet.

"No," she answers slowly. "There is an unspoken understanding about Jase Wade getting what he wants."

"You lost me."

Mandy nods. "That girl is only on this tour because Wade wants her to be. You think she's earned enough respect at her company to head up the marketing campaign for a tour this size?"

I open my mouth to defend Robyn because she really is driven and hardworking and a pretty incredible girl. But before I get a word out in her defense, Mandy continues.

"She's on this tour for one reason and one reason only." My manager goes back to texting after gesturing with manicured fingernails at Robyn blushing beside the stage where Jase Wade is whispering something in her ear. "She's here because he requested her."

*Motherfucker.*

Jase Wade either has brass balls or is just a complete and total arrogant asshole. Maybe both. I heard him telling half a dozen groupies he'd show them his tour bus after the show. I'm pretty sure that's not all he plans to show them. I can't help but wonder if he's in so tight with Midnight Bay that he could honestly just request Robyn to be sent to him like a high-priced escort.

"Lose the hat," Mandy commands, interrupting my internal temper tantrum.

"Excuse me?"

Mandy flicks her hand beside her forehead. "That hat. Lose it. You can't wear it for the show."

I stare at her for several seconds in an attempt to determine if she's serious. She is.

"And why's that?"

Huffing out an impatient breath as if I'm the one making ridiculous requests, she snatches my hat off my head.

"What the—"

"Because. Jase Wade wears a cowboy hat. It's his thing. He throws it to a fan at the end of the show and it's a huge deal. Here. Just throw on one of the ball caps from the sponsor. They sent a box of them over."

She tosses my hat onto a stack of empty crates and retrieves a black Midnight Bay trucker hat with neon blue writing on it. I frown when she hands it to me.

"You're serious about this?"

She nods as I place the hat on my head and adjust the bill. "I am. This isn't a game, Dallas. You want to stay on this tour? You don't get in his way, don't steal his thunder, and do not encroach on his territory."

Right. I'll have no problem keeping my distance from his "territory."

As long as understands Robyn isn't a part of it.

"How the hell are you, Denver?"

The amphitheater isn't packed yet, but it's filling up quickly. I adjust my in ears and I wave an arm as Ty lets loose a riff on his guitar. Lex pounds the drums hard enough that I have to shout into the mic. We've found a rhythm for the most part, touring together for the past couple of months. But Lexington Wilks doesn't have half the skill that Gavin Garrison does and yet he wants twice the attention.

"I'm Dallas Walker and we're gonna play some music for y'all tonight. We hope you like it."

*I'm Dallas Lark and I have no idea who the fuck I'm trying to kid.*

My family surname mocks me from my inner right forearm when I let the first few chords of "Better to Burn" rip.

Fake, it says. Traitor. Liar.

The label thought the name Dallas Walker had a nicer ring to it so after the unsigned artists tour, they dropped my last name as if were an unwanted appendage that could be hacked off.

I belt out a song my sister wrote and try to engage the audience. I don't think about how much I wish I could glance over and see her playing her fiddle next to me. And I don't nod to the drummer who I know always has my back. My sister and that drummer aren't here.

Trying my best not to pay attention to the fact that I haven't written a complete song in nearly three years, I make eye contact with a few women in the front row. One gives me a huge smile and holds up her phone so I wink.

With every song, the seats continue to fill and all I can think is *Holy shit. This is my life.*

It's surreal, the way the lights glow against the jagged outcrops. The crowd is rising up in front of me and it's as if the amphitheater itself just appeared in the middle of the rocks.

It feels . . . bigger than me.

Singing my sister's lyrics in this setting brings my past into my present. I can almost feel her here onstage with me, just as I can sometimes feel my parents and my grandparents even though they're gone. They live on in me—this gift they gave me allowing me to live my dream keeps them alive as long as I'm playing.

No matter how confident I seem on the outside, on the inside there was always this fear—this voice of self-doubt that said I'd never make it and that I should've just settled down in Amarillo and gotten a regular job like the rest of the world. But when I hear a few girls in the front singing along with some of my songs, and the stubborn spirit of the men who raised me fills my soul, the music takes over. The energy from the audience and the amphitheater is alive, fueling the show I put on. By the time I finish my set to a stadium full of applause, I can't hear that voice of self-doubt anymore.

# 8 | Robyn

THERE SHOULD BE A RULE ABOUT EX-BOYFRIENDS. THEY SHOULD have to get fat. Or bald. Or just . . . boring. Something.

They should not be allowed to become sexy country music singers who put their perfect bodies on display while singing seductive ballads on stage night after night.

Seriously.

His voice booms through the amphitheater like a seductive lightning show. Crew members chat around me, equipment is moved from one place to another, vendors bring in more booze, but all I hear is him. The man who used to sing just for me. The one who let me belt out my favorite songs in the car as loud as my heart desired.

The hypnotic sound of his voice lures me toward the stage, where I stand captivated through the first half of his set.

After Dallas's first few songs, I do my best to shake off the dream-like reverie his singing caused and return to the Midnight Bay display to make sure fans are still getting pictures with the Jase Wade cutout and the lit-up bottles. They made one for Dallas, too; it's to the right of the display and while there aren't as many people stopping to take a photo with it, the ones who do are female. And gorgeous. And making entirely audible comments about his ass in those jeans and how sexy and intense his eyes are.

After roughly the fifteenth comment about Dallas, I can't take much more.

"What do you say we just pack it up?" I smile at Katie and Drew. "I think we're good for tonight."

Katie gives me a knowing half smile. I'd never said much about my personal life, but one drunken night in my office a few days ago I poured most of my heart right out. All over the place.

"How about Drew and I handle the tear-down? See you back at the room?"

I glance up at the stage, where Jase is performing his last number. I should stay. I should stay and schmooze because it's my job. But I just . . . can't.

I haven't told Katie about Dallas's enticing pancake offer and I'm not going to. Because I'm not meeting up with him tonight.

"Are you sure?"

Katie nods and shoos me with her hand. "Get out of here. Drew and I have everything under control."

"You're positive?"

"We are." She nods at me again. "Pinky swear. We're going to check out what Denver nightlife has to offer anyways. Don't wait up."

"Don't forget we have an early flight tomorrow. I'll take a cab and y'all can have the rental car to haul the display in."

"Got it," Katie says. "Now, go, before Wade struts out here and tries to lure you onto his bus of dirty debauchery."

I giggle as I leave, but the sad truth is, I can't even remember what dirty debauchery looks like. My mom got sick while I was in college and taking care of her plus landing the internship at Midnight Bay took up a lot of my time. Even once my mom was healthy, I was hired full-time at the distillery so I threw myself into my job—attending every event, catering to the needs of every potential celebrity endorser, and sitting in on strategy meetings that ran well past the hour the company was named for. I haven't had a lot of time for dating, much less debauchery.

It will all be worth it one day. At least that's what I keep telling myself. Sacrificing my social life for my career will pay off eventually. Once I'm settled into my plush corner office, I will find time to get a life if it kills me.

As I ride back to my hotel in a cab, I hear my mom's voice in my head.

*"Robyn, have you eaten? Are you getting enough rest? Have you lost weight?"*

I take decent care of myself. I jog three miles every morning. I make healthy food choices. I get as much sleep as my job allows, which, okay, isn't a ton. Surely I'll live long enough to see the fruits of my labor. Despite my mother's constant concerns.

But then there's another voice in my head.

My dad's.

Before an accident on the oil rig where he worked took him from us my senior year of high school, he had these little sayings. He loved Yogi Berra, used to quote him all the time. I didn't know much about Yogi except that he played for the Yankees. But after my dad died, I online-searched him. Like my dad, he had this charmingly innocuous way of giving advice.

*"You have to be careful if you don't know where you're going, Pete. You might wind up someplace else."*

My dad also called me Pistol Pete because I was kind of a wild child when I was little. I blame the red hair. As I got older he dropped the Pistol and just called me Pete. I can't even count the number of times I had to explain that when I had a friend over.

With my dad, well, Yogi's advice constantly in mind, I set my goals for myself extremely high. In high school, I was the valedictorian on my way to college. In college I was president of Pi Beta Phi and made damn sure we won the award for the most community service. I worked my ass off to get the marketing internship with Midnight Bay and once they hired me full-time I set my sights on a promotion.

That's my thing. I know where I'm going.

"*There's Robyn Breeland*," people say when I walk down the street. "*That girl knows where she's going.*"

Okay, so maybe they don't say it *out loud,* necessarily. It's enough that I know.

Or at least, I usually do.

When the cabdriver pulls up to the Hyatt Regency, I don't get out right away. I weigh my options.

Pancakes with Dallas or lying in bed staring at the ceiling all night wondering how long he sat at that diner alone.

Neither option is particularly appealing. But at least with one of them I might actually get some sleep tonight.

"Um, did we happen to pass a diner on our way here?"

"A diner?" The driver turns in his seat to face me. He's attractive, younger than I first realized. His head is shaved and there are tattoos on his arms that look like military insignia but it's too dark to be able to tell for sure.

"Um, yeah. A friend of mine said there was a diner near the amphitheater where you picked me up and I was thinking of meeting him there instead of calling it a night. Would that be okay?"

He shrugs. "It's your dime, lady. But there are two diners between here and the amphitheater."

Crap.

"Is one of them open all night by chance?"

"That'd be Rosa's. You want me to take you?"

*Do I? Should I?*

My head says sure. My heart is too pissed at me to even weigh in right now. I pray for a sign. Usually I look for them in songs on the radio or street names. But tonight the radio is off, and I haven't paid any attention to the street names. So I go with my gut instincts.

"Sure. That'd be great."


*I* *should've changed clothes.*

It's the only thought I can hold on to as the cabdriver drops me in front of Rosa's Diner, a small fifties-themed place tucked between a run-down hardware store and an all-night pharmacy.

For God's sakes, I still have my Kickin' Up Crazy tour sponsor pass dangling from the Midnight Bay lanyard around my neck.

*Nice, Robyn. Very sexy.*

I yank it off and shove it in my purse knowing that I should not care about being sexy. This is just pancakes with an old friend. An old friend who might not even show.

Just as I whip out my compact to check my makeup, I see him out of the corner of my eye. Dallas beat me here, probably because I took a twenty-five-minute detour of indecisiveness. Snapping the compact shut, I pace for a few minutes.

"*It's not a big deal, Robyn. Stop acting like a teenager having lunch with the varsity quarterback. It's just Dallas,*" I whisper-yell at myself. "*You're being ridiculous. Cut it out.*"

I close my eyes and take a deep breath. I don't know why, but it feels like this particular decision is much grander than its outcome warrants.

It's pancakes. He's a friend. No big.

But as I open the diner door and a bell chimes overhead, his eyes meet mine and the moment feels monumental. I check the steel cage I erected around my heart the moment I learned he was going to be on this tour. Seems fairly sound, no major breaches so far. That I can feel anyway.

I give Dallas Lark the best I-am-so-over-you, this-is-totally-casual-and-it's-all-good-in-the-neighborhood smile that I can.

His answering smirk tells me that one thing definitely hasn't changed—even after all this time.

I'm still a crappy liar.

# 9 | Dallas

The way I see it, I have two options.

Freeze Robyn out the way I've tried to do since she dumped my ass three years ago, or man up and accept the fact that I'm glad to see her on this tour.

Sitting alone in a diner wondering if she'll show, I decide to quit being a pussy and let go of the anger and confusion I've held on to for so long. She ended things for one reason or another, reasons I may never know, and I have to shove my macho bullshit aside and deal with that like an adult.

I drum my fingers on the table impatiently while I wait.

*"Patience, Dallas,"* my granddad used to say when he was first teaching me to play the guitar. I'd get so damn frustrated when my fingers wouldn't cooperate. *"The music isn't going anywhere,"* he'd remind me. *"Be patient with it, with yourself."*

I've just made up my mind to relax and let her know that I've put our past behind me when she breezes into the diner. A bell chimes at the door and all the progress I've made vanishes like a figment of my imagination.

Robyn Breeland is the kind of woman who steals your breath away just by entering a room and gifting you with a smile.

I shouldn't be surprised—she's pretty much always had this heart-stopping effect on me. But I thought the high from tonight's show might curtail my reaction to her a bit.

It didn't.

"Hey," I say, standing to greet her. "You made it."

"You know me," she says with a shrug. "Can't resist pancakes."

I fake a wounded look. "And here I was telling myself you might've come for the company."

I add "come" to my mental list of words not to say around Robyn, for my dick's sake. He has some cherished memories of her that are fairly easy to evoke.

Robyn blushes as if she might be thinking something along the same lines.

"It's good to see you, Dallas." She says it like she means it and I grin like a lovesick jackass when she barely lets me give her a one-armed hug before we slide into the booth. "And I caught part of your show tonight. The crowd seemed really into 'Better to Burn.' I read that it's been getting some radio play, which is great, right?"

I nod at an approaching waitress and avoid Robyn's eyes. If I look directly at her, she'll see the truth burning in them. She always could see right through me.

"Yeah, Dixie wrote that one. It's doing well."

Thankfully before Robyn can inquire any further into my song-writing, a waitress comes over to take our order.

"What'll it be, kids?" Our waitress's name is Kay and she has pens stuck in her hair, her shirt pocket, and her apron. Maybe if I kept pens handy like that I'd actually get a decent lyric or two written.

"The blueberry oatmeal pancakes and an orange juice, please," Robyn answers after barely glancing at the menu.

"I'll have the double bacon cheeseburger with loaded cheese fries and a large Coke."

"Holy cardiac arrest on a plate." Robyn reaches for the waitress before she turns away. "He was just kidding. He'll have the black and blue steak salad with the dressing on the side and a Diet Coke."

My mouth drops open and I am literally at a loss for words. Kay looks to me for confirmation. I shrug because what else can I do? Throw a tantrum and demand my fucking cheeseburger? That seems like a good way to make Robyn regret meeting me here.

Once Kay has corrected my order on her notepad and walked away, I make a face at Robyn. "Well, that was . . . emasculating. Thank you."

She bites her lower lip and creases appear in her smooth forehead. "Are you trying to kick the bucket before thirty or what? Your grandfather just had a fatal heart attack, which probably means heart disease runs in your family. So maybe you should, I don't know, have something other than a cow topped with a pig dipped in grease for dinner."

"Well, when you put it that way, sure, Robyn. A salad sounds super filling. Can't wait."

She grins and a dimple I used to have a habit of kissing every time I saw her pops out in her left cheek. "It will be. Get a glass of water, too. Drink the entire glass before your meal arrives and you'll be full in no time without all that trans fat clogging your arteries. And if that doesn't work, I might even let you have one of my pancakes."

"Since when are you so health conscious? God, you'd freak out if you saw the way we eat on the road. Half my meals have come from places with wheels and a walk-up window."

She cringes. "I wondered about that. Not that you look bad or anything, just, um, I don't know . . . tired, maybe."

I arch an eyebrow at her. "I look tired? Did I look tired onstage?"

She shakes her head. "No. You looked great onstage. I mean, you know, like you're supposed to look." She blushes again and all sorts of images run through my mind. I want to tell her she looks great. And that she'd look even more great naked in my bed. But that would not be appropriate. At all.

"Well, thank you. I think."

Robyn lets out a loud breath. "I just meant that when I walked in here I noticed you had dark circles under your eyes and you obviously haven't shaved in a while. I know you've been on the road even before this tour and I wondered if you were taking care of yourself. That's all."

"Ah." I nod and contemplate the many hints she's thrown at me. "How did you know I'd been on the road before this? Dixie tell you?"

"Uh, no. Not exactly." The rose-colored hue deepens on her creamy cheeks and I ache to see it on other parts of her body. When Robyn blushes, she blushes all over. "I had to do research for my job, because of the sponsorship. It was on your website and social media stuff. Plus I'm an All Grown Up fan and I saw that you were touring with them. I just didn't make the connection and realize you were going by Dallas *Walker* now until the new Kickin' Up Crazy tour promo materials showed up at my office."

"If you ask me to get Afton Tate's autograph for you, I'm going to be seriously offended."

The tension that's been holding Robyn rigid finally eases and I grin.

"Well . . . Christmas *is* just a few months away, so if you wanted to get me something, that'd be an excellent gift."

I let out a low chuckle. "I'll see what I can do. But if you keep hijacking my food orders, I'm going to reconsider giving you anything at all."

"I might survive," she says without cracking a smile. "And if you let me order for you more often, you might, too."

I can't stop watching her eat. The way she cuts her pancakes into cute little squares and slides them around in circles in the syrup before bringing her fork to her full pouty red lips is like foreplay I can't get enough of. She's letting out these tiny little moans with each bite and I'm rock hard beneath the table.

She's obviously trying to kill me.

Except, she doesn't even seem to notice the effect her carnal seduction is having on me.

"You have to try these," she says, her bright eyes shining with excitement. "Seriously."

My steak salad thing wasn't terrible, which was surprising. But I am still hungry. Fucking starved, actually. But not for food.

"Sure. I basically had grass for dinner, so why not add some oats to it," I say, teasing her just a little because I know she can take it. "Maybe I'll sprout bunny ears and a fucking tail."

"Here. Open up," she commands, aiming a forkful of pancake squares dripping with syrup my way.

I do as I'm told and she presses forward into my mouth.

If any other woman on the planet ordered for me and then hand-fed me over the table in a public place, I would bail out before she could blink twice. But this is Robyn . . . and Robyn is . . . special to me. So I guess part of the special privileges package includes allowing her to do whatever she wants to me. And I have been a spectacular asshole version of myself the last few times I've seen her, so I owe her this much.

"So? Good, right? And they're gluten-free." Her face is lit up with excitement as she waits for my response, but I'm too focused on her to really pay attention to what was in my mouth. My train of thought has derailed into a dirty part of town and all I want in my mouth is her.

"Not bad," I tell her as I swallow. "I have no clue what gluten is and they're not as good as Nana's were, but they aren't completely disgusting."

"True," she says, nodding in agreement. "But no one could top Nana. They'd be crazy to even try."

The mention of Nana prompts Robyn to offer her condolences again about my grandfather passing and we reminisce for a few minutes about meals we'd shared when she'd come over, before I can't keep quiet anymore.

"So . . . you and Wade. There something going on there I should know about?" He mentioned her a few times after the show and I saw them during the meet-and-greets. The way he watched her like he was stalking prey put my blood pressure at a seriously nuclear level.

Other than the shit in my head, there's no segue that leads me to blurt this out and I can plainly see the surprise on her face at my invasive inquiry.

Her eyes narrow as the surprise turns to anger.

"That *you* need to know about?" She lowers her fork and leans back in her seat. "Tell me, why exactly would *you* need to know if there was anything going on with me and Jase Wade?"

I know one thing. I fucking hate the way his name sounds in her mouth.

"Well," I begin, sitting up straighter and clearing my throat. "For one, I'm on tour with him. And for two, I—"

"Mom! Oh my God! Mom, look! That's him! That's Dallas Walker!"

Hearing my name—well, part of it at least—I turn to see a group of girls who appear to be around twelve assaulting their moms with the announcement. A few of them have their cell phones out and are already heading this way.

Robyn looks as if she just remembered there were other people on the planet with us.

"Can I have your autograph?" A blue-eyed blonde with a pink-streaked side braid hands me her iPad mini in a Hello Kitty case and a stylus. My how times are changing. So much for napkins and Bics.

"Of course you can, darlin'. What's your name, pretty girl?"

"Rebecca," she says, smiling at me with bright pink braces. Girl likes pink apparently. "I play guitar, too."

"Do you now? That's awesome. I—"

"I am so sorry, Mr. Walker," a woman interrupts as I'm signing Rebecca's tablet. "We were just at the concert and the girls convinced us to stop in for cheese fries. I told them to leave you be, but they—"

"It's fine. Really." I hand Rebecca's tablet back and a few others hand their items over to be signed. "I've always wanted to meet my prettiest fans. And here they are." I wink at the group and giggles fill the diner.

Five concert tickets, two iPad minis, and a Rosa's Diner menu later, I've signed and smiled and had my picture taken to their hearts' content. The two moms thanked me profusely. One of them slipped me her number.

"Looks like you have that effect on women of all ages," Robyn mutters under her breath. "Well, most of them." She nods to a girl lagging behind the group.

She seemed shy, more reserved than the others, and she didn't hand me anything to sign. Her dark curly hair in a low ponytail reminds me so much of Dixie, of how she had to wear my hand-me-downs, of how withdrawn she was after mom and dad died, and how I swore to myself that somehow, one day, I would make it better, that it's almost painful to look at her.

"Can I sign something for you, sweetheart?" I ask her once the other girls have followed the two women with them toward the door.

She regards me warily, like I might bite. Then she shrugs, clearly not as impressed with me as the rest of the group was.

"Actually I'm more of a Jase Wade fan. But thanks. Great show tonight." With that, she turns and leaves and I gape at Robyn. Who immediately bursts out in hysterical laughter.

"She just . . . totally . . . put . . . in your place," she barely chokes out.

"Nice. Sheesh. And here I was finally feeling better about not writing and Dixie junior goes and puts me down."

Robyn sobers almost instantly. "You haven't been writing? But what about the songs you sang tonight?"

I cringe. I hadn't meant to throw myself a pity party.

I grab a salt shaker and spin it back and forth between my hands. "Egh. Some of it was old stuff. I threw in a few covers, and Dixie wrote 'Better to Burn.'"

"So . . . how long has it been since you've actually written anything?" The concern in her voice matches the way her eyes are watching me.

I focus on my salt shaker.

"A while. Six months maybe. More since I've actually written a full song. The band was working on one. Leaving Amarillo, I mean."

I hate that I have to clarify because I have a new band now. Feels like infidelity somehow. "But we never got the chance to finish it."

"I'm sorry to hear that." She uses the same tone she used to say she was sorry about Papa's passing. I finally look into her eyes and see the genuine sympathy in them.

Robyn cares about me. I know this. I've always known this. I care about her, too, I do. As much as the only other women I've ever cared about, which is a short list limited to my mom, Nana, and little sister. But my life isn't going to be the kind that allows for a wife and two kids and a picket fence, and she deserves that. So it's time I got to the point, told her we're cool and I'm going to put my big-boy pants on and call it a night, despite my dick's dire protest.

"You don't want to talk about it, I'm guessing."

"No. I don't. I actually asked you here because I wanted to let you know I'm going to do my best impression of a grown-up while we're on this tour together. We both have jobs to do so let's just do them." Something akin to pain flashes in her eyes and I hate that my self-loathing bullshit is messing up our time together. I know that it's almost over and I don't want to end on a pissed-off note. "Sorry. It's just that the writing—or lack thereof—is kind of a hot button issue right now. Mandy's all over me about it, the label wants a single that can drop alongside the tour, and the goal is to launch an album immediately after so that I can headline my own tour."

"Mandy's all over you all right," Robyn says without looking at me.

"What?"

Her eyes cut to mine. "Don't act like you don't notice, *Superstar*."

Her lips are pressed together tightly and her arms are folded over her chest, forcing her ample breasts up just enough to shift my focus for a second.

I chuckle lightly, but the thoughts in my head are dark and dirty. God I get off on her jealousy.

I've never really seen it before, not like this. In high school everyone knew we were together, and while a stray cheerleader might have offered to do me a *favor* from time to time, I ignored them and Robyn knew I ignored them.

I'll happily ease her mind about Mandy as well, but that's a two-way street I don't plan to travel alone. "You never answered my question about Wade."

Kay places our check on the table and I lift it without taking my gaze from Robyn's.

"And I'm not going to. Like you said, we both have jobs to do. I think we need to set some boundaries since we're going to be working together."

"Boundaries?" I fish a twenty and two fives out of my wallet. "Such as?"

"Appropriate topics of conversation, for starters. No more late night dinner dates, especially not where you pay as if we're on a date. And no more looking at me like you're . . ."

My mouth quirks up on one side. "Like I'm what, darlin'?"

"You know," she hisses from across the table. "Stop it. Stop with the drawl and the darlin' and the smoldery looks."

"Or else?"

"We have a history, Dallas. And this isn't easy for me, okay? There. I said it. This isn't easy and I have to deal with it professionally or risk a career I've worked really hard for. You have no idea what I've sacrificed to get where I am. So stop toying with me for your own amusement. We've hurt each other enough for one lifetime, don't you think?"

# 10 | Robyn

THIRTY-THREE MINUTES.

That's how long I made it before I said everything that I shouldn't have. *Loudly.* And in a public place.

Fabulous.

At least I finished my pancakes before making a complete fool of myself. I can't even look at him. He already put enough cash on top of the ticket for the bill and a generous tip so all I can do is slide out of the booth, dragging my dignity along with me. Pretty sure it's somewhere around my ankles near the same location where Dallas Lark used to manage to relocate my panties.

"Robyn," he calls out, but I don't stop. I make my way out of the diner, clutching my purse for dear life, and try to hail a cab.

It's nearing midnight and cabs aren't exactly plentiful in this partially deserted area. I take out my cell phone and am in the middle of asking Siri where the nearest cab company is, which she hears as lab testing company because she's an evil bitch that likes to screw with me.

"Cab company!" I'm screaming into my phone, enunciating as much as humanly possible, when I feel a hand on my shoulder.

"Robyn." His voice is rich and gravelly and warms my insides like a shot of whiskey. Damn it.

As if our little scene isn't quite dramatic enough for Mother Nature's liking, fat drops of rain start to splat down between us.

"Great. That's just fucking great," I practically yell.

"Tell me what you've sacrificed. I want to know," Dallas says evenly, completely unfazed by my obvious psychotic break. "Because I know a thing or two about sacrifice myself. But I can tell you this much, I would never sacrifice my dignity and I sure as hell didn't get where I am on my back or by putting anyone else on theirs."

What the hell?

"Excuse me?"

"Mandy. She's my manager. Our relationship is strictly professional, and it will stay that way, regardless of what her intentions may or may not be."

"Okay." I don't want to feel relieved. I shouldn't care. But my tightly wound nerves loosen a fraction.

"Your turn," he informs me, folding his muscular arms over his broad chest.

"My turn for what?"

"To tell me if you're fucking Wade! If that's how you got on this tour, I want you to end it. He's a grade A piece of shit who doesn't give a damn who he—"

Dallas doesn't get to finish his sentence.

Because I slap him. Hard. So hard my hand is still stinging.

Our faces must be matching masks of shock and I see the replay in slow motion. I've never struck another human being in my entire life. And I just slapped the only man I've ever loved with everything I was worth.

"If you ever, *ever*, even *think* to insinuate that I got where I am on my back, I swear to God, Dallas Lark, I will make that seem like a love tap."

I am so immensely infuriated that everything in my line of sight is tinged in red. But more than that, I'm hurt. Hurt that someone I once cared so much for, and still care about more than I'd like to admit, would think that of me. Stitched-up lacerations on my heart that were on their way to being pretty pink scars are opening wide and angry. He didn't invite me here for pancakes to catch up or spend time with me or figure out how to work together or even attempt to make amends. Nope. He's just jealous and arrogant and a raging asshole.

"I didn't mean to insinuate that—"

"Get the hell away from me." I whirl around and step right into a fresh puddle. Great. Wonderful.

"No," Dallas says, pulling me toward him and catching me off guard. "I need you to hear me out."

"What's to hear? You're an arrogant ass and I hate you."

He gives me an infuriating smirk. "No you don't. If that were true, you wouldn't be this pissed."

I struggle to find a reasonable argument to this so I say, "Fuck you, Dallas."

"Yes, please. Come back to the hotel with me. The car service is already here." I yank out of his grasp, causing a painful friction between our skin.

"Ouch."

He pulls me to his chest and my anger is fading, too diluted by his scent and his intensity.

"I'm sorry, baby. I'm so damn sorry," is all he says before kissing me brutally on the mouth. Mine pops open in shock when he pulls back to breathe. His gaze presses into mine as my mind tumbles over itself trying to process the abrupt turn of events. His thumb grazes my cheek gently. "I never meant to hurt you," he says before devouring me again.

And Lord help me, I don't even know which thing he's apologizing for—the past or the present—because I'm melting. The rain, his fiery hot mouth, his hands scorching a trail over my body. I'm drowning in Dallas and I can't stop.

Worse, I don't even want to.

"You taste like maple syrup. I'm never going to be able to look at pancakes the same way again." Dallas's tongue tangles with mine and I can't get enough. We're spiraling quickly out of control. I need to breathe before I pass out.

"Dallas," I mumble against his mouth. "We shouldn't do this. Not here."

The driver can hear us, could glance in the rearview and get an eyeful.

"It's a ten-minute drive to the hotel. I'm probably going to spontaneously combust before then."

I laugh against his lips. "You're a big boy. I think you can handle it."

I slide off his lap, leaving my legs draped over it, though, and lean my head on his shoulder.

"I can't wait to show you just how big of a boy I am, and how well I can handle it."

"Behave yourself," I whisper in the darkness.

"Can't," is all he says, sliding his warm fingers beneath my skirt and between my thighs.

"Dallas." I squirm as he dips beneath my panties.

"I haven't forgotten, baby," he murmurs against my hair. "I remember exactly how tight and hot and wet you are. I remember each and every place you like me to touch you. I am a dying man waiting to hear those sweet whimpers you make when I slide inside you."

I whimper right then, because damn. He feels so good, smells so good, tastes so good. He's familiar but at the same time, new, different from what I remember. Rougher around the edges, broader, and behaving more boldly than he ever has with me.

The boy version from my memories was sweet, polite, and somewhat distant. The grown-up version of Dallas Walker Lark is all hard edges, and intensity—sin wrapped in sugar sprinkled with lust. And I want to savor every single bite.

I am a throbbing, aching, needy mess and everything I should be thinking about—the past, the future, the insurmountable pain that this likely will cause—has fallen away. All I can concentrate on is the pleasure.

Because I know he can give it to me.

I've dated a little here and there when my job allowed. I've even fooled around pretty seriously with a few guys and had a one-night stand with a friend of a friend. But none of them ever managed to make me feel the way Dallas does.

Completely out of control.

I am at his mercy and while I should be terrified, all I feel is the thrill of adrenaline, as if a needle shot him into my veins.

Maybe that's why I can't stop this, because I know this is a sure thing when it comes to orgasms. I'm going to have them, lots of them, and Dallas is going to provide them in reckless abundance as he always has. He's matured a great deal, but some things never change. Thank God.

When he sinks a thick finger into me, curling it forward at just the right spot, I arch my back and cry out. At least there's a glass partition between us and the driver. Because I want to give in. I want to let go and shatter the way only he can make me.

"I hope you're rested, sweet girl," Dallas rasps with damp heat in my ear.

The town blurs by us, the city lights melting like I am in the rain.

"W-what? Why?"

"Because it's going to be a long night."

# 11 | Dallas

I'D BLAME THE PANCAKES, OR THE INTOXICATING COMBINATION OF blueberry and maple syrup that assaulted my senses when I put my mouth on hers, but it's the sweet, sinful taste of Robyn that tosses me carelessly over the edge.

Seeing her tonight—those legs taunting me from beneath her dress, that mouth that spewed those angry declarations, gleaming eyes that told me what she was saying and what she was feeling were two very different things—has brought a man to life inside me that I forgot existed.

I'd invited her out for pancakes to try to make peace, to let her know that I wasn't going to act like an asshole on this tour. She'd fucking slapped me. The sweetest girl I've ever known slapped me hard enough to make my ears ring and I'd never been more turned on in my life.

She said she hated me. Not that she was pissed or still holding a grudge—fucking *hated* me. I knew she didn't mean it, but there was something about the challenge in the words, the defiance. I knew she didn't mean it and I needed to hear that sexy mouth say sweeter words.

I couldn't leave it like that, couldn't leave *her* like that. Years ago I'd let Robyn go, walked away because she'd asked me to. Then I'd behaved like a complete ass afterward. And Robyn, my tough girl, had always just said it was okay. It was fine. She understood. She could handle it.

She could handle anything, always. Nothing rattled her or set her off. Robyn liked to be in control.

But tonight I'd caused her to lose that control, watched her let loose on me and everything I'd held in from the moment I saw her came roaring to the surface, possessing me and propelling my body to hers in a fusion of frustration and lust-filled fantasies come to life.

Tearing at her clothing as we make our way to my hotel room, I have no regrets.

"I want you so fucking bad, Robyn," I tell her, because it's the truth. "I barely made it through that fucking meal."

"You have me," she tells me before sucking my bottom lip into her luscious mouth.

I don't even want to admit to myself how long I've waited for her to say those words.

"Not yet. But I will."

Pulling apart long enough for me to slide my key card through the slot on the door, we both take the opportunity to catch our breath.

The last thing I want to do is to rush this. I want to take my time with her, show her my passionate appreciation for every inch of her body until the sun comes up. But I'm afraid if I give her too much time to think, she'll remember all the reasons why this is a bad idea and the past will become a roadblock we can't overcome.

The second she steps into the room, I pin her against the wall and tear the blazer, jacket, whatever the hell it is, from her shoulders.

Taking advantage of its absence, I fasten my mouth hotly to her neck. The gratifying noises she makes in response send shocks of pleasure through my chest and straight down to my dick.

"You still smell and taste like strawberries." My tongue ventures to the sensitive spot behind her ear that always rendered her boneless in my arms. Thank fuck it still does. "Let's see if you taste the same everywhere else, shall we?"

Either she's cold without the jacket or my words make her shiver. I don't take the time to ask. Instead I drop to my knees with every intention of worshipping her in this position for as long as she can stand, both literally and metaphorically speaking.

"Dallas." There's a wary edge to her voice. She's afraid. I don't blame her. I'm the furthest thing from a safe bet that there is. I'm starved for her and she has to know that by now.

"Shh. I got you, baby. Tonight, I got you."

I can't promise her anything beyond that and we both know it. She doesn't protest when I hook my fingers between the lace and cotton parts of her panties and pull them down. Without a word, she watches me while stepping out of them.

"Good girl," I murmur, placing my mouth on her bare inner thigh.

Her head lolls back, bumping gently against the wall as I tease a circle around her petite folds with my tongue. Though she's certainly trimming a little more these days, her sweet center is nearly the same as I remember. Delicate and delicious. Her scent calls to me, awakens the possessive streak in me. I want to strip her bare and fuck her hard against the window, shouting to everyone in hearing distance that she is motherfucking mine. But that might be frowned upon by the hotel, so I do my best to smother that urge.

Each stroke of my tongue opens her wider for me until I am dead center, lashing relentlessly into her, gripping her ass with flesh-denting fingers while she calls out my name.

Fuck. Yes.

I need more of her, need her spread out on the bed for me, so I stand and lift her in my arms. Her breathless cry drives my efforts as I practically sprint to the bed. Once I've lowered her as gently as I can manage, I divest her of the pretty lace dress that's been taunting me all night. Robyn must sense that my patience is wearing dangerously thin because she unhooks her bra and flings it across the room like a grenade.

"You are so fucking beautiful," I tell her, the words exiting my mouth without my permission. "It shouldn't even be legal to look this fucking delectable naked."

She blushes all over like I'd hoped she would and I want to lick every single flushed inch of skin. Supple breasts tipped with pale pink nipples beg me to devour them. Who am I to deny them?

My mouth descends on the left then the right, and all I can think is *What does she put on her skin to make it taste so fucking sweet?* I don't often indulge in dessert but I'd help myself to an entire meal of Robyn Breeland every single day if my life allowed.

Her fingers rake hard into my hair and she uses the leverage to pull my face to hers.

"Please, Dallas. Please, now." It's a blatant plea and her voice is shaking.

Fuck me running, she's begging.

Robyn is literally begging me to fuck her and I am adrift in a sea of hedonistic pleasure-filled waters I don't know how to navigate. All I can do is give in to my need for her, the need to part, fuck, and fill her right this moment.

My arms wrap her upper body and drag her roughly up the bed. We're on top of the covers but there's no time to remedy this. Robyn's hands pull greedily at my shirt and I help her yank it over my head. It goes the way of her lacy white bra to an unknown corner.

Her fingers deftly begin unfastening my jeans and I can't help but let out a low chuckle at how eager my girl is tonight. We've passed the point of no return and I am so fucking relieved she isn't the type to play games with me or start spouting shit about what this means or change her mind at the last minute.

Her eyes are filled with fiery desire burning brighter by the minute. They drop to my cock when it springs free from my boxer briefs. I kick those to the floor along with my jeans, realizing a second too late that I need my wallet.

"Fuck."

As if she's reading my mind—hell, maybe she is—Robyn twists beneath me and leans over the side of the bed.

"I'll get it," she rasps out.

Her bare ass is like a juicy apple I want to take a bite of. Before I can act on that particular impulse, she's back up and thrusting the condom wrapper at me.

I tear the foil with my teeth and toss it aside once I've plucked the contents out like a precious pearl from an oyster.

"Was it always that big?" Her eyes are round as she watches me roll the latex over myself.

"I'll be careful with you, baby." I part her legs with one hand and I can feel how stiff her body has become. "Promise."

"It's, um, been a while, Dallas. So just, you know. Go easy at first, please."

I nod, knowing my caveman behavior probably scared the shit out of her. Or maybe it really is the size of my dick or the fact that she hasn't had sex in a while. Another possessive surge of testosterone powers through me and I'm suddenly feeling competitive, which is not a sensation I've ever associated with sex. It's not a sport, nor should it be treated like one, and yet, something about her admission makes me want to claim her, imprint myself all over her so that no one else will ever measure up.

"Dallas." Her hands come up to either side of my face. "Stay here, in this moment, with me. Please."

I nod again because I can't seem to find words.

She arches up to brush her lips against mine and the kiss turns dirty in an instant, pulling me down onto her and in the next instant, into her.

*Fuuuuuck.*

I don't know if I thought it or said it out loud.

I forgot this. Somehow in the years of struggling to make music while making ends meet, I forgot how perfectly I fit inside her, how her body was always seemingly molded for mine. It's a tight fit, but the friction only serves to massage my dick while I slide all the way inside.

"Goddammit, Robyn. It's like you were made for me."

She moans into my ear and it only encourages me to keep talking dirty.

"Were you waiting for my cock, baby? Needing me to fill that perfect pretty little pussy of yours, sweetheart? All you had to do was ask."

She rocks hard against me, all requests for taking it easy seemingly forgotten.

"Go deeper, Dallas. I want all of it in deep."

Lord have mercy on my soul, this woman will be the death of me. I ram hard into her and the blunt force of impact shoves a noise from her throat I could hear while being stabbed and die a happy man.

"That's it, good girl. Take it all." I go in deep and hard a few more strokes before I have to back it down or risk embarrassing myself. Even though I didn't volunteer the information, it's been a while for me, too.

Her legs wrap my waist and in an acrobatic move we've never before performed, I lift her up onto my dick and impale her again and again like we're training for a sex triathlon while she clings to my body.

"Oh my God," she moans into my ear. "You feel so good inside me. Don't stop. Please don't stop."

I rake my teeth across her throat because I am really and truly gone from the world of right and wrong and acceptable behavior while fucking.

"I have no intentions of stopping until you beg me to. And maybe not even then."

Her walls clench around me in a quivering throb of warning. She's close.

"Can you take it, Robyn? If I keep on fucking you right through your first orgasm?"

"I don't—" She interrupts herself to let out a moan and grips me tighter. "I don't know."

"Only one way to find out."

With that, I pull out and lower her back onto the mattress. Her expression twists into one that tells me she's unhappy with this development. I let out another low, dark laugh, realizing I can read her mind a little, too.

"Don't pout, pretty girl. I'm going to make it all better."

Sliding my slick erection down her center and back inside of her eases the tension in her facial features. Placing my thumb on her damp clit and my mouth on her left breast I begin the divine torture that is drawing out her orgasm. I rotate fucking, sucking, and circling until she screams my name. Then I move to the right breast and begin again, nipping the tips of her breasts with my teeth just hard enough to hurt.

"Louder, baby. I think there are hotel guests at the end of the hall that still can't hear you."

An incoherent string of supplications for me to stop, don't stop, harder, punctuated by ohmygods and fucks and more of my name slip out of her mouth like adulations she's memorized for this specific occasion.

I'd been confidently assuming I'd make her come at least twice if not more before I took my own release from her body, but I am caught off guard when Robyn's walls begin launching an aggressive assault on my dick. Her pussy becomes a tight fist determined to milk me dry, and I lose myself in the push and the pull of it, coming right along with her as she spirals out into oblivion.

Letting go never felt so good.

# 12 | Robyn

DALLAS COLLAPSES ON MY BARE CHEST, OUR SWEAT-SLICK BODIES melding together like liquefied metal. My previously erected steel façade obviously had some weak areas I forgot to address. Particularly in the area around my vagina, it would seem.

As much as I want to chastise myself for letting this happen, the residual euphoria from being so thoroughly fucked won't allow it.

Life is short and for the most part made up of experiences that fall into two categories: mind-blowing and non-mind-blowing. This one definitely falls into the former, so I can't even bring myself to feel guilty.

"You okay?" Dallas is still catching his breath and so am I, but his voice sounds a lot steadier than mine likely will so I just nod my response. "I'm going to take care of this real quick. Be right back."

He places a chaste kiss on the side of my mouth before hopping out of bed to deal with the condom.

" 'Kay," I mumble in my half-conscious stupor to his bare-assed retreating figure.

We should probably talk, or I should at least reassure him that

I know this wasn't about more than sex. I've known Dallas long enough to know that the moment any talk of feelings enters the equation he'll get all weird and distant on me. That boy spends more time in his own head than anyone I know. Always has.

*He's not a boy anymore,* my subconscious reminds me.

That's for damn sure. The moment I felt his rough stubbled jaw rub against my inner thighs the way I'd been imagining since the first moment I saw him earlier tonight, I knew I was dealing with a much more lethal version of Dallas Lark.

He used to ask permission before doing anything to my body he was anxious to try out but wasn't sure I'd be comfortable with. While that was sweet and considerate of him, this man he's become, one who takes what he wants without asking, is pretty damn hot, too.

I feel the bed shift when he slips back in beside me

I'm shattered. Empty. Drained of all life-sustaining matter.

"Tired, babe?"

I think maybe I grunt something in response. Strong arms wrap around me and I'm cocooned in warmth.

*Beam me up, God. Pretty sure I can die happy now.*

"Sweet dreams, pretty girl," Dallas whispers in my ear.

Maybe I'm already dreaming.

Waking up in a strange hotel room without any clothes on isn't a familiar experience or one I have any requisite protocol for.

My senses come back to me slowly and one at a time.

I'm cold. Naked. And I can hear music playing softly from across the room.

It's still dark outside, but there's a lamp on in the room. I don't see it but I can tell by the golden glow it emits.

My first instinct is to reach for my phone. Not just because that's what I do every morning when I first wake up, but because I'm slightly concerned I might have to call for help.

The décor in the room isn't familiar and just as I contemplate turning to see who's playing music in the barely lit corner, my night comes back to me like a freight train barreling at full speed.

Dallas.

The concert.

The diner.

The slap heard 'round the world.

Okay, maybe just 'round the parking lot at Rosa's Diner, but still.

And holy blueberries on oatmeal pancakes, the sex.

My muscles are sore and relaxed all at once. My entire body feels like it barely survived a Thai massage. Every tension-filled muscle knot has been steamrolled from existence. Naked between expensive hotel sheets I feel sexy and aroused and . . . alone.

I twist to the side as much as my aching body will allow and see Dallas sitting at the table. He's writing furiously while most of his magnificently nude body is blocked by his guitar.

*Hello.*

All of my synapses begin firing away at once, demanding I somehow lure him back to bed. Immediately.

Conflicted emotions swirl into a dangerous storm inside me.

This was a mistake.

This was the hottest night of my life.

I'm going to regret this for the rest of my life.

God, he looks good over there, all bare muscles and music notes.

I want to hear what he's working on.

I shouldn't interrupt him.

Tormented by tumultuously conflicting urges, I rake a hand

through my wild hair—hoping it doesn't look as messy as it feels—and sit up.

I don't want to screw with his process, especially since he mentioned he hadn't been writing. But *day-um*. Why does he have to look so scrumptious? It's like having someone deliver a decadent slice of double chocolate cake drizzled in hot fudge right to your door and telling you all you can do is look at it.

I strain to hear him, but I can't make out the tune or the words he's muttering as he writes.

He's writing.

He said he hasn't written in a while.

Could our night together have inspired a song?

*Stop making this into more than it is.*

Right. Got it. But just in case it was the sex that got his musical mojo flowing, don't I owe it to him, to all people with the ability to hear, to do whatever it takes to make sure he doesn't get blocked again?

That settles it.

If I'm going to regret tonight eventually anyway, I'm going to regret it as much as I possibly can.

# 13 | Dallas

RIGHT AFTER THE MOST AMAZING SEX OF MY LIFE, ROBYN FELL asleep and rolled over onto her side facing away from me. I don't know how long I stared at the smooth curves of her body, her spine, her hip, her shoulder, before growing impossibly hard again. She was resting so peacefully I'd decided not to wake her for round two, but there was too much going on in my head to fall asleep myself.

I'm three verses and a chorus into the most promising song I've written in nearly a year when I hear her stirring in the bed.

Something profoundly fucked-up is happening here and now, and I've decided to ignore it while I still can. But I suspect that after to-night, the inevitable truth will come out whether I want it to or not.

Robyn is more than an old friend, more than an old flame.

She's the one who blows me away and brings me back down only to turn me inside out and send me into a free fall all over again.

She's my muse.

I can't give her what she deserves—the full-time boyfriend, the promise of a picture-perfect life—not without giving up my dreams.

While I once contemplated this back when she ended things be-tween us, I've seen what kind of man I become without music and it isn't pretty.

When my sister went to college in Houston and the band took a breather, I worked in construction for a while—did some roofing with a local contractor. The work was mind-numbing and back-breaking. Night after night I was too tired or too sore to play my guitar. My hands ached and stung with the wrong kinds of callouses. I told myself I'd play a few gigs on my own, but I didn't. I lost the music. I lost myself.

Basically it fucking sucked.

But now the fact that living my dream without Robyn in it would be just as pathetic is staring me in the face and I don't know how to avoid it.

"You're writing," she says softly, barely even loud enough for me to hear.

I scrawl the last lyric, knowing I'll add one more verse later, after I've been inside her again, before I look up.

"Yeah. Couldn't sleep."

She's standing at the edge of the bed with the white sheet wrapped around her and it's like a goddess fell from the heavens and landed in my hotel room.

"Can I hear it?"

"It's not ready yet. Soon, though. Are you traveling with us to Kansas City tomorrow?"

It's my roundabout way of asking her when I'll see her again. Call me a coward, but asking her outright feels like crossing a line I shouldn't. Even after everything that happened tonight.

"Nope," she says with a shrug. "I have to attend an event in Los

Angeles. So you're free of me for a few days. I'll be working both shows weekend after next in the Carolinas, though. And New Orleans and Nashville."

"Ah. Well, I guess I'll try not to inhale too much grease while you're away."

She's coming closer so I set my guitar aside.

"You do that." The words fall from her lips as her eyes flicker to my recently exposed appendage. When she looks up our gazes slam into each other with the force of two Mack trucks behind them.

I need more of her tonight. I don't know how she's going to feel about this. Hell, I don't know how *I'm* going to feel about this. But right now I know that I need more. Neither of us is leaving this room until we are physically unable to seek out any more pleasure from the other.

"Drop the sheet, baby," I command gently. "I need to see you. All of you."

She does so, offering her body up like a sacrifice.

I stare openly, memorizing every inch, every angle and curve in case this is the last time she's laid bare to me this way.

"Dallas, I want—" Her chest rises with an intake of breath I feel like she pulled straight from my lungs.

"Take it." I reach for her, resting my forehead on her stomach and closing my eyes when I make contact with her bare skin. "Whatever you want, it's yours."

I'm completely still when she lifts my chin and straddles my lap.

There's nothing between us, no layer of protection. It's reckless. Risky and pretty damn stupid. But the need to feel her without a barrier is greater than my need for safety or common sense.

She watches me, her eyes seeking permission and telling me that she trusts me. Begging me to be careful with her.

I close mine and let my head fall back so that they don't make any promises I can't keep.

Robyn eases onto me and it's like having my heart ripped from my chest and shoved back in. Her bare breasts brush against my chest, her nipples tightening against my skin. Her pace is torturously slow and my dick begs me to pound into her. But this isn't for me. I let her take what she needs without interfering.

When I open my eyes as much as I can manage, I see the contentment etched into her beautiful face. She begins to move faster, sinking her teeth into her bottom lip, and I hold on to my restraint with a white-knuckle grip. The veins in my neck are probably straining hard enough to burst.

"I'm on the pill," Robyn whispers in my ear. "You can let go."

"You first."

An incoherent word, maybe a curse or maybe my name, slips past my ear and she slams down harder and harder, pushing me nearly past my breaking point.

I almost don't make it, but thank fuck she falls apart around my cock, stiffening then trembling on top of me.

I stand, lifting her limp body and carrying her to the bed.

Once I've lowered her gently on the mattress, she gapes at my still fully hard length. "Oh God, Dallas. You didn't . . . I don't know if I can take any more."

"Oh I think you can, sweetheart. Besides . . . only one way to find out."

I remain standing and run my fingertips down the length of her left foot. Once I reach her ankle, I massage my way to her inner thigh before starting over on the right side, this time placing openmouthed kisses in the trail left by my hands.

Robyn moans when I reach the apex of her thighs with my tongue.

"You taste so damn sweet. Always have, always will." The kisses I place on her swollen center are gentle at first. Almost innocent aside from the location. But the more she writhes beneath me, the less I'm able to control myself.

She's throbbing against my mouth, causing me to ache to be back inside her. I need to be inside her again, need to feel that cresting wave hit hard and break over my cock. But I want to prolong the sensations for as long as I possibly can.

Placing one last hard lick up the length of her pulsating flesh, I inhale her scent as deeply as my body will allow and then stand upright. Taking each of Robyn's ankles, I place them on either of my shoulders and stroke her center with my dick.

"D-Dallas," she moans on a shaky breath.

"I got you, sweetheart." My view is fucking incredible as I watch my cock disappear into her tight, wet heat. Her entire body bucks from the intrusion but I'm done going slow, done taking it easy on her. I want to soak up every second with her that I can in case this is all I ever get. "I got you."

I need every last ounce of pleasure she can give me right now. So I take it.

My alarm is ducks quacking today. I have to change it up from time to time so I don't become immune to it. The irritating sound propels me upright in an attempt to find the offensive device.

Once I locate it and hit snooze, I realize I'm alone. The bed is empty beside me. Robyn's purse is gone and so is she. Glancing back at my phone I realize it's 7:45 in the morning. So either she had to catch an earlier flight than mine, or she hightailed it out of here as soon as I passed out.

I replay last night's events to determine if I might've done something to make her upset. After multiple orgasms, she was fairly malleable in my arms.

Our last conversation comes back to me—the whispered one we had in the darkness just before we fell asleep.

I yawned, a huge, wide-mouthed, groaning, back-stretching yawn, and Robyn giggled in my arms.

"Did I wear you out, Grandpa?"

"Cute. No, but you slept for several hours, thank you very much. I stayed up and wrote."

"Well, if it makes you feel any better, I'm probably going to walk with a limp tomorrow."

I grinned into her hair. "Fuck yeah, that makes me feel better."

"I told you it had been a while. I didn't know you had a sex marathon in mind."

I tightened my grip around her body. "Me, either. Two in one night's not something I normally do."

"No? No all-night orgies with groupies then?"

For some reason, her tone pissed me off. Or maybe it was the accusation itself. "I don't sleep with groupies."

Robyn twisted in my arms so that she could face me. "Seriously? Never?"

"Never. Is that really what you think of me? That I'm just in this to hook up with my fans?"

She stared into my eyes for a full minute before answering. "No," she said slowly. "But I think you're a human being and most guys wouldn't be able to resist a ton of girls throwing themselves at them night after night."

"I'm not most guys, sweetheart. You know this."

She settled back into my arms, nestling her pert little ass against me in a way that nearly necessitated a third round. "I'm glad."

"I'm still me, Robyn. No matter what's changed between us, I'm still me."

That was it, the last conversation we'd had before I passed out. I couldn't figure which part had sent her running.

But I damn sure intend to find out.

# 14 | Robyn

"I'M STILL ME," HE'D SAID BEFORE FALLING ASLEEP.

I'd been about to snuggle down into that blissful murkiness of sleepy time when he'd said it.

No matter how much he'd changed, Dallas was still Dallas. And maybe I had a college degree and a big-girl job, but I was still the same girl he couldn't forgive. I'd been an idiot, pushed him away so that he wouldn't let my mom's illness stop him from chasing his dreams. By the time I realized how unfair it was and how much I needed him, the damage was done and Dallas Lark had moved on.

I was the one who'd needed space, but Dallas ended up being the one to walk away for good.

Forget being on the same page; Dallas and I had been reading entirely different books when it came to our relationship. In mine, there was a happily ever after that involved making a life together. He wasn't just in my story—he was my story. In his I was merely a chapter.

*I'm still me.*

I wanted to smack myself. Hard. Of course he was still him. And he'd still walk away, dragging my battered heart behind him while I watched him leave. I'd hurt him, deeply. And I'd live with that regret for the rest of my life. He'd still be the guy who chose music over me, over us. He had even more reason to now that he was on this tour.

I waited there in his arms, forcing my steel walls back up between us while he drifted into unconsciousness. Once his breathing was deep and the light rumble of a snore settled into a steady rhythm, I slipped out of his bed and gathered my things as quietly as I could. Dressing quickly, I watched him, memorizing that peaceful look on his handsome face and promising myself this was a one-time thing. I wasn't going to obsess over it. It was a life experience, one I didn't regret but knew I'd be crazy to repeat.

I chanced one last look as I left, before I shut the door completely. The light from the hotel hallway sliced across him and he looked so . . . alone.

I closed the door and told myself this was for the best. What would having breakfast together or sharing a cab to the airport change? Nothing, that's what.

This time, I'd been the one to leave. For the sake of my sanity and my heart, I could never fall into bed with Dallas Lark again. Here I'd been hoping that one day we could be friends, and our first actual attempt turns into . . . I don't even know what. I've never been a fuck-buddy type of girl. Not that I don't see the appeal to an exclusively physical mutually beneficial relationship, because I do. But it always seemed like a silly distraction, a waste of time that could be better spent finding something stable long term. But that, last night . . . I may not know exactly what it was, but it sure as hell wasn't a waste of time.

I couldn't stop thinking of him, of the way he looked at me, the smell of him, the way his calloused fingers felt on my skin, that stubble on his jaw, and dear Lord in Heaven, those sexy as sin whispered confessions. But now I was in Los Angeles getting ready for the National Business Bureau's award ceremony, where I was accepting the award for Most Successful Family Run Business for Midnight Bay and I needed to focus. I called Katie to run through the reminders for the Kickin' Up Crazy show she was handling in Kansas City and she wasn't going to just let it go. Even though I was desperately trying to.

"Come on, Robyn. You never came back to the room last night. You expect me to believe the two of you spent the night reminiscing about the good old days? Have a sing-along, did you?"

I laugh at Katie's pouting. I did get to hear him sing a little and her words conjure the erotic memory but I shake it off the best that I can. "No sing-alongs."

I'm not like her. I didn't have a lot of female friends growing up. I had Dixie, but she definitely didn't want to hear about my sexual exploits with her brother. I had sorority sisters in college but mostly I kept my private business to myself.

"You're really not going to give me any details?" Katie whines as I step into my four-inch heels.

I can already tell how badly my feet are going to hurt later. Between these shoes and my night with Dallas, I'm starting to wonder if maybe I'm a masochist.

"I'm going to give you lots of details. That's why I called."

She squeals and I grin wickedly in the mirror above the bathroom sink.

"First, make sure the VIP sections are spaced far enough apart for separate lines. Jase's line will be crazy long so make sure it doesn't interfere with any of the entrances or exits or crowd flow into the amphitheater. Second, make sure you upload the pictures Drew takes to the cloud so that I can access them and get them to the social media guys. Third—"

"You are no fun," Katie interrupts flatly.

"I was plenty of fun last night. Today is about business."

"I don't think I like you anymore." There's a smile in her voice so I'm not too worried.

"Yeah, yeah. You love me. Anyway, I need to go but I'll text you the rest, okay?"

"Got it." Katie's quiet for a moment before she says, "Hey, Robyn?"

"Yeah?" I give my hair one last tousle with my free hand.

"Um, it really is none of my business. And I am totally not judging you because I don't think a girl in the world would've been able to turn that guy down after the show he put on last night, but . . ."

I freeze where I'm standing, hand still in my hair, while I wait for her to finish.

"It's just . . . it's *him*. So . . ."

I sigh and let my hand fall. "Just say it, Katie-O. Whatever it is, just say it."

"I hope you know what you're doing. And that you don't get hurt like before."

Staring at my too-wide eyes in the mirror, I ask myself if I know what I'm doing. My brain morphs into a Magic 8 Ball that only answers me with "outlook not so good."

"Me, too, Katie. Me, too."

> *I woke up alone.*
> *Feeling cheap and used.*
> *I had a great time, girl.*
> *But you left me sore and abused.*

Song lyrics. Dallas is texting me song lyrics in the middle of the ceremony that has already dragged on entirely too long. I smile at the screen and place my phone on my lap beneath the tablecloth so I don't appear rude to my table companions.

> *You rocked my world, turned it upside down.*
> *Now you're nowhere to be found.*

The alert chimes again. More lyrics.

> *Do you miss me, girl? Remember how you kissed me, girl?*
> *'Cause I have to speak the truth, there's not much I wouldn't do*
> *to wake up holding you.*
> *I should wrangle my dignity. Should play it cool for a while. But*
> *I miss those lips. I miss that smile.*

I type out a quick response text. *This your next hit? Do I get a cut?*

His response comes almost immediately.

*Maybe. I'm still trying to find a word that works with "slapped."*

I laugh out loud, stifling it the best I can, when an older gentleman to my left startles at my outburst. No one can see my phone so I don't look rude, just crazy.

*I told you I was sorry about that,* I type out quickly.

*It was pretty hot. I'm tough. I can take it if you like it rough.*

Well now he's just being inappropriate. I'm not sure if it's an actual response or a lyric. And I'm squirming in my seat.

I don't have a witty comeback yet so I just text him that I need to get back to my ceremony.

*I'll keep you posted on the song.*

I stare at his words, my eyes zeroing in on the first three. I have got to get a grip on myself.

*Thanks. Have a great show tomorrow night.*

After that, I ignore my phone and focus on the speeches and awards. But Dallas Lark is holding a blowtorch, steadily burning a hole in my steel wall—one I don't know how to protect myself against.

# 15 | Dallas

I'M SEEING SPOTS. BRIGHT ONES. BLINDING ONES.

Cameras flash from directly in front of me as I pose with fans.

Fans.

I have fans.

It's kind of hard to wrap my head around. The band had a few regulars who attended shows at certain bars, but I think that was more about the bars than us.

"Thank y'all for coming out," I say to two girls wearing matching If Lost Return to Dallas Walker T-shirts. Melissa and Jessica, I think they said their names were. But I still can't get over the fact that I have shirts. "Love the shirts, by the way." I wink and they laugh, the blond one turning a little red in the face.

Some fans are sweet like that.

And some are a little more than sweet.

"Remember me?" A brunette with a wide smile stands beside me for her picture.

I try to place her face but I can't. "Um . . ."

"Chandra. I saw your band play in San Antonio last year. I was in town visiting a friend. We hung out after your show."

"Did we?" I put my arm around her shoulders like I'm supposed to for the picture. "Sorry. It's been a crazy year."

"I can imagine," she says softly, pressing her full breasts firmly into my side. "Congratulations, by the way. My sorority sisters and I are your number-one fans. Your album is going to blow Jase Wade out of the water."

"Thanks." Taking a deep breath while we smile for the photo, I rack my brain trying to remember playing San Antonio last year. Nothing memorable comes to mind, but judging from the knowing look in her eyes and how forward she's being with my body right now, she might have carnal knowledge of me.

Damn. This is not good.

I make a mental note to ask Mandy what I should do in these situations. I haven't exactly been a saint and the last thing I want to do at this point in my career is get a reputation as a player or an asshole.

She bats her eyelashes at me. "Will I see you after the show tonight? Some of us are going to a bar called Kelly's. You should come."

Her eyes meet mine on the last word and I'm pretty sure I don't imagine the innuendo.

"Um, I don't know."

After an awkward pause, she says, "I'll text you." Then she gives me a lingering look full of dirty promises and moves aside so the next person in line can get their picture made.

My phone buzzes a few times in my pocket and I check it once the line has subsided.

Someone with the number 555-213-9857 has sent me several messages. One of them is a picture of me and Chandra, the overzealous fan, at a bar. My arms are around her and she's kissing me on the cheek. I'm holding up a beer and from the looks of it, I'm blitzed.

There's no telling what happened after that picture was taken. Well . . . fuck.

M y set went well, amazing actually, and Wade pulled me back out onstage to sing with him at the end of his, which was new.

"We're gonna do this, we're gonna have to get to know each other," he says to me after we finish the encore. "Come grab a drink with me."

"All right."

"Relax, man," he says, thumping me hard on the back. "We'll have a few beers. Talk a little. Think of it as an icebreaker."

I'm too amped up to go pass out on the bus anyway. But I wasn't prepared for male bonding, either. I like to let my music do the talking for me. If Jase Wade wants to stay up and paint each other's nails, he's on tour with the wrong guy.

"I could go for a beer," I say, because what the hell. One beer won't hurt. And I'm not an idiot. Jase Wade didn't get voted last year's Entertainer of the Year for nothing. There's probably a lot I could learn from him.

Arick, the drummer in Wade's band, high-fives us as he passes. "Hey, man, great show," he says to me. "Y'all heading to Kelly's?"

"Yeah," Wade answers him.

Aw, hell.

"You know, I just remembered I have to—"

"Shave your legs? Call your mama? Come on, Walker. It's a few beers at a bar. We promise not to slip you anything." Jase Wade eyes me warily.

I'm coming off like a prick. I hardly talk to anyone and I'm being a pussy about grabbing a beer.

I swallow hard and nod. "Right. See y'all there."

"Don't be crazy," Wade tells me. "Ride with us."

I follow him onto his bus and take a seat on one of the black leather couches. Wade grabs two beers from his built-in fridge, uses the counter to pop the tops off both of them, and hands one to me.

"Thanks," I say, taking a nice long drink. I didn't realize how thirsty I was until the crisp fizzy liquid hit my tongue.

"So, tell me about yourself, Walker."

I set my beer down as the bus rumbles to life. "What do you want to know, Wade?"

He grins and tips his own beer back. "Oh, I don't know. Where you from?"

"Amarillo. You?"

"Lake Park, Georgia. It's tiny. You haven't heard of it. How long you been playing guitar?"

"Since I was twelve or so."

"Sorry, I haven't been keeping up with your birthdays. How old are you?"

He's fucking with me. But I'm not that easy to rattle. "Twenty-four. You?"

"Thirty-two."

I thought he was younger than that for some reason. I tell him so.

"I'm young at heart," he says with a grin. "You like football?"

"College football mostly. But I catch a Cowboys game now and then."

He nods like he's really interested in my answers. "I'm a Bulldogs fan myself. You hunt? Fish?"

"My grandpa took me a few times when I was a kid. I didn't have a hell of a lot of patience for it."

He laughs. "Yeah, me, either. Mostly I drink beer and shoot at trees when we go. Not that I have much time for that these days."

"I bet."

We take an almost simultaneous drink to fill the silence that follows. Fuck this is awkward. This is why I don't socialize with people.

"Well, hell. I'm out of questions." Wade shrugs then his eyes light up. "Nope. Just thought of another one."

"By all means," I say drily.

"You got a girl back home?"

Robyn's face flickers in my mind. Mandy's words about Wade requesting her on this tour accompany the image my head. "Nah. I got a sister and that's the only woman I answer to."

"She hot?"

"She's a lesbian."

"Ah."

"I'm kidding. But I'd break both of your legs before letting you near her." Maybe I should've broken my best friend's before he got anywhere near her. I try not to think about what Gavin and Dixie may or may not be doing back in Amarillo.

Wade nods. "Good man. I got a daughter, so believe me, I get it."

Well, this is news. "I didn't know that. That you had a kid."

"Yeah, well. I don't advertise it. No reason all this insanity should keep her from having a normal life, you know?"

"Makes sense."

"You don't like to talk much, do you?"

"Not particularly."

He grins again and tosses his empty bottle in the trash before grabbing another one. "You know, I was you once."

"Excuse me?"

"Young. Hungry for this. For the road and the fame and the music."

I frown at him. "You're not anymore?"

Jase Wade takes a deep breath and a long look around the bus. It's a nice fucking bus. His band is at a back table playing cards and drinking beer and joking around loudly.

"It's hard to be hungry for something you get force-fed every day, you know?"

I don't know, so I shrug and finish off my beer.

"You'll see. One day. You're a talented kid. Won't be long until you're sitting in my place watching some guy remind you of yourself and wishing you could give him the advice you wish someone had given you."

"You're not going to give me any advice?"

He smirks at me. The bus comes to a stop so he stands. "Would you take it?"

We both know the answer so I don't bother saying no out loud.

"That's what I thought. Let's go get shitfaced."

The bus is parked in a lot across the street from the bar and I catch sight of Mandy coming off my bus. I jog over to her.

"Hey. Sorry. I rode with Wade."

She barely glances up from her phone. "I know. He told me he was going to talk to you. Everything okay?"

"Yeah. Everything's fine. I had a question, though?"

Mandy stops walking. "About?"

"Women."

She laughs. "Really? You seem like you understand women just fine." She steps closer to me, letting the members of my band pass us. "But I'm happy to answer any questions you have, Dallas. Shoot."

I clear my throat "Not what I meant, exactly. I mean, like, fans who . . . um . . ." I'm not comfortable saying this kind of thing to a woman—not one I have no plans to be intimate with, anyway.

"Offer to suck your dick?"

All right then. "Yeah. I mean, I don't want to be an asshole to them. And some have met me before and I don't remember if—"

"Oh, Dallas. Brace yourself, Superstar. All of your slutty skeletons are about to come out of the closet. The more attention you get, the more aggressive they'll get. Everyone will know you somehow and they either want something or they want to give you something. Their demo. A song they wrote for you. A blow job. You just have to decide which favors you want to accept."

"Um, okay. So if I don't want their favors? How do you suggest I handle that?"

"We'll meet with your new publicist after the tour to discuss this further. But for now, I'd say just be your polite, gentlemanly self." She pauses to give me a salacious grin. "You've managed to keep out of my bed for this long. I'm sure you can handle a few groupies."

She nudges me as if she's just kidding, but the wicked glint in her dark eyes suggests she isn't.

"Right. Okay. Thanks." *For making this as uncomfortable as possible.* Oh how I wish Mandy Lantram would stop screwing with me and just be my manager.

Wade gives me a knowing look as I follow him into the bar. I don't know his history with Mandy, but he certainly has one. Maybe I'll ask him about it during our next Q&A session if there is one.

Kelly's is a decent-sized pub-style bar and it's packed. I check my phone once we're inside.

Robyn hasn't texted me back. It bothers me more than it should. Because I'm obviously a chick now.

I scroll through our previous messages while waiting in line to order a drink. I was just messing around earlier, texting her stupid lyrics about ditching me. But as I read back through them, I can almost hear the beat in my head.

"What can I get ya, handsome?" A woman with curly copper-colored hair is waiting for my order. I start to get a beer and a burger, but I remember what Robyn said about Papa and heart disease so I order a light beer and a buffalo chicken wrap instead.

"For someone who doesn't have a girl, you sure are worried about that phone," Wade says from beside me. I hadn't noticed he was there.

"You really this interested in getting to know me? Or is there something specific you want to ask?"

*Please do not ask me about Robyn Breeland.*

He narrows his eyes, but before he can ask anything else, a body crashes into mine, nearly spilling my beer.

Thin arms wrap around me and a mouth fastens to the side of my face. *What the fuck?*

I steady myself, pulling back far enough to see Chandra attaching herself to me like an octopus.

"Dallas! Oh my God! You made it!" she squeals in my ear. "We have to get another picture together. My friend Allie is gonna take it. Smile!"

I force a quick grin just in time for the flash.

"Thanks! Come sit with us." Her fingers clasp my free hand and she tugs.

"Actually I'm going to hang out with these guys," I say, pulling free and nodding toward where Wade is.

"Nah. We're good. Go ahead, Walker. We'll save you a seat." Wade winks like he's doing me a favor. There's amusement playing on his face.

"Will you sign some stuff for us? Pretty please?" Chandra pouts surgically enhanced plump lips at me. A few other parts of her appear to be surgically enhanced as well.

"Sure," I say, relenting, and let her lead me to the table where her friends are.

It's probably for the best that Robyn didn't answer my texts. It's not like I can ask her out on Friday night, take her to a movie, and all that for as long as we both shall live. I tell myself to be thankful for the memory of something real while I'm facing a future full of something fake.

As much as I hate to admit it, there is something flattering about the fact that Chandra wants my autograph and didn't seem the least bit interested in Wade.

I'm just asshole enough to care.

# 16 | Robyn

When Katie texts me that she's uploaded the meet-and-greet photos from the show in Kansas City, I can't resist opening them on my flight back home.

My flight back to Dallas.

You know what's a dumb idea? Living in a city with the same name as your ex-boyfriend.

The first set of photos is Wade and a long string of posed pictures with his adoring female fans. I forward the best ones to Harvey on the social media team with a note to post them to the Midnight Bay website, as well as the Facebook and Twitter accounts.

The next group shows Dallas and there are nearly as many fan photos. A candid shot Drew took of his line shows that it's nearly as long as Jase's. I'm happy for Dallas and I'm relieved to see he's not the tour underdog. But a few of the women in some of the photos have my insides twisting into knots.

Some of them are drop-dead gorgeous and have their bodies plastered onto Dallas like cling wrap. One in particular wears an expression that makes me cringe.

*He's not yours, Robyn.*

Right. He's not.

As much as it pains me to do so, I include the smoking hot brunette picture in the ones of Dallas that I send to Harvey. It's a really good picture and it shows how very desirable he is. I can do this. I can be an adult about working with my ex.

But I might print myself a copy of that photo and throw darts at it in my office just for fun.

"Eleven percent. How crazy is that?"

"What? What's eleven percent?" I lift my head off my desk when Katie barges in. Thank goodness it was her and not one of the Martins that caught me napping.

"Were you asleep?"

"No." My answer is negated by the giant yawn that follows.

"You all right?" Katie's round blue eyes are filled with concern.

"I'm fine. Just tired. Between Denver and L.A. and my layover getting delayed, I got in really late last night. I'm just a little drained."

"I wondered why I didn't hear you come in. I might have some ginseng tea in the break room. Oh, and I have ginkgo drops in my purse."

"Thanks. I promise I'm good. Just need some good old-fashioned caffeine and more rest."

"You sure?"

"Yeah. You were saying something about eleven percent when you came in and caught me drooling on my desk?"

Katie laughs. "Oh yeah. I just ran into Louis from the finance department. He said they've been tracking the numbers closely since the tour kicked off so that Mr. Martin could evaluate the effectiveness of sponsoring it. And apparently, since the ads started running the week before the Denver show, sales are already up eleven percent."

"Wow." Eleven percent is a much larger increase than what our standard advertising typically generates. And it's only been a few weeks since the promos went out that showed us as a tour sponsor, so it's even more impressive.

"Apparently Jase Wade fans are big bourbon drinkers." Katie plops down in the seat across from my desk. "Who knew?"

"That's fantastic. I'm going to email Louis really quick and see if I can get a copy of the exact numbers. Are we running any other ad campaigns right now?"

"Just the 'Make the Right Call' spots about calling for a ride if you're too drunk to drive. And the print and digital promos we've been doing every month."

I send a quick email to Louis with my request. But if this is correct, if being a sponsor on the Kickin' Up Crazy tour is upping sales this much this quickly, it's one of the highest returns on advertising investment we've ever seen.

Which means a few things. One being that this is a route we definitely want to continue taking, sponsoring tours. And the other I try not to think about. Because if I value this company and my job at all, the last thing I should be doing is engaging in an inappropriate relationship with someone on the tour.

If it got out that Dallas and I had a history, there would be all kinds of questions about why Midnight Bay was sponsoring the tour he just happened to be on. The nature of relationships between artists and sponsors should be of a strictly professional and business nature. The public discovering that we'd slept together in Denver would reflect poorly on Midnight Bay. It might not get me fired necessarily, but it would probably cause me to at least be questioned by my boss and possibly his sixty-two-year-old uncle about topics I never want to discuss with either of them. Ever.

I say a silent thank-you to the universe that Dallas isn't currently famous enough to have paparazzi following him around. Then I feel bad for feeling glad that he isn't famous yet.

"You are so in your head right now," Katie says, startling me as I chew my manicure to hell while waiting on Louis's response. "What's the deal? I thought an eleven percent bump in sales would be great news."

"It is." I nod. "I'm just a little worried about . . . you know."

"Your little fling with Mr. Hotpants?"

I roll my eyes. "Very funny. Not exactly. I'm more worried about our history coming to light. I'm the one who pushed us to sponsor this tour and then I outright begged Mr. Martin to put me on the promo campaign. If it comes out that I have a prior history with Dallas, it might get complicated."

Katie looks at me like I've said something ridiculous. "How so?"

"There were two acts previously scheduled to be on the tour that were asked to leave for undisclosed reasons. Dallas took the open spot. It might look like I was involved in that, or like I used company dollars as leverage to get him on the tour."

"But you weren't and you didn't. You worry too much, girl. You want to get a drink after work?"

Katie stands to leave, and while I could probably use some girl time, I really am exhausted. "I think I'm just going to go home and crash. Tomorrow, though, I'm in."

"Sounds good."

Katie leaves and the email I've been waiting for comes through. I'm lost in sales numbers when my phone chimes with a text notification.

I tear my eyes from my computer long enough to locate my phone to my left.

> *She won't answer my texts. Won't take my calls. It's probably all my fault.*
> *What I don't know is what I did to get myself on her do not answer list.*
> *Hit me up, girl. Or just hit me.*
> *I can take it, whatever you have to say. Anything you wanna throw my way.*
> *Whether it's a call you back soon or right hook. Give me what you got.*

More lyrics courtesy of Dallas.

At least he's writing, I guess.

I set my phone down and rub my temples for a few minutes.

I'm not avoiding him. That would be childish. I'm just avoiding . . . it. This thing between us that I can't explain or contain.

My travel-lagged brain is too tired to compute a response.

I'll text him after work.

I will.

Or maybe after I get home and take a nap.

I just have to figure out what in the world I'm going to say.

*Thanks for the hot sex but I don't think we should make it a habit* seems kind of harsh.

*I'm ignoring you because I don't want to lose my job for sleeping with you* doesn't really work, either.

*Should I just book one room for us to share from now on?* is what actually comes to mind.

No. It was a fling. A temporary rekindling of a flame that has long since burned out and nothing more. Because that's all it can be.

A drink with Katie is suddenly sounding a whole lot more appealing. And necessary.

# 17 | Dallas

"I WAS STARTING TO THINK YOU'D DROPPED OFF THE EARTH."

"Yeah, well, some days that would be an improvement."

"You all right, Garrison? The man gettin' you down?"

Gavin huffs out a breath and then I hear him tell someone in the background to hang on a fucking minute. Okay then. Clearly he isn't hanging out with my sister at the moment. Or he has a death wish.

"I'm fine. Working at the Tavern. Still trying to get shit handled with my probation officer. I can't really talk right now. But hit me up later. We'll grab a drink when you're in town."

"It'll be almost two months before the tour hits Texas. Quick question."

"Shoot."

"Robyn works for the tour sponsor. I saw her. I'll be seeing a lot of her actually."

"No shit?"

"No shit," I confirm.

Gavin laughs. "And you're asking *me* for advice about Robyn? I know as much about relationships as I do—"

"No. That's not what I'm asking about." Though a part of me

does wonder if he could give me some insight into why she blew me off after our night together, I know it's best if I appreciate it for what it was and let it go. I'm partially relieved she never responded to my texts because the last thing I need to be on this tour is distracted. I'm partially pissed-off, too, but I'm ignoring that part of me.

"You're losing me."

I huff out a breath while doing a quick check of the bus to make sure it's empty. "That's not the issue exactly. The problem is I'm also running into some of my former . . ." I don't know what to call them without being disrespectful.

"Questionable choices?"

"Yeah."

Gavin chuckles low into the phone. "I bet, Big Timer. Probably coming at you by the truckload these days."

"If it was funny I'd be laughing. I'm serious here. I don't want to be known as the manwhore of country music."

"I don't mean to be dick, D. But really, what did you expect? This is the reason half the guys we know play music."

"That include you, Garrison?" *Dude who swears he loves my sister but has yet to tell me if he's seen her.*

"Nah. For me it's about channeling aggression so I don't walk around beating the fuck out of people on a daily basis. But for most guys, it's about pussy. Period."

"Well, I'm not most guys." Why do I have to keep reminding people of this? Do I have "Johnny Guitar Player" tattooed on my fucking forehead?

"Right. So what's the question exactly?"

"When you run into your . . . *questionable choices,* what do you do about it? How do you let them know you're no longer interested without coming off like an asshole?"

Gavin laughs again. "There's one major difference between you and me that you forgot to consider when consulting me for advice."

"What's that?"

"I don't give a flying fuck who thinks I'm an asshole."

"I can think of one girl we both know who adamantly swears you're not an asshole."

"You obviously haven't spoken to your sister lately. Look, man, I gotta get back to work. Keeping a job is part of my probation arrangement."

"Hold up. Why? What happened to make Dixie change her mind? I thought you were running off into the sunset together and that's why your ass isn't on this tour with me."

"It's complicated, brother. Right now, she isn't exactly speaking to me."

I knew that was a possibility once he'd told her what happened while she was in college in Houston, but I figured they'd work it out eventually. "Christ, Garrison. Am I going to have to beat your ass when I come to town?"

Silence.

"I'll take that as a maybe. Six weeks, man. I'll be there in six weeks. You should probably get your shit straight with Dixie before I get there."

"And here I thought you called me for advice."

"That's not advice. Or even a suggestion. You really care about her like you swore to me you did, then you do whatever it takes."

"Working on it," he says before I hear someone yelling at him to get the fuck back inside.

"Don't get fired. I'll hit you up later."

"Later."

After I disconnect the call I promptly dial my sister's number.

She doesn't pick up so I leave her a voice mail asking her to call me. She's going to be pissed that I didn't tell her Gavin was home. But I thought he was going to tell her. I thought he was getting his life together and that she'd be a part of that. Apparently I was wrong.

I hate being wrong.

# 18 | Robyn

THE AMPHITHEATER IN GREENVILLE IS LARGE AND HAS A SLIGHTLY different setup than we're used to so Katie and Drew and I get creative. Or rather, I plot.

Placing Dallas's meet-and-greet on the east end of the stadium seating means I won't have to interact with him as much. So I set up the red line bottles for his display and take the blue line ones to the west end.

I tell Katie she's in charge and leave Drew with her. For Jase's side of the display I will have to be both organizer and photographer, but that's fine. Drew loaned me his spare camera so I familiarize myself with it while I wait for the venue to start letting fans in.

Jase joins me while I'm testing out the flash.

"Whoa, darlin'. How about not blinding me before the show?"

"Sorry, Mr. Wade." I lower the flashbulb.

"You can call me Jase. You're Robyn, right? I think we'll be spending enough time together to refer to each other on a first-name basis."

"Right. Of course. Whatever you prefer."

"Well, that's a dangerous thing to say. I don't think you could handle what I would prefer."

He nails me with a wicked grin and I can't even pretend to contain my shock. Apparently Dallas can't, either.

"The fuck did you just say to her?"

I practically twitch out of my skin in surprise. I didn't hear him walk over. But Jase just grins and holds his hands up. "Easy, killer. I was just being honest."

Dallas clears his throat harshly and redirects his attention from Jase to me. "So where do you want me?"

The hard edge in his voice and the loaded question itself sends heat up my neck.

"Um, you're over there. On the other end with Katie and Drew."

Dallas regards me with anger and apprehension in his intense stare. I blew him off and now I'm separating us as much as I can in the one place we actually should be together. Maybe it's immature, but I'm not in a place where I can watch women fawning all over him right this moment.

"You lost, kid?" Jase says to Dallas when he makes no move to leave. "She just said your display is over there."

"You got a problem, Wade? I don't recall her asking for your—"

"Okay, boys," I interrupt, moving between them. "Everybody has an equally big . . . guitar," I say. "To your corners. Fans are coming in."

I place a hand on Dallas's chest and shove him toward where his meet-and-greet is.

His fingers encircle my wrist reminiscent of the way they did in the bedroom not too long ago. "So this how it's gonna be with us now?"

"We're not discussing this now, not here," I say, nodding toward the steady stream of fans pouring into the aisles.

"After the show then?"

"We'll see."

After I've wrangled him over to Katie, I head back to Jase, where fans are waiting impatiently for me to take their pictures. I apologize half a dozen times and get started. But the entire time, I can feel his eyes on me. More so when I have to step closer to Jase or when Jase comes over to talk to me between pictures.

*I'm just doing my job, Dallas. Back off.*

I try to send the message telepathically to him, but judging from the hard glare he gives me when he has to leave to take the stage, the message was not received.

"You cannot ever do that to me again." I corner Dallas backstage after his show, having had time to grow angrier about his Neanderthal behavior. "How would you feel if I stormed into your meet-and-greets and snapped at your fans the way you went after Jase? Do you even know what could happen if you piss him off?"

"First of all," Dallas begins, whirling on me, "I am not afraid of him. And second of all, he was out of line. If one of my fans got out of line like that and you called her out, I'd probably sport wood for a month from that memory alone."

"You so do not get it. And here I thought you took this seriously."

He zeroes in on me with the precision of a hawk. "Oh I take it very seriously. The question is, does he?"

"It was one night, Dallas."

"Bullshit. Maybe it was one night *recently,* but we both know it's a hell of a lot more than that."

"You do not own me," I state firmly, planting my hands on my hips. "So stop acting like you do."

Dallas's chest expands and he opens his mouth, but before he can say whatever asinine thing he has planned, Jase lets out a loud guitar riff onstage and the drums take off like a thousand helicopters.

"Come!" Dallas shouts over the din, reaching out and taking me by the elbow.

I follow because otherwise my head is going to explode from the noise.

Once we're back behind the buses in a relatively quiet area, Dallas leans back against a trailer. "Look, I get why you blew me off. You're right, it was one night and I don't own you. But I don't want to see you get hurt, either. How well do you know him? I mean, really know him?" He nods at the giant rendition of Jase's face

"I don't know. I know a lot about him. I had to. For my job."

"But you don't really know him as a person? Like you know me?"

"Are you looking to get slapped again, Lark? Because every time you insinuate I am screwing my way into—"

"Stop. That's not what I meant."

"Then say what you mean, Dallas. Quickly."

"I hear him with fans. He propositions them. And Mandy says that's why the two guys before me got kicked off the tour. Because they encroached on his female territory or some bullshit."

"Okay. But I heard differently. I heard they got grabby with some girls, thinking they were owed a piece of ass just because they were on this tour so he kicked them off. Either way, I just work with him. I don't have to approve of his values. I'm not planning to date him or whatever it is you think. I'm here to do my job . . . despite what happened in Denver."

Dallas gives me this look, his blue eyes darken a shade, and his long, sleepy lashes lower as he blinks slow and takes a step toward me. "He treats women like objects. Like disposable playthings for his amusement. Do you know why you're on this tour, Robyn? Do you know why you were handpicked to run this campaign?"

I fidget with the sponsor pass around my neck. "Because I worked my ass off and I asked to be a part of it. Because I gave a kick-ass presentation that blew everyone away."

Dallas nods. "Maybe. But word on the street is you're here because he requested you. Specifically." He nods to Jase's smirking face on the trailer. "And if he requested you, I don't think it was your hard work that appealed to him."

I have paced up and down the length of Wade's tour bus for the past hour. When he finally returns to it, he isn't alone. A tall thin blonde and a curvy chick with hair similar to the color of mine flank him on each side.

"Hey, Robyn. What can I do for you?" Wade whispers something to each of the girls and they walk past me onto the bus wearing matching confident smirks. Ugh. Maybe Dallas was right.

*Stop judging, Breeland. Not your business.*

"We need to talk. In private, please."

A few guys from Wade's band have walked over to see what's going on. He tells them to give us a minute so they meander off.

"You look pretty pissed, but I can't imagine what I possibly could've done to make you so angry with me." He scratches his chin and adjusts his cowboy hat.

"I need to know something. The truth, preferably."

"I'll do my best. What do you need to know?"

I take a deep breath and just lay it out there. Either way, it's better to know. Even if it will sting like hell to know I didn't land this job on merit. "Did you request me specifically to head up the tour promo?"

Jase grins at me. "I did. Is that a problem?"

"Yes," I practically yell at him. "Of course it is. What the hell is wrong with you? You can't just go around requesting women like you are King Pimp of the universe. Just because your shameless groupies fall at your feet doesn't mean all women are fair game. I am a professional, damn it. I work really hard at my job and I wanted to be on this tour because I was excited. I was a fan of your music and I hoped partnering with Midnight Bay would be the kind of opportunity that—"

"Whoa, darlin'. Rein it in a sec," he says, throwing his hands up. I didn't even realize I was charging toward him.

"What?" I demand, wondering what in the hell he could possibly say to justify his behavior.

His smile widens but his hazel eyes cloud over with a troubled expression. Like I hurt his feelings. Like that's even possible.

"I did request you, Robyn. But not for the reasons you've obviously assumed."

I take a deep breath and fold my arms across my chest. "Then why?"

"Because you're young and smart and driven. Because you were the only one at Midnight Bay to mention social media integration in your presentation. Those were the words I was waiting to hear. You said them. So I thought you'd be the right person for the job. You also happen to be beautiful and I wouldn't kick you out of bed if you were interested, but that had absolutely nothing to do with my requesting you for this tour. Scout's honor."

"So the comment earlier about what you'd prefer?"

"If my teasing you made you uncomfortable, I apologize. It's a habit I just sort of fall into when I don't know what else to say. I'll make an effort to cut that out where you're concerned. It's unprofessional and uncalled for."

"Well . . . thank you. I'd appreciate that."

I feel two inches tall and if I had one wish right now, it would be for the ground to open up and swallow me whole.

"So . . . we good?" He nods toward his bus. " 'Cause I got—"

"Go. Sorry. In the future I'll ask any questions I have without taking your head off first."

Jase laughs good-naturedly. "It's fine. You're a woman in a mostly male-dominated business. I can imagine the shit you have to put up with. My hat's off to you." With that, he tips his hat. "And for the record, my groupies are pretty shameless. God bless 'em." He turns and gets onto his tour bus, leaving me shaking my head and contemplating the many ways in which I could murder Dallas Lark.

# 19 | Dallas

THE KNOCK ON THE THIN DOOR TO MY ROOM ON THE BUS IS SHARP and angry sounding. So naturally I assume it's Mandy here to make some lewd suggestion about how I owe her my dick or something.

I sigh and open it, pleasantly surprised to find Robyn on the other side instead. My guitarist, Tyler, is standing behind her looking concerned for my well-being. I give him an I've-got-this nod and move aside for Robyn to come in. She blows past me without a word.

"You okay?"

"No. I'm not." She shakes her head and looks off into the distance, paying more attention to the modest furnishings in the room than to me. "I confronted him. Because of what you said. And guess what?"

Now her eyes do meet mine and I'm nervous about what I see in them. Matching glinting emeralds of hatred is what they most resemble at the moment.

"I can't even begin to guess."

"No?" Her voice rises an octave or two. "You can't? That's funny considering a few hours ago you were an expert on the subject."

"Clearly you're upset with me." I state the obvious because I know her well enough to know that when she's in this mood everything I say will be fuel to her fire.

"You think?" She purses her sexy little mouth and shakes her head at me. "I was ranting on and on about being a professional and the whole time I was acting like some stupid teenager freaking out over gossip. Because guess what, Dallas? Whoever your *source* is got it wrong. Jase Wade didn't request me on this tour because he wanted to get into my panties. He requested me because of the social media pitch I gave in my presentation."

"Okay. Well, then I'm glad I was wrong."

"You're glad you were wrong? Since when? Since when are you ever wrong, Dallas? You just decide how things are and that's how it is, right?" She runs her hands through her tangled hair, then gapes at me. "Dead God. I said he thought he was King Pimp of the universe."

I fold my lips inward to keep from laughing. Laughing would be so bad right now.

"Do not dare laugh at me, Dallas. I cannot believe you said that stuff to me. But you know what's worse? I *believed* it. And do you know why?"

*Do not speak.*

In lieu of a verbal answer I shake my head.

"I believed it because that's how you make me feel. Like all I'm good for is getting you off when you need it. Right? Bang out a few orgasms and hey, maybe a song, too, for good measure. Good old Robyn. She'll just take what she can get. That's all you want me for, so of course, that must be all any other guy can see as well." She takes these gaspy little breaths that make me hate myself.

The urge to laugh has passed.

"Baby, I—"

She slaps my hand away when I reach for her. "No. No, we're done with that. Do not touch me. You could've cost me my job tonight, riling me up with your jealous macho crap. And I am so done."

"Robyn," I call out, pulling at her waist before she twists out of my arms. "Listen to me. That's not how it was."

"How was it then? Tell me. Because I feel cheap, and used, and played. And I do not deserve that."

"You're right." I nod like a fucking bobblehead. "You don't. I swear to God, making you feel that way was not my intention." I sit on my bed and look up at her. Her pain is mine now, and it's weighing heavy on my chest. I hurt her, deeply, and I'd kick my own ass if I knew how.

"Then why, Dallas? Why say those awful things to me? Because it sure seemed like you meant them."

I clear my throat and give her the most honest answer that I can.

"Because I got caught up. I was worried that he wanted you here so he could use his authority over you and pull with your company to take advantage. I should've just confronted him myself instead of telling you. But we used to tell each other everything and old habits are hard to break."

"Well, get un-caught-up. Just stay out of it from now on, okay?" She takes a shaky breath that throws me off balance. "Just stay out of my personal and professional business and worry about you."

"Ask me anything, Robyn. Ask me to back off, to keep my hands to myself, to stop wanting to pummel every guy who looks at you sideways. I can't make any promises, but I can try. But please, babe, don't ask me not to care. Because I can't not care about you. I've tried. I failed. I will always care. And anytime I see someone who I think might try to hurt you in any way, I probably won't be able to stop myself from stepping in even if you don't want me there."

For a split second I see something in her eyes that makes me think she's going to say she understands. That's she'll try to be patient with me because I'm a jackass and she knows I can't help it.

But then her expression hardens and her shoulders stiffen and she shakes her head.

"When you get up on that stage, Dallas, I am so proud of you. I remember watching you play at dive bars and catfish weigh-ins and wherever else they would let you. I knew from the first time I saw you play that you were something special. I couldn't wait for the rest of the world to see it. And now that they do, I am so honored to get to be a part of that. But I need you to at least respect my job even if you don't think it's as important as yours. I may not get up on a stage night after night, but I work really hard, too. And it would've been really nice if you could've been proud of me back."

"Robyn—"

"Don't. I acted like a psycho in front of a client tonight because I let you get in my head. That's not okay, Dallas. Just leave me be. You focus on your career and I'll focus on mine. Got it?"

She doesn't even wait for my answer.

After she walks out, I toss a chair against the wall and watch it splinter into pieces. For the rest of the night I feel even more alone than I did before she came by to yell at me.

She's right. We can't do this second-chance romance shit right now. We both have careers to focus on and neither of us can afford to get caught up in something that could cost us everything we've worked for.

Just because I know she's right doesn't mean I have to like it.

My phone rings sometime around sunrise. The bus isn't moving so I assume we made it to North Carolina. Glancing over on the nightstand that's strapped to the wall, I find my phone and see my sister's face on the screen.

Sitting up, I slide the bar to accept her call. "Hey, Dixie. Everything okay?"

"Yeah. Why wouldn't it be?" I can hear the challenge in her voice. She's pissed and she has every right to be. I'm two-for-two then where women are concerned.

"Oh . . . I don't know. Did you know Robyn was going to be on this tour with me?"

My sister sighs loudly, which means yes, she did.

"Sorry, big brother. It didn't exactly come up and I wasn't sure how you'd respond if I dropped it on you at the last minute. Seemed like it might be best to just let you find out on your own. Kind of like how you knew Gavin was in town and not on the unsigned artists tour with you and you kept it to yourself, I suppose."

She's got me there. And now I know why she sounds pissed. "I'm sorry. It just wasn't my truth to tell, you know?"

"I do know. And ditto, I guess."

I run a hand through my hair and lean back on my headboard. "Can you tell me something else, though? Something important? Even if you think it will hurt my feelings."

"I can try."

"Am I an asshole? Be straight with me, Dix."

"Dallas," she scoffs at me. "What kind of question is that?"

"If a guy's sister can't call him out for being an asshole, who can?"

"I don't think you are—not really anyway. You might impersonate one from time to time, but I think we both know there's more going on beneath the surface. But it doesn't really matter what I think. Why do you ask?"

"Do you think I've been terrible to Robyn?"

Again my sister sighs. I contemplate sending her an inhaler.

"I think you could be more up front about your feelings for her sometimes instead of pushing her away. I think whatever happened between the two of you was complicated and that it left a mark on you. You tend to go overboard sometimes trying to keep people from getting too close. That can be hurtful, you know?"

"I see. So what do you think I should do about it? Send her some flowers with a card that says, 'Sorry for being such a dick'?"

My sister laughs at me as if I'm kidding. I am not kidding.

"I think you should apologize in a more meaningful way. One that says more than just sorry but lets her know that you're going to try and do better in the future."

"Right. I'll see if I can get that iced on a cake."

"You sound tired still. Get some sleep, Dallas." With that my sister pretty much hangs up on me.

I should sleep some more. The show will run late tonight. But there's a song in my head, one Robyn inspired, so mostly I write. When I come to a lyric I can't make fit, I pick up my guitar and try to play through it.

"Patience isn't enough," Papa used to say when I'd get tired of a song I couldn't master. He'd hand me my guitar time and time again after I'd set it aside. "Persistence is just as important. It's what sets you apart from the quitters."

I'd huff and puff and pout, but I'd take the guitar and try until I got it.

"Life is what you make, boy," he'd tell me. "You get back what you put in. You quit on life and it will quit on you right back."

I don't go back to sleep until I've finished the song.

# 20 | Robyn

By the time we reach Charlotte, I have cooled down considerably. Both from my humiliating encounter with Jase Wade and my anger at Dallas.

Katie talks me through it as we follow behind the convoy, reminding me that it's sweet that Dallas cares, though he could certainly demonstrate that concern in more appropriate ways. But then he wouldn't be Dallas. After a hot shower and a good night's sleep in the hotel, I decide it's a new day and I'm not going to let my past cast a shadow on it.

At least that's the Kool-Aid I'm drinking until I see him.

Dallas is in the middle of sound check when we arrive at the amphitheater. He's wearing a Midnight Bay trucker hat and his black T-shirt fits just snug enough to make me jealous of how close it is to those muscles.

He's performing a new song, one I haven't heard before. "Tough All Over" must be the title because it's repeated several times in the chorus. I catch a line about how she can throw anything at him she wants, a kiss, a hug, even a right hook. If she wants to cry, he'll be her shoulder. 'Cause he's tough all over.

I'm frozen where I stand, setting the Midnight Bay free sample boxes around the stage for the drink girls to distribute.

I have twenty dollars in my pocket that says that song is about me. And deep down, I have always been a Dallas Lark fangirl.

A few of the women who are working for the venue stop what they're doing to listen, too.

This is Dallas in his element. Strong. Seductive. Charismatic and hot as asphalt on a sunny day.

Damn him. Damn him to hell in his tight jeans and his cocky country boy swagger.

*Look away, Robyn,* my subconscious warns me. But I can't. He's up there in all his glory and I have the ideal view.

When the tempo ramps up and he launches into a cover of a song called "Take It Out on Me," I practically have to wipe the drool from my chin. It's not until a few of the workers step over and ask for his autograph and he quits playing to sign their stuff that I manage to tear myself away.

Katie hangs back with a knowing look.

"Not a word, Katie-O. Not a word," I command as I walk by with my now-empty boxes.

She laughs. "I didn't say anything."

"I could hear your thoughts."

She nods. "Uh-huh. And I could hear yours. You, my friend, are a naughty, naughty girl." She shoves me lightly as we walk over to the VIP area.

"Yolo," I say, using the phrase we both make fun of that means You Only Live Once.

"So true," Katie says, pretending to ponder the sentiment deeply. "So very true."

\* \* \*

don't know if it's how well the meet-and-greets go, or just how much fun Charlotte folks are, but I'm in a fantastic mood when the show ends. I'm not even as tired as I normally am after running around for hours. So when Katie and Drew ask me if I'm up for grabbing a drink at a college bar nearby, I say yes.

It becomes abundantly clear about half an hour in that I am very much a third wheel, but as long as they don't mind, neither do I. I knew they were hanging out a lot when we were on the road, but I didn't realize how serious it was until I saw them dancing.

Talk about sexual tension. Hot damn.

Drew is quiet. He pretty much hides behind his camera for the most part. I don't know much about him except that he's from Portugal, a retired athlete in his thirties turned photographer, but when I see the way he moves with Katie on the dance floor I am seeing the guy in a whole new light.

When the bump-and-grind makes me blush, I finally have to look away.

"You still mad at me?"

The voice is deep, male, and the one that rolls over me like melted caramel.

"No," I tell Dallas, because I'm not. I'm embarrassed that I was so distracted by Katie and Drew that I didn't even notice him sitting there.

"Promise?"

"Do I lie?"

He grins and leans closer, close enough that I can smell that woodsy, now liquor-infused scent.

"You try to. But your face gives you away."

I arch an eyebrow in his direction, having lost interest in my fruity drink. Should have stuck with bourbon. "Oh yeah? What am I thinking now?"

"You're thinking that watching your friends get it on over there on the dance floor got you pretty hot and you're extremely glad that I'm here to handle that five-alarm situation for you."

He winks and I let out a small awkward laugh. Maybe all of my thoughts are being flashed in neon lights above my head. As close as he is to the truth, I am not going to be one of those people who keep repeating the same mistakes.

*I'm not, I'm not, I'm not.*

"Great show tonight," I say, my pathetic attempt at changing the subject.

"Yeah? Did you catch the new song?"

I focus on the bottles lined up behind the bar. God how I wish someone would turn them all the right way. "I might've heard a lyric or two."

"What'd you think?"

"It was all right."

I turn around in my seat, so that I can focus on the dance floor. I'm out of things to distract me behind the bar. Drew has his hands on Katie's hips now, holding her body from behind, and the way they're moving together makes me question if they've already gotten it on. Their bodies seem awfully familiar with one another's. I make a mental note to ask her.

"Just all right?" Dallas scoffs, taking mock offense at my lack of enthusiasm.

The truth is it's an amazing song, one girls all over the country will be listening to wishing their boyfriends or husbands would sing to them. It's about being her rock, her solid pillar of strength or her punching bag, whatever she needs whenever she needs. And I've had my hands all over his body so I know the title is true. Dallas Lark is the walking, talking, living, breathing example of tough all over.

"Eh," I say with a shrug.

"You're a terrible liar, sweetheart," Dallas says in my ear, bringing on those damn sexy shivers he induces. "You want to get out of here? Or you want to sit on this bar stool and lie to me some more? I'm good with whichever, so long as you're not still mad at me."

"So you'd be just as happy to sit here with me as you would if I let you take me back to your room?"

*Who's the bad liar now, Lark?*

He takes a long drink of his draft beer and nods. "Yep. Just so long as you're talking to me."

I stare at him, losing myself momentarily in his eyes. The way they're silver on the edges, almost wolflike, and cerulean in the center with a pale sky blue threaded through the irises.

"I almost believe you."

He chuckles, snapping me out of my lust-filled fog. "I didn't say I didn't have a preference. But I am truly happy with either."

"Gee, thanks." I nudge him and he uses the contact to deepen the moment, catching my gaze before I can look away.

"I owe you an apology, Robyn. About the way I acted. Not just with Jase, but ever since that summer, when you ended things between us. I was surprised and hurt. I took what I had for granted. Afterward, when you tried to make nice and I acted like an asshole, that was my own stupid bullshit getting in the way and I'm sorry. And I'm sorry I let my macho male crap interfere with your job. I'm going to do my best to make sure that doesn't happen again."

I am officially stunned. Dallas Lark doesn't do humility or apologies. Maybe Dallas Walker does. Hell, now I'm confused.

"Well, um, thank you. Apologies accepted." I smile and he grins back in a way that scrambles my brain.

"Anyway, I think you were right," he tells me. "About boundaries."

No I wasn't. Screw boundaries, I want to say. I sip my fruity waste of a drink and nearly choke. "You do?"

"Yep." His voice is low and husky, raking over my skin as if I'm sitting here naked. "I think our problem is that we haven't communicated what we each want. This isn't a situation where we can afford to get caught up and confused about what's going on. The first boundary should be we only have sex when you want to. I won't initiate our sleepovers anymore. I'll wait for you to tell me what you want."

I huff out a breath. "Hope you enjoy waiting."

One corner of his mouth lifts. "Sometimes I do. When the reward is worth it."

It's like he speaks the language of my lady parts. Stupid traitorous lady parts.

"Any other boundaries I should know about?"

"I won't interfere with your job anymore, swear it. But that goes both ways. We both have to accept that sometimes our jobs might mean interacting with people that make us uncomfortable or even damn near blind with jealousy. But at the end of the day, we both know whose bed we're going to."

"And you think I'm going to yours?" I should not encourage this behavior. I really shouldn't. But his confidence has always been the sexiest thing about him. Besides his eyes. And his hands. And his ass in those damn jeans.

"A man can hope," he says softly. "You want to dance, pretty girl?"

He's followed my line of sight back to Drew and Katie.

"I'm fine, thanks."

"The offer is there," he tells me with a noncommittal lift of his shoulder. "Just sayin'."

I have a feeling the "offer" is about a lot more than dancing. I decide to go with that feeling. "If we were going to, um, *dance,* we'd need more than boundaries. We'd need some hard rules. Ones I'm not sure you can follow."

Dallas grins, clearly feeling victorious since I'm playing along. "Lay 'em on me, darlin'."

"You suck at sticking to boundaries, Dallas. And I'm serious, this gets out or you pull any more of that crap on me about Jase, I could lose my job. It could cost us both our place on this tour and I really, really would not be happy about that."

"Me, either," he agrees. "So we agree to be discreet. Keep it casual. And to give each other space if needed regarding work obligations."

"Except when it comes to your manager," I amend. "I kind of want to cut her every time she comes near you."

Dallas chuckles and the sound rolls through me, massaging my tense muscles from the inside out. "Stake your claim then, baby. Whatever you need to do."

I glare at him and he throws his hands up.

"Or don't. Totally up to you."

"Dallas . . ." It sounds so simple, but we both know it won't be. I am jealous of Katie and Drew for far more than their sexual chemistry. They can date. They can hook up. They can do whatever they want. Dallas and I have all this . . . messy history in the way.

"Don't back out on me now, sweetheart. The way I see it, this is a win-win. You don't have time to meet new guys right now, and I don't need some groupie throwing herself at me so I can screw up and get her pregnant in a moment of weakness. You think some of those women don't pull that shit on purpose so they can trap guys in my situation in hopes of tying themselves to the money and the fame? I wish that wasn't true but that's my reality. Most of my fans are amazing and loyal and precious to me. But some . . . well, you've met my manager. So tell me what to do to make you see that I mean what I say. I know I've been an ass and I am truly sorry. But we're not kids anymore. We can do this. We *should* do this. I can behave like an adult. I can."

"Prove it," I tell him, not sure if that's even possible.

"You got it." He dips his head and stands. I'm expecting him to reach for my hand, either to lead me to the dance floor or out the door, but he doesn't. Instead he marches his crazy self directly up to the stage and says something to the band that's playing. The music stops and everyone turns their attention to him.

"Evenin' y'all," he says into the mic as he straps on the guy's guitar. "My name's Dallas Lark, and I have to prove something to my girl tonight. So bear with me, folks."

Katie makes a face at me and I just shake my head. With Dallas, you just never know what to expect. I gave up trying to figure him out long ago. It's more fun to be surprised anyway.

When he plays the opening chords and the band chimes in, I laugh out loud.

Dallas strums and sings, entertaining the crowd like the professional that he is and the entire bar is mesmerized.

His rendition of "I Walk the Line" is a hit and I wonder how many people know that the man on the small stage before them is the same one who played to a sold-out amphitheater a few hours ago.

When he starts toward me with his guitar, I close my eyes.

*Fight or flight, Robyn.*

This is it. Dallas is on one side of the chasm that's been growing between us for years and I'm on the other. When he reaches me, I know I have to make a choice. Now. Either I can play it safe and walk away, again, or I can jump down a gaping black hole with him.

I chew my lip as he serenades me in a crowded bar, am contemplating, weighing my options, and pitting the pros against the cons. They stack up pretty evenly. This tour will end and I'll either have some scandalous memories of being young and reckless that will leave another scar on my already wounded heart or a list of regrets that come from playing it safe.

I glance around and see the carefree smiles of the bar's unsuspecting patrons. To them I just look like a lucky girl a sexy singer is flirting with. And damn it, I want to be that girl—the one who gets to have an impulsive fling, even though I know it can't last and I'll eventually have to go back to being me.

God help this man. God help me.

I let my protective shield fall to the ground and shatter at my feet as I meet Dallas's intense stare and give him an almost imperceptible nod. He smiles and the relief in his eyes hits me in all the weak places I've left exposed.

*Yes,* I think so loudly it's a wonder he doesn't hear my thoughts over the music. *I'm going to risk a world of hurt for experiences that might become painful memories. Because I'm pretty sure it will be worth the pain.*

I add one more thought in case he really can read them. *Be careful with me, please.*

For better or worse, I am his, and he is mine—even if only for a little while longer.

# 21 | Robyn

"WHERE IN THE WORLD ARE WE GOING?"

Dallas showed up at my hotel room right at lunchtime and said we were going out to dinner and that I didn't need to bring anything except myself. We never made any official plans for today so I'm a little surprised to see him. He apparently wasn't kidding about waiting for me to initiate the sex in our new arrangement because he walked me to my room last night and left me without so much as a good-night kiss.

We're supposed to be heading to New Orleans tomorrow morning. I'd spent the afternoon getting some work done in my room so I'd have time for sightseeing in New Orleans.

"You'll see," he says, tugging me by the hand to the hotel lobby. He's still holding my hand when we exit the hotel. He waves the driver off and holds my door open.

Tossing him a questioning glance of apprehension over my shoulder, I slide into the backseat.

"Do I at least get a hint?" The car pulls into traffic once Dallas is all the way inside.

He rubs his chin thoughtfully. "Remember that trip the honor society took in high school? The one that included Italy and Spain that you didn't get to go on?"

I nod. I do remember. I didn't get to go because my dad had died.

"You said you were really just upset because you were excited about the food."

I smile. "This is true. But what does this have to do with where we're going?" Surely he realizes we don't have time to hit Italy or Spain before tomorrow morning.

"We're going to get the food."

B lue Restaurant and Bar is exactly what Dallas promised. The menu is divided into locales and there are even more countries on the menu than there were on the National Honor Society trip. I don't even know how he remembered that. We order dishes from all around the world. Some of them are amazing and some are, well, kind of gross. But we try it all and we laugh a lot. It's the best date I've had in . . . forever. And I'm not even sure it's a date.

I stare at the table full of half-eaten food. "I can't eat any more. I'm so full it hurts. The dessert menu is tempting, but I can barely breathe." Dishes with names I can hardly pronounce fill the table. Foie gras, a fish that's pan seared, and soup referred to as bisque. It was amazing.

"That's okay. We're going to do a little walking, then I have other plans for dessert," Dallas informs me.

"Oh do you?" I sincerely hope his dessert plans include sex, though I might need a nap first after all the rich food.

He pays the tab, then stands to help me up from the table. "I do."

"Since when did you become such a planner?"

He makes a low satisfied noise in my ear. "Since now."

\* \* \*

After a gallery crawl in the North Davidson arts district, I am delighted when we stop in front of a French bakery I've wanted to visit since I saw it on Food Network.

It's gotten late and I didn't expect much of anything to still be open. But Amelie's is open twenty-four hours a day.

"I've always wanted to come here," I tell Dallas, squeezing his arm as we step inside. The menu is a giant chalkboard and the vibe is trendy and upbeat despite the late hour. "How did you know?"

"Seemed like a Robyn-type place," he tells me with a self-congratulatory grin. "So I did good?"

I feel like a little kid at Christmas. "So good," I gush, barely managing to tear my eyes from the display cases full of sugary confections.

Once we've ordered, we both descend on our coffees and sweets. Mostly I do a lot of inappropriate moaning, stopping just short of having a *When Harry Met Sally* moment.

"So you never told me," Dallas says before shoving the last macaron into his mouth after I turned it down.

"Told you what?"

"What your dream is." He meets my amused smile with a serious stare. "I'm serious. You know mine. We talk about it all the time. Hell, you're watching me live it. So what's yours?"

I take a bite of my caramel apple tart and chew slowly while I contemplate this. "Mine's not as exciting as yours."

"What? It doesn't have to be exciting. Your dream is your dream and fair is fair. I showed you mine, now you show me yours."

I feel the heat that sweeps across my cheeks. "Pretty sure I've shown you mine more times than I can count."

Laughing, Dallas shakes his head at me with amusement sparkling in his blue eyes. "There's my dirty girl."

I roll mine. "I don't know, Dallas. I don't think of it as a dream, I guess. More like a goal."

"Okay," he says slowly. "Tell me your goal then."

I take a sip of my coffee and decide to buy a French press ASAP. "I have way more than one."

He smiles like he knows this about me already. "I'll text the driver and let him know we're walking back to the hotel from here. These goals of yours, let's hear 'em."

# 22 | Dallas

"WELL, FOR STARTERS," ROBYN SAYS, HOLDING UP ONE FINGER, "I want to be successful. I want to be the best at what I do. I want to be recognized for my sacrifices and hard work but not with like, a Grammy, or anything. Just with raises and promotions. So I can buy lots and lots of shoes." She winks and I shake my head.

"Well, I think you're the best damn marketing events promotional person there is."

She's grinning when she corrects me with her official title. "And I want to be happy, you know? Not just content. But full-on happy."

"Full-on happy?" We've almost reached the hotel but I want to hear her explanation of this so I slow our pace.

She nods and her voice is soft when she speaks. "Yeah. I want to love and be loved and I want to smile and laugh and be grateful for all that I have every single day." Her eyes don't leave mine as she continues. "I understand what you meant about getting caught up in the tour and the interviews and the media stuff. Sometimes it's easy to just shift into autopilot and go through the motions. But I don't want that. I don't want to just 'get through' my life. I want to really live it and enjoy it. I want to experience everything that I can while I can."

Her words flow out of her mouth and into me.

Is this what this is? An experience? One with an expiration date because I've set it up that way?

There's a convincing smile plastered on my mouth but Robyn listing her life goals is doing something strange to me. It's like listening to someone tell you what's going to happen after you die.

We've had a fantastic night and I'm happy for her, but knowing I won't be a part of this future she's so excited about has me twisted up inside in knots I don't know how to untie.

"I want to go hiking and sailing and travel the world," Robyn continues, her enthusiasm growing as my trepidation about the entire state of our relationship consumes me. "I want to eat a meal that costs way more than it should in Europe, and have pasta in Italy that fills me so full I look like I'm pregnant with twins. And, oh! I want to go to that toy store in New York. The one in that movie with the giant piano, you know?"

"FAO Schwarz," I say because it was in a Tom Hanks movie she and I used to watch on my grandparents' couch on lazy Sunday afternoons.

"Right." Her eyes are gleaming with excitement while I am wrestling with my own selfish shit. She's practically skipping ahead while I trail behind.

*I* want to be the one to take her to the fucking toy store to play on the giant piano, damn it. I want to take her to Europe and Italy. I want to be the one who gets to watch her have these experiences she's so excited about.

But I won't be. Because I'll be on the road, on some bus living like a gypsy while she moves on with her life. With some other motherfucker who'll get to kiss her sweet mouth and see that light shining in her eyes when she dances across that damn piano. I won't be the one who gets to watch her dreams come true and that hits me in a place I don't let anyone affect, ever.

"Ready to call it a night?" I gesture toward the hotel.

Robyn tilts her head at my abruptness. "Yeah. I guess so."

We ride the elevator to her room in silence. She has this look on her face that has me wanting to kick my own ass. She opened up and I shut her down.

When we reach her door, I see it, the hopeful look of invitation.

I'm going to be invited inside. But I don't deserve it. And even though I do want this, want her, my head is in the wrong place for this right now.

Before she can say anything I take a step back. "I'm beat, babe. Get some rest and I'll see you in the morning, okay?"

Wounded surprise flashes in her eyes but she nods. "Okay." Just as I'm about to turn away, she touches my arm. "Dallas?"

"Yeah?"

"Tonight was . . . really great. It was pretty much the perfect date—for me, anyway. Exotic food, art galleries, and dessert at the coolest place I've ever seen. But I know you and none of those are really your idea of a good time. And now you're not coming in so . . ."

I don't answer her unspoken question because I'm not entirely sure what it's going to be.

"I guess I'm just wondering what you got out of tonight." She averts her eyes in a way that makes me feel like I've embarrassed her by making her spell it out for me. I place a finger under her chin and lift so she has to look at me.

"You had a good time?"

"A great time," she says softly.

"That's what I got out of tonight."

I kiss her lightly on the mouth, but I step back before she can wrap her arms around me. Tonight wasn't about casual sex or getting off and we both know it.

If this goes any further right now I'm going to tell her that we can do this every night. That I would do anything to take back the time we lost. That being on the road would not be nearly as much fun if she weren't here. That I want more than casual sex. I want to be the one to see her dreams come true, fuck, I want to *make them* come true.

It wouldn't be possible and it wouldn't be right to say any of that, so I place one more kiss on her forehead and let go of her hands. There's only one way this can go and I need to wrap my head around that and accept it.

Sometimes you don't get your dream exactly as you wished it. Sometimes you get a solo deal instead of one with your band. And sometimes a woman you are realizing you're in love with has dreams that don't include you—that *can't* include you.

So I do the only thing that I can.

I walk away.

# 23 | Dallas

EITHER SOMEONE IS KNOCKING ON MY DOOR OR I CHANGED MY alarm to the sound of hammers on my skull.

"Go away!" I holler, though it's muffled by my pillow.

The past week has been a blur. I can't even remember exactly which city I'm in and I don't necessarily want to yet. I just want to sink back into blissful sleep.

"Dallas Walker Lark, I know you do not think you're going to just sit in your room alone in New Orleans and not go out and see the town." Robyn's voice fills my hotel room. "Move your ass and answer this door. There is fun to be had."

Ah yes, New Orleans. I make a groaning sound with my face still half in my pillow. Scrambling out of bed and remembering that I decided to sleep nude last night, I wrap the bedsheet around my waist. I stumble to the door and open it, greeting Robyn with "I'm tired. I need sleep, woman."

"You can sleep when you're dead," she tells me, following me back inside toward my bed. "You played an awesome show last night. We have to celebrate."

She's right—the show did go well. But it ran so late we didn't get a chance to hang out afterward. We haven't had a chance to spend a moment alone since Charlotte. So I have some ideas about how I'd like to celebrate with Robyn. None of them involve leaving this bed. I dive back in and bury my face in the pillow that mercifully blocks the light from the blinds she's throwing open.

Robyn yanks at my covers so I roll over and grab her wrist, yanking her into the bed with me.

"Wake up, Johnny Cash," she says with a laugh. "I'll even let you wear black and the dark sunglasses all around town."

I inhale her clean, just-showered scent while pulling her in closer to me.

"Get naked, Breeland. Those are the rules of this bed."

"I'm not technically *in* the bed."

"Doesn't matter. You're on it. Still counts."

I reach for her but she pulls back. "Come on! There is gumbo and beignets to be had. Street performers to be seen! I'll even let you order food from something with wheels." She stands up, leaving the reach of my arms, and I groan.

"I will happily perform for you in this bed all day. Just get naked first."

A pillow hits me in the head.

"That's it. You asked for it."

I jump up in my birthday suit and chase after her in all my buck-naked glory. Robyn runs to the bathroom and tries to shut me out, but I'm a hell of a lot stronger than her so I force the door open and wrap her in my arms. She stops giggling, stares at me with this wicked grin of hers, and I am so owned. But there's no need for her to know that.

Reaching around her, I grab the shower lever and turn on the water full blast, leaving it completely on cold.

I lift her inside and she screams and squeals so loud it should shatter the glass.

"Oh my God! Dallas! I've already had a shower! And that is fucking cold!"

She braces herself with her arms, which provide no shield against the frozen stream whatsoever. But when I look down and her hard pearled nipples are protruding from her white tank top, my focus shifts from punishment to pleasure.

"Lose the clothes and I'll turn the warm water on." We've been dancing around each other, flirting and making dirty promises, since we agreed to this new arrangement. It's time to put up or shut up.

"Same rules as your bed then?" The glint in her emerald eyes tells me she's ready. We're ready.

Her teeth are chattering so I take pity on her and shove the lever to the warmer side.

"No, baby. Naked in the shower just makes more sense."

She tosses a rag at me when I step in and I let it fall to the floor in favor of removing her soaked clothing. After I've peeled the last item off her body, I let my hands roam in slow appreciation.

As the water heats, so does the look in her eyes.

"What happened to waiting for me to initiate the sex? I was starting to think you were going to make me beg." She arches an eyebrow and gives me a challenging grin.

"This isn't sex. This is just good morning." I press my gaze hard into hers as my hand slips between her thighs. "I meant what I said. I am going to wait. I'm going to wait right here until you're ready."

I tease her outer folds with my fingertips. A whimper that sounds close enough to "please" for me escapes her lips and I slide my middle finger into her slick, pulsating heat.

"Fuck," I moan, knowing exactly how good that clenching is

going to feel on my cock. But not yet. Not until she's sure she wants this with me.

I kneel down, blinking through the water droplets pelting my face, and stare up at her. She arches an interested brow, and I place openmouthed kisses on her inner thighs.

She slides her fingers into my hair. The heat in her gaze is all the permission I need, but I'll wait for the words.

"Good morning, Robyn."

"Good morning, Dallas," she whispers.

I wait patiently until she nods, giving me the permission I'm seeking. I won't push her past this, but I won't leave this shower until she's sated.

Robyn throbs against my mouth, her hips jerking forward the moment my tongue invades the space between her folded flesh.

"Feel good, baby?"

"Y-Yes. But—"

"But?" I pull my head back to glance up at her again.

"After this, we are going out on the town, Dallas. I'm serious."

I pull her delicate clit into my mouth once more before answering. "You got it, pretty girl. After this."

"I can't believe I've never been here before. I wanted to get Leaving Amarillo a few shows in the area but it just never worked out." I look around at the colorful fabric of culture that is New Orleans. Every corner is painted and decorated like they're prepared for a yearlong festival.

"Same here," Robyn says, grabbing my hand and pulling me into the crowd. "I've always wanted to come, but I just never got the chance. This is why I love my job. I get to travel and see the world."

"That the only reason?"

Her eyes widen and I wink to let her know I'm playing around. Except I'm not sure that I am.

"Of course not." She nudges me in the side. "I have great insurance benefits and a 401(k), too."

I reach for her, tickling her around the rib cage hard until she cries out.

"Okay, okay! Stop! I *might* enjoy the fact that I get to see you. A little."

"You've seen me a lot more than a little." I growl softly, then kiss her below the ear.

She whimpers when I let my hands drift lower. "Dallas, we're in public."

"I don't remember that bothering you," I say, recalling a time after graduation when we indulged in some very public sexual acts in very crowded areas. Thankfully everyone else was too wasted to notice.

"You are so bad," she tells me.

"You love it."

Her silence tells me that I'm right. For the next hour we sightsee like she wanted, popping in and out of little shops and even buying some strange voodoo candles. We feed each other beignets and I kiss powdered sugar from her lips.

We grab gumbo for dinner and eat outside on a patio at a place on a busy street corner.

"It's like it never stops here," she says. "Like the city has its own heartbeat and it's just constantly alive and awake."

Beside us a woman, or it might be a man dressed as a woman, hell if I know, is being shoved into a police car. On the opposite corner a group of young men in tighty whities and wigs and lots of glittery makeup are pole dancing on some building pillars.

"Yeah, it's alive and awake all right. And parts of it are fucking weird."

Robyn laughs at my discomfort. "We're a long way from Amarillo, country boy."

"You can say that again."

She grins at me, then leans forward to run her nose against mine. "We're a long way from Amarillo, country boy." This time her voice is lower, huskier like I like it. The exact cadence that makes me want to spread her on this table and have her for dessert. This morning was just a taste—an appetizer. I'm ready for the main course.

"I haven't been a boy in a long time, darlin'." I wink and give her a light kiss on the tip of her nose. "But I think you know this already."

Before she can respond, a jazz band starts up right beside where we're sitting. Robyn doesn't hesitate.

She jumps up from her dinner and runs to stand beside a dark-skinned gray-haired gentleman playing the saxophone. I watch in wonder as she dances along to the music, twirling until her dark blue dress with the little white flowers on it spins around her. Soon she isn't alone and if it weren't for her red hair, I'd be hard-pressed to find her in the crowd.

When I make my way to her, she collapses against my chest. "This is the best place ever. I love it here. Let's never leave, okay?"

When she looks at up me with so much hope in her eyes, begging me to play along, I can't help but give her what she wants.

"Okay," I say, taking her hand for one more twirl. "We'll never leave."

# 24 | Robyn

IT'S FUNNY, AS A KID, I WASN'T A HUGE FAN OF PLAYING PRETEND.
Yet as an adult I can't seem to get enough of it.

After hours of dancing in the street and then in a swanky jazz club
we happened upon by accident, Dallas and I return to his room like a
couple returning to their honeymoon suite.

We should both be exhausted, but there is an energy pulsating
between us that has a life of its own. There is something truly magi-
cal about this place—it's as if the spirits of the past are charging the
air around us, electrifying everything and everyone with their own
never-ending high-velocity current.

Dallas excuses himself to use the restroom and I step out onto his
balcony. It's nearly four in the morning but the party is still going
strong on the street down below. I'm mesmerized by the lively crowd,
entranced by their energy and so engrossed that I don't hear Dallas
come up behind me.

"What a beautiful view," he says softly, the deep rumble of his
voice warming my blood.

"It is," I agree, taking in the lights and the laughter down below.
"It's an amazing city."

"I wasn't talking about the city."

I gasp audibly when his hands slide up my thighs, raising my dress as they go.

*This isn't real, Robyn. This is temporary. Casual, like he said. Don't forget that. Don't get confused about what this means. It's a good time, that's all.*

But it's confusing and it has been since Charlotte. Because it feels real, as real and all consuming as Dallas's presence enveloping me the way he did when we danced tonight. His breath hits my neck before his lips do and my knees weaken. His solid body supports my weight as his fingers tease the thin cotton barrier between us. I can feel his entire length against my backside and it makes me moan in anticipation.

"Anyone could see, Dallas," I breathe, too turned on to be as panicked as I should be. "They could just look up and they'd see."

"Yeah?" he says, as if this isn't of any concern to him. "You like that, sweet girl? We're supposed to be discreet, though. But what if I take you right now? What if you come apart right here on this balcony?"

His thick warm finger slides beneath my panties and strokes the length of my own slick arousal.

"We can't do this," I whisper. "I mean, we can. I want to. Just not right here."

"I want them to watch," he says into my ear. "I want them to know that you're mine, to see how hot I make you and how hard you come for me. Only for me."

I was right about the spirits of the past inhabiting this city. Dallas is a man possessed.

I can't form a coherent sentence so I agree to his request wordlessly. Spreading my legs farther apart for him, I lean back on his chest.

"Only for you," I whisper, and they're the last words I speak before he slides into me, groaning as he fills me and gripping my hips with both hands.

"Fuck, Robyn. You're so damn hot. I can hardly control myself."

"Then don't."

This is insane. Anyone could look up right now and with a second glance they would know exactly what we were up to. But I can't bring myself to feel anything other than exhilarated. Everything is brighter, more vibrant with him inside me. Time slows and I can hear every breath he takes, see every pinpoint of light down below.

I know the exact moment when he begins to lose himself inside me. I'm acutely aware of the change when hard thrusts become a slow, intense grind.

"Come for me, sweet girl. Let me feel how much you enjoy being a dirty girl out here for the world to see."

My insides clench around him, propelled by his sexy words.

"Dallas," I whisper, because I feel myself falling. Not off the balcony but into oblivion with him.

"Come for me, Robyn. Show me how much you love this, how hard it turns you on knowing they could see, knowing they could watch me fuck you. Show me how dirty you can be, sweet girl." His middle finger hits my clit at precisely the perfect moment and it flings me over the edge. His name rolls off my tongue over and over as he finishes inside me. "That's my girl," he whispers between gentle kisses on my neck. "My sweet dirty girl."

I lie face-to-face with Dallas—his arms wrapped around my naked body—after we've both come more times than I can count. For a while we just laid there, catching our breath, but somehow that turned to satisfied smiles and now he's staring into my eyes and we're both in danger of unleashing the truths of our souls.

"I was starting to wonder if we were ever going to get to this part of our agreement. You kept walking me to my door and saying good night like you couldn't wait to kick rocks."

Dallas gives me a sad smile. "I wanted to be sure you really wanted this. The truth is, I feel like us being on this tour together is the universe allowing me to make up for lost time."

I nuzzle my head beneath his chin so I can listen to his heartbeat. And so I can escape the intense moment where I might say something that I shouldn't. "Lost time?"

"When you decided not to go on the road with us that summer, I was surprised, to say the least. But when you ended things between us, it wasn't something I was at all prepared to deal with. You tried later, to explain, I think. And I handled it like a stupid, cocky kid not used to not getting his way when I should've heard you out."

Lying here in postcoital bliss with him exposes my vulnerable side. This is not the route we should be heading down if we're keeping this casual. Rehashing our past is the opposite of casual.

"I bombed show after show that summer. The tour ended abruptly and we didn't get asked back to a single venue. Want to know why?"

Speaking of bombs, he just dropped one on me. I didn't know this because I spent most of that summer avoiding him.

I take his face in my hands and latch my gaze on to his—needing a physical connection to gather the strength I need to hear this.

Dallas takes my silence for a yes and continues. "Every song I'd written, the majority of the ones on the set list, they were about you. Or at least inspired by you. I couldn't get up there and give it my all when I was singing about a girl who'd dumped my ass."

His confession wedges into a crack in my heart, causing it to take off, beating in triple time.

After kissing him gently on the mouth, I take a deep breath and try my best to explain something I should have told him years ago.

"Dallas, I'm so sorry. I didn't know and I never meant to . . ." To what? Ruin his life? Destroy his dream? No wonder he never wanted to speak to me again. The frustrated anger I saw on his face when I appeared on this tour makes so much more sense now. I try to speak over the lump of emotion constricting my throat. "I should've told you the truth that summer. I should've—"

"It's in the past, Robyn. All of it. And I'm enjoying the hell out of our present so I just wanted to clear the air without having that hanging over us."

"We were so young and I—"

His hands tighten around my hips, cutting me off. "I know. And you were right anyway. I needed to focus on my music and you had a full school schedule to deal with. It all worked out how it was meant to, just like you said it would."

I squeeze my eyes shut and try not to wince at how much that hurts to hear. I tried to tell him about my mom, about why I really ended it, a few weeks after our breakup, but he wouldn't hear me out. He avoided me anytime our paths crossed and practically shut down his ability to hear anytime I opened my mouth in his presence, which is understandable since I ruined his tour that summer. So maybe now isn't the time to come clean, either.

But I wasn't right. It was the wrong way to handle it and I know that now. It occurs to me in the form of tears pricking my eyes that if I hadn't ended our relationship abruptly the way that I did, maybe the band would have gotten recognized sooner. Maybe he wouldn't be Dallas Walker solo act and he'd be living his actual dream with his band.

"So Midnight Bay seems like a decent company to work for," he says, completely changing the subject. I should probably feel relieved and yet I don't. "You happy there?"

I nod, swallowing the guilt his apology unearthed from deep in my soul. "Mm-hm."

"You're a hard worker. They're lucky to have you."

"They might not agree if they knew what we were up to right now. It's a family-oriented business with some pretty high moral standards."

"My lips are sealed, sweetheart. Promise. Besides, I'd never let them fire you. I don't know if you've heard, but I'm a pretty big deal these days."

I laugh softly. "Oh yeah? And is it as amazing as you thought it would be? Performing to huge crowds and being on this tour, getting to live your dream?" I trail a manicured finger in circles on the forearm he has wrapped around me while I wait for his answer. Part of me wants to hear that he's happy, that he's just as happy as he would be if he'd made it with his band intact.

"It is. Or at least, I think it is."

I angle around so that I can look him in the face. "You think it is?"

He pulls me closer, kissing me lightly on the lips. "Yeah. For the most part. It's like there's been an exchange of sorts, one I didn't realize I'd agreed to."

"I'm gonna need you to man-'splain that to me, please."

He lets out a small chuckle, then sighs and I feel his chest rise and fall. "It's like I agreed to be this version of myself I didn't expect to have to be. Dallas Walker. Performer Dallas."

I don't say anything as I settle back into the spooning position so he continues on.

"Dallas Lark is 'real me,' you know? The one that you've known for years. The one who harasses his sister constantly to make sure she's okay. I had a cheeseburger and a slice of apple pie alone in a diner on my birthday and realized that I was actually homesick for a place I'd been planning to leave since the day I arrived. But nobody really knows that guy—the one who has pie alone or gets to come back to you after each show and has the pleasure and privilege of tasting and touching you, of filling you and watching you come undone while I—"

"Dallas!" I call out, interrupting him suddenly. "I get the picture. Either move on or we're not going to finish this conversation."

He laughs low in my ear when I wiggle my backside against him.

"I don't know. It's just, I didn't realize that I'd have to cut myself in half, be the two different guys. But that's the price, apparently. I lose my last name but I get to live my dream every night. I don't know if it's an even exchange either way."

My fingers aren't tracing arbitrary circles anymore. They're following the intricate lines of the tattoo that covers his inner forearm. The one that says "Lark" in script.

"Promise me something," I say so low I don't know if he can hear me. "Promise me no matter what, you'll never lose that guy, the one you really are."

His arms tighten around me like a reverse hug and I'm not sure which one of us needs it more.

"I'll try not to."

# 25 | Dallas

*NOT GOING TO MAKE YOUR SHOW THIS WEEKEND. HAVE TO WORK. Couldn't get anyone to trade shifts. Sorry, man.*

Gavin's text reads like a load of bullshit.

I heavily suspect the coward is avoiding my sister, but I've vowed to let her be a big girl and not interfere with her personal life so I text him back that I understand and that I hope he can drop by the after party.

After five straight weeks on the road, we're playing in Dallas and it feels kind of good to be home or close to home at least. It's nice to see familiar landmarks and highways anyway.

Today I'm doing radio interviews in Dallas. I text Dixie while I wait in the lobby of KGBX, reminding her that her and Robyn's mom's tickets will be at will-call and that the backstage passes will be with them.

"Dallas Walker," a rail-thin slip of a woman in a pencil skirt calls out. "They're ready for you. Come with me."

I stand and follow her down a dim hallway to the recording studio. The publicist Mandy put me in touch with pulled some strings to get me on the nationally syndicated Ricky Ray show while I was in town.

It's a huge opportunity, but I'm nervous because I have no idea what he's going to ask. Ricky is known for asking the tough questions and I've been strictly instructed not to answer any involving Jase Wade or his personal life.

My palms are slick so I wipe them on my jeans before shaking the hands of the folks who greet me when the receptionist opens the door.

"Dallas Walker, nice to meet you," a smiling brunette with headphones on tells me. "Just have a seat right there." She gestures to an empty seat on the edge of the L-shaped table. "Be sure you speak clearly into the mic."

"Got it."

"He can manage, Kim. That's what he does for a living," the man on the other side of the table says. "That's Kim Le. I'm Ricky Ray."

I nod at Kim and then reach across a switchboard and shake his hand. "Nice to meet you both. Thank you for having me today."

"Thanks for joining us. We'll just chat. Forget the listeners. Let's just shoot the bull like old friends. Sound good?"

"Yes, sir."

"First rule of shooting the bull, no 'sirs.' "

I nod, feeling like a complete jackass. "Got it."

A tall blond woman with angular features steps into the small room. "We're on in five, Ricky," she tells him.

"Let's do this," he says, putting in earbuds like the ones I was given.

I press mine into my ears and they fill with the sound of someone counting down. "On in five" apparently means five seconds in radio time.

"We're back with Ricky Ray, Kim Le, and up-and-coming country music sensation Dallas Walker," Ricky says in a completely different voice than the one he used to greet me. "Thanks for joining us, Dallas."

The chorus of "Better to Burn" plays briefly.

"Thanks for having me," I say into the silver microphone attached to a long metal arm in front of me.

"So you're from here in town I hear."

It's not a question, but I answer anyway. "Yes, si—uh, yes. I am. From Amarillo actually."

Austin originally, but I don't feel the need to clarify because it would open a door to my past I have no intention of walking through on the radio.

"You had a band there, didn't you?"

I shift in my seat and it rolls slightly backward. I stop myself before I answer with "yes, sir." "Yeah. My sister and a buddy of mine played around for a while."

"Just played around?" Ricky glances down at several sheets of paper laid out before him. "It says here you took third place in last year's state fair sound-off and that your band, Leaving Amarillo, recently played in Austin MusicFest."

Swallowing hard, I nod even though I know I'm supposed to verbalize my answers.

"Austin was a good time. I met my manager there. If I hadn't, I probably wouldn't be sitting here right now."

It's a lame-ass attempt at redirecting, but it's all I got.

"Well, thank goodness for Austin." Kim breaks in, possibly because she's the closest to me and can likely see how twitchy I'm becoming. "Touring with Jase Wade must be amazing. Has that been a life-changing experience?"

I grin at her, thankful for the change in topic. "It has been. Jase is an impressive performer and I've learned a lot being on this tour. It's

an awesome opportunity and I'm grateful to get to be a part of it."
Most of that is true at least.

"You already have quite a large fan base—much larger than most
new artists," Ricky says, eyeing me as if wondering how I tricked
people into listening to my music. "Do you attribute that to your
time with your band? Have Leaving Amarillo fans followed you over
into your solo career?"

I shrug. "You know, it's hard to say. I mean I *hope* so. It'd be great
if they did since it's pretty much the same sound."

Ricky smirks as if I'm full of shit.

"Well, not exactly the same. You had a fiddle player in Leaving
Amarillo, right?"

Son of a bitch. Why this guy wants to talk about the band so much
is beyond me. But like a dog with a bone, he doesn't seem to want to
let go.

"We did. My sister is a very talented violinist and fiddle player.
She's been playing since we were kids."

"She didn't want to come along on the tour?"

*More like the label wouldn't have ever allowed her to.*

Guilt seeps into my pours, thick like lead that weighs me down. I
take a deep breath before answering in order to maintain my composure. "We had a loss in the family. She had other priorities to handle
when this opportunity presented itself."

"I'm sorry to hear that," Kim says, earning herself another grin.

Ricky doesn't offer his condolences. "So you're out on the road,
right after a devastating loss in your family, without your band. That
takes dedication."

I'm a big boy. I can listen between the lines. What he really wants
to say is that I must be some special brand of selfish asshole to leave
my grieving sister and my band behind.

I can't even argue with him so I just nod. "I think dedication is important when it comes to making it in the music business. The window of opportunity is fairly small, so I had to jump when it opened."

"Definitely," Kim says, chiming in to agree with me.

"And your band didn't want to jump with you?"

I grip my knee tightly under the table to keep myself and my temper under control. Telling Ricky Ray to fuck off on national radio would probably not go over well.

"It had a lot to do with timing. Both my sister and my drummer had other obligations they needed to see to at the time."

Kim's voice is more curious and less accusatory when she inquires about Leaving Amarillo. "Do you think y'all might ever get back together? Or is Dallas Walker a lone road warrior from here on out?"

Good question. "I wish I knew the answer to that." I focus on the mic in front of me. "Right now I'm just taking it one day a time."

"One show at a time," she corrects playfully.

"Exactly."

"We posted about your visit to the studio today," Ricky breaks in. "On our Facebook page. The most frequent comments we're seeing are from local listeners wondering why you left your band to go it alone when it seemed like the natural next step would be for Leaving Amarillo to be on this tour instead of Dallas Walker. What would you say to those critics?"

*It's none of your fucking business.*

Sweat forms on my neck and drips into the collar of my shirt. I shove my shirtsleeves upward on my forearms and take a fortifying breath. "Well, honestly, all I can say is sometimes things don't work out how you expect them to. Sometimes life gets in the way and you don't get exactly what you want. But I am really and truly blessed to be on this tour and I don't take anything for granted. I'm grateful for all of the fans and the listeners and people who've never even heard of me who will hopefully give me a chance."

"There you have it, ladies and gentlemen. Dallas Walker." Ricky is back to using his announcer voice. "We're going to break for some music, including Dallas's hit single, 'Better to Burn,' then we'll be back to take your questions."

Once Ricky takes his earphones out, I do the same. I don't want to sit around and take questions. I want to get the hell out of here before anyone else asks about Dixie and Gavin. Those questions aren't mine to answer anyway.

"Do I have time to get some air?"

Kim gives me a sympathetic look. "Not really. But we're almost done here. A few minutes of questions and you're free."

Ricky laughs like I've asked something amusing.

"Spotlight gettin' too bright for you already, Walker? Better buck up, son. It's only going to get hotter from here."

After this live interview I have several more via phone. He's right. It will only get more intense.

The blonde from before taps on the glass and points at Ricky as soon as he steps back into the booth. She counts down from five on her right hand, then nods.

"And we're back with Dallas Walker," Ricky announces suddenly. "Dallas, we checked out fan feedback and we have another tough question for you."

"Oh good," I say, doing my best to sound like I'm playing it cool instead of letting the dread I feel deepen my tone.

Kim laughs but there is sympathy in her smile this time. "So this question comes primarily from the ladies, but a few fellas wanted to know as well."

I hold my breath and keep my expression blank while I wait.

Kim tilts her head to the side. "We're all dying to know, is there a special girl out there? Someone you're missing while you're out on the road?"

Robyn's face flashes behind my eyes. I can't help but wonder if she's listening. Mandy's warnings about encroaching on Jase's territory come to mind as well and it pisses me off that I even have the thought.

We said we were keeping it casual. Surely Robyn will understand. Even if we were heavily involved I'm not the type to go announcing it on national radio. She knows this. She knows me. She was the one who specified that we keep this to ourselves for the sake of both of our jobs. But it still feels like a lie.

Rubbing my sweaty palms on my jeans I chuckle lightly. "Nah. Not really. Right now I'm just focusing on the music."

"Well there you have it, ladies. And, er, gentlemen," Ricky says with a hearty laugh. "Dallas Walker is a single man."

"I bet that makes a lot of women happy to hear tonight," Kim says. Maybe.

It probably didn't bring joy to one woman in particular, though. I pull my phone out of my pocket as soon as I exit the building, hoping against hope that she's home.

# 26 | Robyn

WHEN THE TOUR HEADS TO TEXAS, I'M GRATEFUL FOR THE TIME to sleep in my own bed. The schedule has been grueling and nights with Dallas haven't included a lot of actual sleep. Not that I'm complaining.

As much as I want to crash for the entire weekend, the first thing I do when I arrive home is have lunch and go shopping with my mom. I fill her in about Dallas being on the tour and she sort of half-yells at me for not calling her with this news sooner.

Sitting across from me at our favorite Tex-Mex place, she adjusts the vibrant pink scarf covering her head and gapes at me. "Are you sure you're okay with this? Working with him after everything?"

I don't bother filling her in on the details of our little arrangement.

"I'm fine. It's been surprisingly okay." Better than okay, really, but this is my mom here. Plus she doesn't know why we broke up and I have no plans of ever telling her.

I was always closer with my dad, but after he passed away, my mom and I definitely bonded. When she got sick, I couldn't stand the thought of losing another person I loved so I became dedicated to making sure I did everything in my power to keep her healthy.

The older I get, the more I realize how much she and I have in common. We're both control freaks with slight OCD tendencies who obsess about plans and lists and agendas. Funny, when I was younger, those things drove me half-crazy about her. Now I get it, though, the need for control in a world of chaos. You have to take it where you can get it.

Once I've convinced her I can handle the tour, she moves on from Dallas and peppers me with questions about Jase Wade. I knew she was a fan, but sheesh. When she asks if he's seeing anyone, I'm almost nervous for him since I got her backstage passes for the show tomorrow night. Maybe I should have them bulk up Wade's security. Dixie will be there, too, though Dallas texted and said Gavin wouldn't be able to make it. It's odd to me that he can't come to his best friend's show, but Gavin Garrison has never been the predictable type.

After a long afternoon with my mom, one that ended with us hearing Dallas on the radio telling the world that he's a single man, I'm thankful when I get home to a note from Katie saying she's staying with a friend and not to wait up.

I've just decided to run myself a hot bubble bath when my phone buzzes in my purse. I retrieve it, smiling when I see Dallas on the screen.

"Hey, you," I say. "Enjoying being home in the great state of Texas?"

"It could be worse, I guess." He doesn't sound like himself. He sounds like someone ran over his dog, or maybe even him.

"You okay?"

"Can I come by? It doesn't have to be for . . . you know. I just want to see you."

"Look at you being all sweet. I kind of like this side of you. Maybe we should come home more often."

"That so?"

"Come on over, Lark. I was just about to take a bubble bath but I guess I can wait. Care to join me?"

"You? Naked? In a tub full of bubbles?"

"Yes, sir."

Dallas is quiet for a second. "Well, I guess if you're going to twist my arm . . ."

I'm still laughing when we hang up.

I open the door in nothing but my robe and Dallas smiles despite the sadness in his eyes.

"Hey," I say, ushering him inside. "What's up with you? I thought you'd be happy to be home, or close to home at least."

"I had radio interviews today. One with Ricky Ray and several with a few local stations," he tells me, taking off his dark brown jacket and hanging it in the corner on one of my bar stools. "Want to know what question they all wanted an answer to?"

I nod. I heard most of the one with Ricky Ray but I still have no idea what has him looking so beat down.

" 'What happened to Leaving Amarillo, Dallas? Why'd you leave your band, Dallas? Did you get too big for them, Dallas? Were they holding you back, Dallas?' "

His tone has turned from mocking to angry by the end of his diatribe.

"That's more than one question," I note quietly.

"Same general idea." He pauses to shake his head. "Basically around here I'm the jerk-off that broke up a beloved local band to go be a fame whore. So to answer your question, no, I'm not all that thrilled to be home."

"They don't know the whole story." I don't even think I know the whole story, for that matter.

"No, but that's why they make assumptions and ask. It was like being pinned into a corner all fucking day. What was I supposed to tell them? Dixie was grieving and the label is run by a sexist asshole she didn't have the energy or the desire to try and persuade? Oh, and Gavin didn't particularly want to spend the next three to five years in jail for breaking his probation? I mean, what the hell, you know?"

"I don't really know," I say soothingly. "But I can imagine. And I'm sorry. I wish I could've been there for you." I step closer to him, hoping to absorb some of the frustration rolling off him and ease his anguish

"Yeah?" He looks down at me with a lifted brow. The heat warming in his gaze tells me I was relatively successful. "Well, you're here now." He reaches for the belt to my robe and I let him tug it off. The sides fall open, revealing my naked body.

"That I am. And so are you."

"So now that we're both here," he says, giving me a sexy grin that has trouble written all over it. "What should we do with ourselves?"

"Bath first," I tell him. "Because I've already run the water and I like it hot."

"I like it hot, too," he says, pushing my robe to the floor.

# 27 | Dallas

STRANGELY ENOUGH, ROBYN AND I DON'T HAVE SEX IN HER BATH-
tub. We talk. And we take turns washing each other's backs, and
though my dick remains mostly hard, it's the most relaxed I've felt
since the tour started.

Lying on my stomach on her bed watching her slather her entire
body in sweet-smelling lotion, I feel like I'm being let in on some
secret female ritual. All I did was dry off with one of her fluffy expensive towels. But she had a strategic five-point process to execute
after our bath. After the lotion, there's deodorant, then some type
of cream for face and another kind for her hair, which she combs
through with her fingers before slipping her robe back on.

When she climbs onto my back and begins massaging me, I
suspect I've died and gone to heaven. I can feel her against me, the
warmth at her center, and the swells of her breasts when she leans
forward. It's erotic and the scent of her filling the room is intoxicating.

Her phone ringing from somewhere else in her apartment breaks
the spell and I groan in protest when she gets up to answer it.

She's gone so long I almost fall asleep. When she returns, she
looks both excited and stressed-out.

"Now you're the one who needs the massage," I say while sitting up. She smiles but it doesn't reach her eyes. "Uh-oh. What happened?"

Robyn steps closer to the bed and I notice her hands are behind her back. "I have good news and bad news. Which do you want first?"

I can't even begin to fathom what either could be.

"Uh, bad news first, I guess. Then maybe the good news can cheer me up."

She nods. "Okay. That was my boss. I won't be at your show tomorrow night. My mom is going to be so bummed."

Fuck. "Why? Because of me? Because of us?" If Midnight Bay is firing her over this, I'll be having words with them first thing tomorrow morning.

She grins in response to my panic attack. "Nope. Actually I'm not supposed to tell you."

"But you're going to," I tell her, because like hell I'm dropping it without an explanation.

"Yeah. I think you've dealt with enough today with the radio interviews. A surprise party is probably the last thing you need thrown at you."

"A surprise party? What am I, twelve? It's not even my birthday."

Robyn laughs softly and produces a bottle of champagne from behind her back. "The numbers just came out. Jase's album went platinum and your single went gold."

Whoa.

I can't believe Mandy or someone from the label hasn't called me. Hell, maybe they have. I forgot I turned my phone off when I got here.

"No shit?"

"No shit," she says. "Congratulations, Dallas. Midnight Bay is throwing you and Jase both a celebratory surprise party next weekend the night before your show in Nashville. I'm in charge of setting it up. I leave first thing in the morning. Act surprised."

I am surprised. I'm in fucking shock.

I have a gold single.

This is huge, and not just for me. Since she wrote the song, my sister will get a nice, fat royalty check, which, in a way, helps me feel like I'm still taking care of her as much as I possibly can.

Robyn is grinning like a maniac and I assume I am, too. But there's something else in her eyes. Worry, or anxiety, or . . . something.

"So you have to go to Tennessee tomorrow?"

"Yep. I have one week to plan this thing so they want me on it as soon as possible. Tell Dixie I'm sorry. Katie will take care of the Midnight Bay and VIP sections tomorrow night. I'm hoping she'll take care of my mom, too. She was really excited about meeting Jase."

I let out a loud groan of protest. "God. Even Belinda likes him more than me? Christ. That woman used to make me grilled cheese sandwiches. I even ate them if she burned them black. Still, I come second to Wade?"

"Er, no, babe. I think you're like fourth on my mom's list. There's Wade. Then Luke Bryan and George Strait."

I hold my hands over my heart like I've been shot. "You are not funny."

"I'm just being honest."

"Kick a man while he's down, why don't ya?"

"You, Dallas Lark, are not down. Your single just went gold. We're celebrating. And anyway, I prefer to lick a man while he's down," she says, catching me off guard by pouring a trickle of champagne down my stomach then licking it off my abs. And then lower. And then mother of all things holy, her sweet lips wrap around my cock and I slide my fingers into her still-damp hair. "Congratulations, Dallas," she says seductively before taking my full length into her mouth.

I know she didn't make my single go gold, but I'm overwhelmed with gratitude just because she exists. I came here feeling defeated and miserable and now . . . now I could take on the world. As long as she's there beside me.

"Come here, baby," I say, using brute force to pull her upward, past my cock, past my abs, and higher than my chest. When she yelps out a small sound of surprise at where I've placed her body, I let out a low, dark chuckle. "I never said thank you for the massage."

"Yeah, it is. I know. I'm still in shock," I say into the phone. "Thanks, Mr. Borscetti. I really appreciate that. Yes, sir. Sounds great."

Robyn is already dressed when I disconnect the call with the head of my record label, which is a travesty since I had plans of reciprocation for how well she took care of me last night. I've never really had anyone else take care of me before. I've always been the caretaker. But last night Robyn bathed me, massaged me, and to celebrate my single's success she blew my mind in ways I never thought she would allow. I'd hoped we could spend the day celebrating my gold single in bed but I'd turned on my phone and had a million missed calls to return.

And now she's leaving, heading for Nashville while I'm stuck behind in Texas.

"This is a switch," I say while walking out of her bedroom. "I'm staying home while you run off to the country music capital. Let me know if you decide to cut a record while you're there."

"I'll do that. Have you seen my keys?"

"I think they were on the kitchen counter last night."

"Thanks. Stay as long as you like but maybe put some pants on because Katie could come home at any time." Robyn leans down and places a chaste kiss on my lips.

"I'm right behind you. I need to check in with Dixie, let her know to be watching for a royalty check, and try to stop by and see Gavin at work since he can't make the show tonight."

"Okay," she says, her voice trailing out of the room as she continues the search for her keys.

"Everything okay, babe?" I ask once I'm dressed and Robyn has her keys in hand. "You late?"

"What?" Her eyes go so wide I feel like I've said something wrong, but I have no idea what it could be.

"You're rushing around like a crazy person when you generally live by a tight and color-coded schedule. I was just wondering if you were running behind or something."

"Oh." Robyn breathes an audible sigh of relief. "No. I'm fine. Just a little stressed about this party. It's a lot to plan in a short amount of time."

"Got it. Well, if anyone can pull it off, it's you."

"Thanks." She smiles at me but she's still behaving kind of strangely.

I lean in for a kiss and she lets me steal one, but then she pulls back. "You know, I was thinking."

I can already feel the kiss of death coming on our arrangement. "Highly overrated, thinking. I don't recommend it."

"I'm serious. We said we'd keep this discreet, so at the party, maybe let's just each do our thing. You mingle with your fans and I'll focus on keeping everything running smoothly. Both of my bosses will be there so it might be in our best interest to just—"

"Pretend we don't know each other?" I don't mean to sound pissed, but when I said discreet I didn't exactly mean hiding, either.

"No. I don't mean that. That would be weird. Just no PDA at work functions. You tell anyone who asks that you're single and focusing on your career and I'll do the same. Like you did on the Ricky Ray show."

"Heard that, did you?"

She nods, but there's no judgment.

"You ashamed of me, Breeland?"

She rolls her eyes, but I'm only half-kidding.

"Don't be silly, Dallas. Of course not. You know how proud I am of you. I just don't want to get in your way at your party and I don't want my bosses to suspect something inappropriate is going on and start asking questions. Technically they could fire me for this."

"But then after the party we can get inappropriate, right? Say midnightish? My hotel room?"

"You're incorrigible, Dallas Lark."

"You're fickle, Robyn Breeland."

"Hey, that's not true," she says, placing a hand on her hip and jutting it out so I can't walk past her. "Take that back, jerk."

"Come on, woman. Last night you practically devoured me whole. Today you're all distance and no PDA and making rules about what's appropriate and what's not."

"I'm not trying to be coy or fickle or whatever. I'm doing you a favor."

I nod. "Uh-huh. Well, for the record, I prefer the kind of favors you did me last night versus this rules-and-boundaries brand of favors."

She shoves at my chest.

"I meant the massage. Why? What favor did you think I was referring to?"

"Check yourself before you wreck yourself, Lark," she teases. Thankfully she lets me kiss her smart mouth once more before she heads out the door. "For real, though," she begins again once I've walked her to her car, a cute sporty black Jetta I didn't even know she owned. Fits her. Sleek, sophisticated, and petite enough to be called adorable. "I don't want to cramp your style, *Superstar*."

She's mocking Mandy but I don't blame her. I mock Mandy in my head all the time.

"You never cramp my style, Red," I say, using Jase's nickname for her just because he bugs me.

"Okay then, bad choice of words. I don't want to hold you back or weigh you down. Lots of people are going to want a piece of you at this party, Dallas, and some of them it will benefit you to get to know. So I'm going to hang back behind the scenes where I belong and let you do your thing."

"Whatever you say, babe." I reach for her hand and pull her toward my truck. "I'll drive you to the airport so you don't have to pay for long-term parking."

"You sure?"

"Yep. Hop in."

When we get to the airport I can only walk her to the security gate. We stop and she gives me a quick hug. "See you in a week. Have a great show tonight. Make sure my mom doesn't run off with Jase Wade."

"Will do," I promise. "And hey, about what you said, about holding me back or weighing me down?"

Her brow crinkles. "Yeah?"

"That's a load of malarkey and you know it, Breeland. If anything, you keep me grounded so all of this craziness doesn't go to my head."

She smiles. "Well, someone has to."

# 28 | Dallas

SOUND CHECK AT THE GEXA ENERGY PAVILION DOESN'T TAKE TOO long and I'm glad. Dixie texted earlier that she'd come early and she's bringing Robyn's mom. I've always loved Belinda Breeland like she was my own mother and I wasn't kidding when I said I was wounded at the thought of her liking Jase Wade more than me. I never claimed to be mature. Blame the testosterone.

I brought Belinda a giant box of her favorite Godiva chocolates. Maybe she's still a little mad at me for not working things out with Robyn back in the day, but I am determined to win her over.

After I've put my guitar aside and cleared the stage so Wade could warm up, I head back to my bus in hopes of catching a quick nap before the show. Feels like I haven't slept in a month.

Halfway there I see my sister and Belinda making their way backstage and I stop dead in my tracks.

"Stop gaping at me like I'm about to faint dead away, Dallas Lark," Belinda says to greet me. "I'm fine. I've been in remission for months now. I just wear the scarves still because I like them and I'm not used to the short hair."

She's about twenty pounds thinner than I remember and even

with the scarf I can tell that her once-long red locks are now cropped in a short pixie cut. She didn't come to Papa's funeral. Robyn mentioned that she was ill and couldn't make it. I thought she meant like a cold or something.

"I'm sorry. I didn't know . . ."

"That I was in remission? Surely Robyn told you." She shakes her head. "That girl acts like I'm going to relapse any second, though. You should see the stuff she makes me eat." Belinda laughs lightly, probably hoping to break the tension I've suddenly created with my inability to conceal my shock. "When the doctors gave us the lists of restricted and recommended foods, you would've thought they were handing her a dietary Bible."

Apparently I could fill a fucking book with the things Robyn hasn't told me. The pieces of the puzzle that is Robyn Breeland are beginning to take shape in my head. The food. The obsession with healthy eating and all her overzealous ordering habits.

"Oh my God," Belinda practically squeals, sounding more like a teenage girl than a grown woman. "There he is. Can we get closer to the stage?"

Dixie and I both follow her line of sight to where Wade is now warming up.

*Grrr.*

For this woman, though, the one who made me homemade chicken noodle soup when I had the flu, I'll endure it.

"Come on," I say, offering her my arm. "I can do better than closer to the stage."

Once I've escorted them both past security and up the stairs to the restricted backstage area, I tug my sister's elbow and pull her aside.

"Tell me what the hell is going on." I nod toward Belinda.

Dixie shrugs. "She's a huge fan of his—"

"I'm not talking about that." My jaw clenches and I have to swallow several times to get my emotions in check. "Remission. When did she have cancer? Did you know? Did Robyn tell you?"

Dixie and I have had our communication issues lately. She keeps the details of her relationship with Gavin off my radar and I haven't exactly filled her in on what Robyn and I are up to. But if she tells me right now that she's known all this time that Robyn's mom had cancer and she didn't tell me, I don't know how I'm going to keep from losing my shit.

"She didn't tell me, either," Dixie informs me, choosing to answer my last question first. "Belinda seems to think we knew. I practically yelled at her on the way here. Obviously if we'd known we would've been there, would've visited her in the hospital."

I watch the woman with stars in her eyes staring at Wade onstage. She turns to me and gives me two thumbs up and she looks so much like her daughter I'm struck with a pang of longing. I want Robyn here. Mostly so I can demand to know why she didn't tell me her mom had cancer, but also because I want to hold her. To kiss her and tell her I'm sorry I wasn't there for her, for both of them.

After Robyn's dad died I made sure to cut their grass, change the oil in their cars, and take out the garbage as often as I could. I wanted to make sure they didn't have to feel his loss in those ways as well. Belinda eventually "fired" me and told me I wasn't the hired help before she hired actual help to take over the landscaping duties. She told me the McKinley boys at the garage could change her oil just fine.

Those Breeland women. Self-sufficient pains in my ass they are. But God help me, I fucking love them.

"How bad was it?"

Dixie's mouth tightens at the corners. "Bad. She had to do two rounds of chemo. Had an awful reaction and didn't respond to the first round well at all."

"When?"

I don't know why I'm asking. I already know.

"That summer," Dixie says softly, almost so softly I don't hear her over Jase's guitar.

She doesn't clarify which summer. She doesn't have to. The summer before I turned twenty-one, Robyn began acting strangely. Up until then, she'd done all the social media and online outreach for the band. She'd gone overboard in her typical way, acting as our manager and our agent even though she didn't know a whole lot about the music business. What she did know was how to reach people and to this day I'm certain she is one of the main reasons we had such a large local following.

We were planning a six-week tour between Dixie's junior and senior year of high school. Mostly just the tristate area, but a big deal for Leaving Amarillo since it was our first time actually going on "tour." Robyn was all set to go with us and she was so excited about being on the road. She had this whole list of places we were going to go in each city we were scheduled to play in, a road trip music mix, and enough snacks stockpiled to feed a football team.

Then she bailed. Said she had decided to take a few summer classes and she stopped answering my calls. Eventually I got frustrated and drove down to see her at school. Except she wasn't there.

When I showed up at her house and confronted her, her eyes filled with tears and she broke down. Said she just couldn't do it anymore. I needed to focus on the band and she had other obligations. I'd assumed she meant school obligations. She'd always been such an academic overachiever.

From that night on her porch until now I have imagined a thousand scenarios that caused Robyn to end it. I can't even count the nights I lay awake wondering.

*Was there another guy?*

*Did she finally decide I wasn't worth waiting for? That I was just going to spend my life chasing a dream I'd never catch?*

I'd refused to leave her porch that night until the sun peeked over the horizon.

"Just tell me what I did. I can fix it, baby. Please."

I'd been fucking pathetic.

"You can't," she'd said a dozen times. "No one can."

The more I'd pressed, the more she'd closed herself off to me.

"Just come with me," I'd begged. "We have a show in Fort Worth tomorrow night. Sunday we can go to that museum like you wanted." I'd never given two fucks about visiting art museums, but I'd suffered through a couple for her. She'd get so excited. While she was looking at paintings I couldn't make heads or tails of, I'd be watching her. The way her eyes would light up and her mouth would drop open just slightly as she stared in awe at each work.

For a moment, I thought I'd had her. She got that look, the same one she got when she looked at her favorite paintings. Then her expression blanked, her eyes lost their light, and she shook her head.

"I can't, Dallas. Life on the road is your thing. Not mine." She wouldn't even meet my eyes when she said it.

I'd wondered briefly that if maybe I had more money, if the band were more successful, if I could promise her fancy hotels and room service instead of leftover pizza and Cracker Jacks in a van, if that would've mattered. But I'd never known her to be materialistic and up until then she'd seemed fine with the lack of luxury accommodations.

But as we said goodbye for the final time, my insecurities took over and I decided that she'd simply gotten tired of my shit and finally lost faith. In the band. In me. In us.

There was always a possibility the band would never take off, never "make it," so to speak.

I'd had a choice to make.

I could let her down or let her go.

Standing here now, staring at the woman she loves most in the world and half-listening while Dixie details the hell that was Robyn and Belinda's life that summer, I know I chose wrong.

# 29 | Robyn

"YOU LATE?"

Dallas's words echo in my head over and over.

Because I am late. And I am never late. My life runs according to a very set schedule and my body cooperates with this most of the time.

I try to reason it away. I'm stressed. I've been traveling a lot. My body is just out of whack.

After hours of hanging decorations and lights and chasing down everything from extension cords to building permits, my feet and lower back ache like I spent the morning beginning my career as a barefoot carrot farmer. To make matters worse, I feel like I'm coming down with something. Something I am hoping and praying has nothing to do with the fact that my monthly visitor from Hell had yet to arrive. The nausea has mostly subsided but a wave blindsides me and while Katie handles the rest of the setup I am in the bathroom, sitting on a closed toilet seat holding a wet paper towel to my neck.

After a few minutes the soggy texture of it against my skin threatens to bring the half a turkey sandwich I had for lunch back up, so I throw it away and lean on the cool marble wall, concentrating on taking deep breaths until I regain my equilibrium. That is, until the scent of the bleach-based cleaner they must use to sanitize the ladies' room hits my nostrils and nearly doubles me over.

Tonight's party is one of the most important of my career, the one Mr. Martin will use to decide if I can really pull this off as well as I've said I can. I might as well be wearing a T-shirt that says, "Don't believe the hype."

The two-story historic home is fully decorated by the time I feel steady enough to leave the restroom. Guests are pouring in and it looks like I pulled myself together just in time. The main room is alive with neon blue lights streaking the blackened ceiling and our LED-lit displays are strategically placed by each minibar. Maneuvering my way through the crowd in search of Katie, because I basically owe her my life for covering for me, I crane my neck in search of her blond head. The second I think I've caught a glimpse of her, a solid mass slams against me, sending me careening toward a waiter in a tux carrying a tray of the signature cocktails Midnight Bay created for Jase's tour. Just before I crash into him and his tray full of glasses, a strong hand grips my upper arm and yanks me back to safety.

"Shit, Robyn. My bad." Jase Wade stands with one hand still holding tightly to me and the other wrapped around his cell phone.

Taking a steadying breath I give him a wavering smile. "No worries. I'm fine."

Sort of. Minus the constant urge to vomit making me wish I could go home and curl up in old sweats. Wade is usually so much smoother. From the bags under his bloodshot eyes and disarray his shirt is in, he looks as bad as I feel and I can't help but wonder if *he's* okay.

"You all right? I think there's something going around."

He looks at me strangely, as if I've asked if he's interested in nuclear physics and the atomic properties of space. "Yeah. Fine. Thanks."

"You sure? Because the one-word answers don't exactly scream 'having the time of my life.' Congratulations on the album going platinum, by the way."

He releases my arm and shrugs, giving me a halfhearted grin. "Thanks."

A modest Jase Wade isn't something I've seen before. If anyone has the cocky country-boy swagger down to a science, it's him. Dallas has been garnering a lot of attention since "Better to Burn" went gold. Both happening at the same time has likely created some competitive friction but I'm afraid to ask, for fear I'll hear something I shouldn't.

"Well, um, I should go check on the hors d'oeuvres, so . . ."

"You want to get some air? You look like you need it as badly as I do." He rakes a hand roughly over his head and glances around for the nearest exit.

"You sure know how to flatter a girl."

He rolls his eyes. "Stop. You know you're gorgeous. You just look a little . . . I don't know . . . out of sorts or something."

"Or something," I say, taking his arm and leading him to the French doors that open to the balcony. Thankfully no one stops us as we make our way outside. Fresh air is actually starting to sound pretty good.

"I'll make you a deal," Jase says as we step over to a deserted section of balcony. "You tell me why you're green and look seconds from chunking on my shoes and I'll tell you why I was barreling through the room like a runaway truck that nearly took you down."

Sighing, I take a few minutes to breathe in the crisp, cool air around us.

When I turn to Jase, either he missed his calling as an actor or he's genuinely concerned about my well-being.

"I either have the flu or food poisoning. I've been feeling off since New Orleans and I can't shake it."

"Did you go to the doctor?"

I gesture toward the party I had all of six days to plan. "When? In all of my spare time?"

He nods like he gets it. "That sucks. I hope you get to feeling better. Can I get you something to drink? Ginger ale or club soda or something?"

"Thanks. I'm good. For now."

"You should go home if you're feeling bad. The party is pretty much handling itself here. Hell, I'm the guest of honor and I don't think anyone even cares if I'm here." He rests his elbows on the balcony ledge and looks out over the courtyard.

I tilt my head. "That's not true. All of this is for you, you know. To celebrate your hard work and success."

"My success," he huffs out under his breath.

"Whoa. I didn't realize you'd invited me out here to your pity party." I nudge him with my shoulder. "Who peed in your Wheaties?"

He chuckles, but it's devoid of the lighthearted happiness that typically accompanies laughter.

Suddenly he turns to me, nailing me with an inquisitive stare I'm not prepared for. "You're a hardworking girl, Red. You ever wonder if it's worth it? The long hours? The traveling? Missing out on time with your family? Missing out on having a life, period?"

I regard him warily. He probably doesn't realize how revealing his questions are. Or how much I can relate to them.

"Sometimes. I guess I tell myself that one day all the sacrifices will be worth it."

"When?" he demands, growing instantly angry at my answer and catching me off guard. "When do people just sit back and say, 'Okay. You did enough to deserve to just get to live your life. Now go enjoy it.' Because I gotta tell you, in my experience, that day is never fucking coming. Your single hits number one and that puts more pressure on the album to do the same so they add more tour dates. More promotional appearances. More radio interviews and talk show appearances. Sell out venues? They add sixteen more shows. It's all about feeding the machine. Put your heart and body and soul into it, and poof, money comes out. Too bad you won't have time to spend it." He shakes his head. "I'm not complaining."

I arch a brow at him.

"Okay. Yeah, I am complaining. But I'm also trying to caution you from making the same mistakes I have."

"Which are?"

"Too many to name. But most importantly, don't use each goal you reach as a reason to set another, higher, less attainable one. Because I can tell you from experience that a life of chasing the next number one, the next promotion, the next opportunity, without ever taking the time to sit back and enjoy what you've accomplished is exhausting. And empty."

I blanch at his declaration. Jase Wade is sad. I can see it so clearly now. Why he puts up the front. It's a defense mechanism, same as my own. I completely understand what Dallas was talking about now. About "Performer Dallas" and "Person Dallas."

Performer Jase Wade is on top of the world right now. But Person Jase is lonely and full of regrets. Who knew?

"You want to talk about it?" I coax gently, leaning against him just to let him know he's not alone.

Performer Jase would make a comment laced with innuendo at the contact. But this version of him just gives me a shrug and pitiful puppy-dog eyes.

"Not really. Nothing I can do about it, anyway."

"You sure? Sometimes a fresh perspective helps with—"

"My wife got remarried today." He lets out a soft breath and continues speaking more to himself than me. "My album goes platinum and I get to celebrate on the day my wife marries a fucking accountant."

If he had thrown me over the balcony, I don't think I would've been more surprised than I am now.

"You're married?" I don't even bother keeping the incredulous apprehension out of my voice.

"Not anymore."

"But . . ."

"But no one ever mentioned me having a wife? That's because we separated several years ago and she filed for divorce when my career took off."

"I'm sorry. What happened?" I shake my head. "Jesus. My mama would smack my mouth for prying. I'm so sorry."

"I made choice, choices that hurt the two women I loved more than anything in this world."

"Two?"

Jase turns his attention to his phone and when he holds it up I think it's my cue to leave him the hell alone to wallow. A gorgeous auburn-haired little girl with startling green eyes and angelic curls smiles into the camera. She can't be more than three or four and she's holding up tiny hands covered in finger paint.

"That's an old picture, but that's my McKenna," he says softly. "I call her Mac. She'll turn thirteen soon." There is reverence in his voice and it hits me hard in my chest.

My hand lifts to my mouth and inexplicable tears fill my eyes. "God. Sorry. I don't know what's wrong with me. She's beautiful."

He pulls up a more recent picture of a smirking twelve-year-old girl who looks a lot like him. A tear escapes my left eye, then one from my right follows and I feel like a complete jackass. First of all, it was my job to research Wade and all of his history so that I could make sure this tour was the right opportunity for Midnight Bay. Second, he's Jase freaking Wade. How does no one know he has a wife, well, ex-wife, and a kid? Third, why the hell am I crying?

If Jase notices my emotional breakdown, he's gentleman enough to pretend he doesn't.

"I wanted joint custody, or scheduled visitation at least, but Aubrey fought me hard. I had the expensive lawyers but she had all the proof that she is Mac's sole caretaker. There was no denying that the life I lead isn't a great place for a kid. She won't even let me pay for anything and that's the whole reason I work so damn hard. So that Mac can have whatever her heart desires. Oh, hey, look at this one. Doesn't she look like a superstar?"

He scrolls to another picture and I am barely in one piece at this point. McKenna is wearing a leotard and tights, standing in what I think is first position.

"She's beautiful, Jase."

"Right?" He shakes his head. "I just wanted . . . damn it." Now his eyes are beginning to water.

"We are one hell of a pair of party animals."

He puts his phone away and shakes his head. "Sorry."

"Hey, listen. I won't say anything. This is your personal business and no one else's."

"The only people that care about that part of my life are the vultures anyway." Jase looks like a man with the weight of the world on his shoulders.

I wish I knew how to comfort him, but there isn't a go-to response for situations like this one.

Turning around, he faces the party and leans back on the railing in a way that makes me dizzy. If I looked over the banister right now I'd likely puke all over the people below.

"You know, when this all started, moving to Nashville, cutting a demo, signing with a label, it was all for them. For my girls."

"You have another daughter?"

He shakes his head. "I mean Mac and her mom." He swallows hard, his Adam's apple bobbing in his throat. "Aubrey," he says softly. "We were crazy in love. She stood by me through everything . . . and we had some hard fucking times, you know? Bank repo'd my truck. Nearly lost our house. And then . . ."

I hold my breath in anticipation of having my heart further broken on his behalf. I don't know when I became so vulnerable to everyone else's pain but I'm an oversensitive mess lately.

"My career took off. It got bigger than me. Bigger than us. The things I had to do to really make it here—the demands and the schedule and building a brand and a fan base—it didn't leave any room in my life for them. And I just let it happen. I told myself there would be time to fix it later. That once I was on top of my game and killing it on the charts, we'd figure it out."

I'm quiet because I don't know what to say and because I get it now. What he's trying to tell me. I'm sacrificing everything for a "one day" that might never come.

"I'll stop boring you with my bullshit. It's a great party, Robyn. I don't say it enough, but I appreciate all of your hard work."

He gazes at the crowd through the glass doors with a look of detached amusement on his face.

"You're not boring me," I assure him. "I was just thinking."

"About?"

"About whether or not it's worth it," I answer quietly.

When he doesn't speak, I glance over to see him looking at his phone again.

"It isn't," he says evenly.

A waiter steps over and offers us our choice of champagne in flutes or highball glasses of bourbon and another is close behind with chocolate-covered cherries on the music note sticks I ordered.

I skip the booze and take a few of the cherries. Jase lifts the squat glass full of amber liquid to his lips while I place the dessert in my mouth. Something about the combination of bittersweet dark chocolate and the sickly sour cherry hits me wrong and I spit it out over the balcony.

"Oh my God," I say once I realize what I've done. "I cannot believe I just did that."

And I sincerely hope my half-chewed cherry didn't land in anyone's hair.

Jase laughs at me. "And here I thought you were some classy broad. You could enter a chewing tobacco spitting contest and give some boys I know a serious run for their money."

"I'll add that to my resume." I wrap the remaining cherries in my cocktail napkin. "I usually love those. But lately chocolate has been making my stomach turn. And I need to go see someone about those cherries. I think they might be rotten."

Jase gives me some intense side-eye. "I had some earlier. Tasted fine to me."

"Well, that batch had to be bad. They even smelled weird."

"You think so?" He's still scrutinizing me as if I am an alien life-form to be studied beneath a microscope. "You know, when Aubrey was pregnant with Mac, she couldn't stand the smell of oranges. It was the damnedest thing. She used to love them. Then she got pregnant and said they smelled like kitchen cleaner and I had to keep her out of the produce section for fear she'd get a whiff and puke all over aisle five. We couldn't even keep OJ in the house anymore."

My mouth gapes open. What the hell does my spitting out a rancid rotten cherry have to do with his wife's pregnancy and aversion to—

I feel as if my head is detaching from my body and floating up into the sky like a wayward balloon.

I don't want it to be true but it's entirely possible. I know it is. I knew the day I stood in my bathroom realizing I had two more birth control pills than I should have had after getting home from weeks of traveling for work. After having unprotected sex with Dallas. More than once.

I doubled up my next two doses but then I googled that and saw that it wasn't necessarily effective or even a good idea.

Likely noting my distress, Jase takes my arm much more gently than he did when he almost knocked me over. "I think you've had enough fun for one evening, darlin'. I'm going to call us both a cab so we can get—"

"No. I'm fine. It's just this stomach bug. I need to get back inside. Excuse me."

Without another word, I stride quickly away from him and toward the throng of people flowing in and out of the ballroom.

Halfway across the room, I run smack into a couch where Dallas is sitting surrounded by executives and half-dressed women snapping pictures with him. A bottle blonde in a sparkly blue dress is in his lap. She looks comfortable. Like she's been there awhile.

The small amount of lunch I've managed to keep down rises in my throat and I have to get to the ladies' room or risk covering the entire couch and its occupants in puke.

On second thought . . . no. I'm better than that. I clench my jaw and try to swallow the excess saliva filling my mouth.

"Robyn, hey. There you are. You did an amazing job with the—"

I hold a hand up and shake my head. I can't talk to whoever is trying to get my attention. Dallas looks up when they call my name but I avert my gaze.

I can't do this right now.

All I can hear is Jase Wade in my head telling me about his pregnant wife as I run through the crowd, elbowing people out of my way in hopes that I make it to the bathroom in time.

I didn't even eat that much today. Apparently my stomach decided to hang on to a week's worth of meals to toss into the toilet.

Leaning against the side wall of the bathroom stall, I place a trembling hand to my forehead.

My head pounds and my throat is raw, but that's not what's concerning me the most. Jase's words play over and over.

Then Dallas's question at my apartment.

*"Are you late?"*

I kept telling myself it's the stress. The traveling.

It isn't the first time I'd skipped a period or two. But I've never felt like this before. Weak. Drained. Constantly nauseated and repulsed by smells that I barely even noticed before.

For a fleeting second, I wonder if maybe it's something else. Cancer runs in my family on my mom's side. Jesus Christ. If my brain is trying to reconcile this by reassuring me that it could be a fatal disease instead, I am even more screwed up than I thought.

Stepping out of the stall, I see one of the girls from Dallas's estrogen-filled entourage heading into the stall beside me. I ignore her and turn on the sink in front of me. Rinsing my mouth and checking my hair for puke, I catch a glimpse of my ashen skin in the mirror.

My face looks gaunt, the skin beneath my eyes sallow and puffy.

If I get fired for blowing off my responsibilities at this party I have a promising career as a corpse on any crime show that will have me.

My purse is checked in the coatroom so I can't really do anything about my horrifying appearance except splash some cold water on my face and dab at my smudged eye makeup with a paper towel.

"It reeks in here. Don't you work here? Can't you do something about that?"

Dallas's groupie has joined me at the sink. Oh goody.

"Yeah I'll get right on that."

"Oh, and there are no more of the little blue shots. They're so good. You might want to get on the waiters to send more of those around."

"Thanks for the tip."

She begins adding more black eyeliner to already overly lined eyes. I silently hope her hand slips and she stabs herself right in the retina.

I frown at my own reflection. First I cry all over Wade's tragic turmoil, then I fantasize about gouging some random chick in the eye. I am so not this person.

*Am I?*

I have to get out of here.

After drying my hands briefly, I shove the door open.

"Hey." Dallas stands there as if he's waiting for someone.

"Hi." I narrow my eyes because I don't know if it's me he's out here for or the girl coming out behind me.

When she winks at him on her way by and he doesn't so much as glance in her direction, I have my answer. But I can't do this with him. Not here.

His button-up dress shirt is so dark blue it looks black and seeing him in perfectly tailored charcoal-colored dress pants is confusing. Dallas is flannel and denim for the most part. Hoodies and backward ball caps. Maybe I'm still confusing him with someone that I used to know instead of who he is now. Maybe I don't know him at all anymore.

He takes a long pull from his beer bottle, the light glinting off his shiny black and silver watch, before stepping into my path. "Can we talk, please?"

I shake my head. "Pass. You need to get back to your groupies and I have to find my boss."

"Hey." His fingers are warm beneath my chin. "What's going on? You look like hell."

"Thanks. So much for chivalry, huh?" I jerk my chin out of his hand and turn away from his searching gaze. "Feel free to return to your non-hellish-looking fans now."

"Wait a second. That's not what I meant. Robyn?"

I can hear him and I can feel him close behind me in the crowd but I keep going, walking toward the coat-check room without acknowledging anyone as I weave through a sea of overly perfumed bodies. My stomach threatens to turn on me again and I decide to text Katie instead of trying to find her or Mr. Martin to let them know I'm not feeling well.

No one is manning the coatroom so I walk in and begin searching for my black leather jacket and matching bag.

The door clicks shut from across the room, where Dallas stands glaring at me.

"You want to tell me what that was about?"

"I have no idea what you're talking about." I return to shuffling through coats on the rack.

"Well, you were busy having a moment with Wade out on the balcony so I mingled like you told me to do. After which you run by shooting me a death glare that should've killed me on the spot. Then you come out of the ladies' room looking like you're recovering from a three-day drinking binge. Now you're behaving as if speaking to me rationally is beyond your limits of capability. So I'll ask you again." Dallas comes closer, plucking my jacket from a rack and holding it open for me. "What the hell was that about?"

"I'm just stressed. And tired. This party was a lot of work. But I'm fine now."

"Well, I'm glad. Because we need to talk."

"Can we talk later? I'm beat and I'm just going to—"

"Just going to what, Robyn? Lie to me? Keep something huge from me, like, oh, I don't know, your mom having fucking cancer? Because let me tell you, finding out something like that just before a show wasn't distracting at all."

I close my eyes to shield myself from his wrath.

Shoving my own ire down deep, I turn and let him help me with my jacket. Dallas can't let it go at that, though. He lifts my hair gently from beneath my collar and lays it over my right shoulder, giving him full access to the left side of my neck. He places a soft kiss on it and my traitorous body shivers.

"I'm not going to pretend I'm not angry, but seeing you all sick and fragile is softening my resolve to yell at you. Come back to my hotel room tonight. Stay with me. I missed you and we need to talk about this. About that summer."

It's tempting. I feel like death walking, and seeing that girl on his lap opened old wounds I'd been holding closed with all my might. But the thought of slipping so easily into the warmth of him, letting him hold me and make it all better, is enticing.

This must be similar to how drug addicts feel. I know it's wrong. I know it will only cause more problems. I *know exactly* how much it will hurt the next time I have to see women groping him at a publicity event. But so help me, I am still tempted to crawl through the valley of the shadow of heartbreak. Naked.

I toss up a silent prayer for strength and step away from him. "There's nothing to talk about. She was sick so I stayed home to take care of her. I didn't want you to cancel any of your shows so I kept it to myself. Besides, I think I've got the stomach flu. I'm sure you can find plenty of willing bed-buddy candidates for the evening."

"Maybe I would've wanted to be there for you, Robyn. You didn't even give me a fucking chance." Dallas snorts out a noise of frustration. "Don't blow this off, like you actually give a shit about a bunch of girls hanging around the next big thing for all of five minutes until the next shiny new guy comes along? Come on. I thought you knew better by now. You're the one that told me to play the part and keep what was going on with you and me under wraps. Remember?"

"The one on your lap looked dedicated. She seemed willing to hang around a lot longer than five minutes."

"Cut the crap, Robyn. You know I'm not interested in any of them."

"Don't," I say, pointing a finger at him. "Don't make me seem crazy. I'm not overreacting or making a scene. You're the one chasing me down here. They were all over you and you were lapping it up like a stud in the pasture."

"That's a lie and you know it."

I gawk at him in disbelief. "Are you fucking kidding me?"

"Are you?"

We're yelling now but I can't figure out how to defuse the situation.

"No. I'm not. I'm supposed to be here to do my job and that's pretty hard to do watching the person I'm sleeping with getting molested in front of me. I'm having a hard enough time trying not to gag all over the place as it is. You were right. We shouldn't have crossed that line because now we can't go back."

"I'm here doing my job, too, damn it. And what the hell is that supposed to mean? Go back? You want to unfuck me?"

"I want to unknow you. I want to go back in time and never freaking speak to you. It always ends like this, no matter how hard we try or how many things we try to do differently."

"What do you want me to do, babe? Tell the next woman that touches me to keep her goddamn hands to herself? Do you have any idea what that would do to my career? Who do you think buys my music? Have you paid attention to who's filling those seats at every show? This is part of it. This is the gig, sweetheart. You're the one who planned this fucking party for this very reason. I thought you got that."

"No." I shake my head and wipe the tears threatening to spill from my eyes before they can fall. "The party is to celebrate the music, the sales, and—"

"It's the same damn thing!" Dallas throws his hands up, looking at me like I'm brain dead and he's tired of dumbing everything down for me. "It's me. That's what I'm selling here. Me. I need them to buy into me as an artist. I can't do that by being an asshole to them."

He's about to reiterate his whole "Performer Dallas" versus "Person Dallas" spiel but I just can't hear it right now.

"Go on and get back to your party, Dallas."

"You want me to leave?"

I nod. "I do."

"You sure? I just want to be clear so if I go you don't hold it over my head for the next five years."

I have no words.

None.

The bile burns too hot, sending an acidic searing sensation through my chest and into my throat.

When I finally find my voice, it's eerily even. "Do not throw our past into my face. I have never held anything over your head. If anything, I let you off the hook too easily."

Dallas smirks and shakes his head. "What fucking hook, Robyn? You dumped me, remember? Instead of letting me be there for you, you lied to me—kept something huge from me. And *you're* the one who gets to be pissed? I'm throwing the bullshit flag on that one."

I blow past him and out of the room like a wayward hurricane of hellfire. I am not doing this at a work-related event. Moreover, I can't. Because I'm about to be sick again.

I make it outside to where valets in red vests are retrieving cars before I vomit in the bushes beside the building.

The entire world spins, kind of how my life is spiraling out of control while I'm powerless to stop it. All I can do is kick my purse out of the way, brace my hands on my knees, and let it come.

# 30 | Dallas

WHY I'M FOLLOWING A WOMAN OUTSIDE WHO CLEARLY WANTS nothing more to do with me, I can't be certain. But I do know that something is wrong.

I've never seen Robyn that pale or that hateful. She's been pissed at me before, sure, but this was a whole new level that felt dangerously close to actual hatred.

I don't know if I could live with myself if Robyn hated me. And I know I definitely couldn't live with myself if I let her go home alone looking the way she did. I'm almost positive the anger was the only thing holding her upright. The protective instincts I've honed from years of being an older brother kick in and I press on through the partygoers.

If I could go back in time and stand up so that Carly or Callie or whatever the hell her name was wouldn't have sat on my lap, I would do whatever it took to get there. The last thing I ever wanted was to be the reason for that wounded look in Robyn's eyes. She can put on her angry face all she wants; that was pure unadulterated pain I saw while she yelled at me.

Once I'm outside where people are getting in and out of cars, I look around but Robyn is nowhere to be seen. Someone obviously had too many of the Midnight Bay blue shooters because I can hear them retching even over the music. When it continues to the point that I'm fearful for their life, I jog over to where the sound is coming from.

"Oh, baby," I say once I see who it is. Robyn is bent over yakking into the bushes. The force is jolting her body forward hard. I grab her hair with two hands and pull it out of the line of fire. Once I have it secured to the nape of her neck with one fist, I use the other hand to rub circles on her back. "You're okay, sweet girl. Just get it all up. It's okay. I'm here."

"I don't want—" She surges forward again and heaves but I think she's out of ammunition. "You here," she finishes.

"Well, tough shit, sweetheart. I'm here and I'm not going anywhere."

"Don't want anyone," she begins, pausing to stand and wipe her mouth, "to see me like this." I release her hair and she glances around. Noticing her purse on the ground, I pick it up. At least it didn't get puked on.

"Come on. We'll take one of the sober cars back to the hotel."

I wrap my arms around her and guide her to the nearest valet. Once they've located a car for us, Robyn slides in and I follow.

The driver is a gray-haired man with a gray wool cap on. "Where to, kids?"

"The nearest urgent care center or ER," I answer.

Robyn looks like I've slapped her. "No," she practically shouts. "Just take us to the Hutton, please."

"Are you serious right now?" This girl. She's practically turning green right in front of my eyes. "We need to get you checked out."

"The Hutton, please," she tells the driver while ignoring me. "I swear I'm fine."

"You say that, but you don't look fine," I tell her. "And if you think I'm just going to dump you off in your room, you're crazy."

The driver ends up taking us to the hotel, where I take Robyn to my room so she doesn't keep Katie up all night.

After a pack of saltine crackers and two Gatorades, she takes a shower and comes out looking like a new person.

"I'm telling you, it's just a stomach bug. It's on its way out." Robyn promises me she's on the mend and that if she gets sick again like that she'll make an appointment with her doctor.

She's nearly asleep in my bed when she blinks her sleepy eyes up at me and says, "I'm sorry you had to leave your party. And that I didn't tell you about my mom."

"I don't care about parties, Robyn. But can you just tell me why? Why you didn't tell me about your mom that summer? I could've—"

"You could've canceled the shows you were so excited about. You would have." Robyn sighs against my chest before raising her eyes to mine. "Your grandma had just passed and you'd already put everything on hold once. I didn't want to be the reason you sidelined your dream again."

"So you didn't actually want to break up, you just couldn't go on the road and you didn't want me to stay?"

"I wanted you to stay," she says quietly. "I just didn't *want* to want that. It was selfish and unfair. And I wanted you to have your shot at your dream more than I wanted to have you hold my hand in a waiting room all summer."

My whole life I've put everyone else first. My sister. My grandparents. Gavin. I'd never realized someone had been putting my dreams before their own needs.

I can't explain how her confession makes me feel right now so I don't try.

I lean down and kiss her on the forehead. "Get some rest, pretty girl. We can talk about this later."

She surprises me by grabbing my shirt. "Spoon me for a while? Until I fall asleep? Pretty please?"

"I never could turn down 'pretty please.'"

She rolls over, curving into me with her backside, and I drape my arm over her body.

More of my granddad's wisdom comes to mind. *"A woman's like a guitar, son. It's all in how you hold her."* After that he'd added, *"Get comfortable with her but never take her for granted, appreciate every single inch and curve. The imperfections are what make her unique, what make her yours."*

"Please don't hate me, Dallas," she whispers. "I couldn't stand it if you hated me."

"I could never hate you, Robyn. Go to sleep, sweetheart."

Jesus. I was mad as hell that she didn't tell me about Belinda, but I didn't say anything about hating her. Watching her drift off to sleep so peacefully after her night full of outbursts and erratic behavior makes me wonder if she's a pod person or secretly has an evil twin.

But it was a sexy jealous evil twin and when she dozes off in my arms, I stay awake watching her to make sure the vomiting really has passed. By daybreak I've decided to keep her, evil twin and all.

Robyn is still recovering from food poisoning or whatever the hell she had so she isn't coming to the show in Nashville tonight. She texts me a "have a great show" message but when I respond by asking if I can come by her room and check on her after, she doesn't answer.

Mandy told me to meet her on Wade's bus before the show at the Woods Amphitheater at Fontanel. After making sure that Katie was in their room to keep an eye on Robyn, I left the hotel and joined far more folks than I expected on Wade's fancy-ass bus.

The built-in furniture is all black leather and sleek marble surfaces. There's a flat screen against the wall that's nearly as big as the bunk I sleep on in my bus.

Wade sits leaned back in a booth across from his manager and a few guys from his band. Mandy, Ty, and Lex are here as well.

Barry Borscetti's face is on the computer in front of them and he's talking when I walk in.

"He's here," Wade's manager, a husky guy named Rick, says when Mandy and I make our way over. "We're good to go."

"What's going on?" I look to Mandy for an answer and she grins like someone with a secret.

"Dallas, we're glad you're here," Barry says, drawing my attention from my manager. "Your agent has been filled in so the paperwork is already being processed."

I feel like I'm missing the punch line to an inside joke. "Okay. Someone want to fill me in now?"

"It's about the tour," Barry says. "Jase has signed on for an international leg of the Kickin' Up Crazy tour and we couldn't be more excited. With the success of 'Better to Burn' and the enthusiasm for your upcoming album, we've decided to include you as well. Congratulations. This is going to be an amazing opportunity for both of you."

"The exposure alone is going to skyrocket your career, Dallas," Mandy whispers from beside me, wrapping her arm around mine and holding on tightly.

"Mexico is confirmed for three dates. Five shows in Canada," Barry is saying as I tune back in. "Two shows in Rio de Janeiro and two London venues have committed. There's a foundation supporting a campaign called Bring Country Music to the UK that is ec-static about having you boys over there. We'll have two shows in the Philippines, which will provide some photo ops with service groups that you'll be visiting while you're there. We're still working with Australian vendors and should hear back from Tokyo today."

"Sounds great, Barry," Wade says. He sounds as tired as I feel but we both know how huge this is. Not just for us, or for this tour, but for country music.

Once upon a time, it was only in the southern United States, then it expanded to reach the rest of the country, and now it's taking on the world. It's surreal to be a part of that and I can't even think straight as I imagine visiting those parts of the globe.

"Have a great show tonight, fellas," Barry says before signing off.

"Well, this calls for another celebration," Mandy announces. "I'll have someone bring in some party favors for after the show tonight. We'll see if Midnight Bay can help us out with that."

The mention of Midnight Bay reminds me of Robyn. I hope like hell she'll be joining us for this leg of the tour. The craziest part? I can't even imagine it without her.

# 31 | Robyn

"MISS BREELAND?"

I glance up from the magazine I've been perusing. I'll have to finish the article on the benefits of breastfeeding some other time. Or maybe not. Maybe I'm some crazy exception to the chemistry of home pregnancy tests. That could happen.

*Suuure it could.*

Ignoring my subconscious as it openly mocks me, I smile at the petite blonde in pale pink scrubs as she holds the door open for me.

"Right this way. You're in here," she says pointing to a door that's ajar.

I step into the room and try not to have a panic attack. "Thanks," I mumble.

She smiles again and I try to focus on her face. She's giving me this sympathetic head-tilted, eye-creasing expression and I read more into it than I probably should. I'm not even wearing an engagement ring, but here I am. Hoping against hope that I'm not knocked up even though I suspect we both know that I am.

"Just undress completely and put this gown on." She leans down to retrieve a pale yellow paper gown that's practically see-through and then hands it to me. "Have a seat on the table and the doctor will be right in."

I swallow and nod as she leaves me alone with my gown in hand. My tongue is thick and foreign in my mouth. Maybe I'm allergic to this place. Or this ridiculously thin gown. Why do they have to be so freaking thin? Couldn't I open a flannel robe just as easily? Once you're in the stirrups, it hardly matters.

Oh God. The stirrups.

I glance over and there they are, screwed to the end of the table like a medieval torture device. With all the advances in technology, surely there's a better way.

*You can do this. It's fine. You have a great job, fantastic medical benefits.*

I console myself with this information as I undress in what has now become a freezing cold meat locker instead of a warm and cozy doctor's office.

*But what will Mr. Martin say about traveling? What if I can't? What if I can't find a nanny willing to travel with me?*

My breathing has accelerated to a dangerous level. I can see my chest heaving and I can't remember if I was supposed to take off my bra. Surely I can leave on my bra.

I'm leaving my bra on.

It feels like a strange act of defiance but my breasts are sore and the idea of freeing them right now in this frigid room seems like cruel and unusual torture.

In just my bra, I slip the gown on only to realize it ties in the back. And I can't reach.

*That's what husbands are for, Robyn. Duh.*

My subconscious is an asshole. And stuck in archaic gender and societal roles that I will not succumb to.

I've thrown every excuse I have at Dallas. Telling him repeatedly that I think what I have is contagious so he won't come by. He's called to check on me half a dozen times and I just keep telling him I'm tired, which hasn't been a complete lie. I blink back the tears and twist the stupid offensive ties together the best that I can.

I can do this myself.

My mind churns through the many changes I'll have to make, checking off each one as totally doable. I can turn my small home office into a nursery. I can explain to Mr. Martin that I need maternity leave and to reduce travel for a while. I can put a crib together. How hard can it be? YouTube should tell me exactly how to do everything that I need to.

Shouldn't it?

The magazine I was reading had articles on antibiotics, immunizations, vaccinations, breastfeeding, and several other topics that hadn't yet occurred to me to worry about.

*Fuuuuck.*

But I can do this. I can. I will.

I got this.

"We got this," I say while patting my still-flat belly.

If there's no one in there, well, I'll laugh at my own ridiculousness and go celebrate with a drink. Or two.

"Good morning, Miss Breeland. I'm Dr. Lassiter." A gentle female voice accompanying a fair-skinned woman with shoulder-length auburn hair interrupts my mental breakdown. "How are you feeling today?"

I suck in a deep breath and smile. "Great. I'm feeling great today, actually."

"Actually? Have you not been feeling well?"

"Um, well . . ." Licking my lips, I say it out loud for the first time ever. "I've been feeling kind of sick, not in the mornings, though. Mostly around dinnertime. And I'm a few weeks late. I also haven't had a Pap smear in, uh, a while. So I thought it would be a good idea to come in and—"

"How many weeks?"

"Ma'am?"

"How many weeks late are you?" Dr. Lassiter looks down at the folder she's holding. "Better yet, just tell me when your last menstrual cycle was."

I know the answer, but I pause like I have to do math in my head.

"My last period ended September thirteenth," I tell her on a sigh, because I know, I *know* that was two months ago and anyone who is two months late and thinks they might not be pregnant is half-crazy. Or completely delusional.

Thankfully Dr. Lassiter doesn't pin me with a judgmental frown. She just jots something down before meeting my apologetic gaze. "Taken any home tests?"

"Three," I answer honestly.

"All the same result?"

"One negative that I probably took too soon, one positive last week, and one that didn't have a clear result."

"I see here that you've been on Loestrin for a while now. Have you taken it regularly and at the same time every day?"

I take another deep breath. Maybe this will be good practice for explaining my situation to my mom.

"I travel a lot for work from time to time. I have missed a few doses. I tried to double up to make up for a few missed pills but then I read online that it isn't a good idea to do that."

She nods but her mouth turns down. "If you'd just missed one day, I'd say it would be okay. Missing multiple doses, however, not so much. Let's go ahead and run some tests and see if we can figure out what's going on with you. If it turns out that you aren't pregnant, though I heavily suspect that you are, we'll look at alternate forms of birth control. Ortho Evra, for instance, which comes in a patch you change weekly or possibly an implant that lasts even longer. I typically recommend those to women who travel or have unpredictable schedules."

"Okay," I say meekly.

"A nurse will be in to collect a urine sample and some blood shortly."

With that, she smiles at me once more and exits the room, slipping my chart casually into a plastic bin by the door as if she didn't just deliver huge news with the subtly of a deathblow in a George R. R. Martin novel.

If I ever own my own gynecological practice, which is unlikely, but still, if I do, I'm going to make sure that all rooms are stocked with cupcakes and expensive boxes of chocolates. Maybe a big screen connected to Netflix or with a Nicholas Sparks marathon constantly on repeat. Because this is seriously the most emotionally draining experience of my life.

Time doesn't actually move when you're waiting on the results of an official pregnancy test. Or maybe it moves backward. Hell, I don't know. But I have been sitting on this table for what feels like forever after being poked, prodded, and forced to pee on command. My boobs hurt, my back aches, and the fluorescent lights overhead are giving me a migraine.

"Miss Breeland?"

I have never been so simultaneously thrilled and terrified at hearing my own name.

"Yes," I croak out because my voice is hoarse from disuse.

"Results are in," Dr. Lassiter says, waving my chart at me. "Congratulations. You're going to be a mom."

This is the part where I'm supposed to panic. Or where I'm supposed to turn to my husband and cry while he showers me with kisses.

I do neither. I take a deep breath. Right now, breathing is about all I can manage successfully.

I'm pregnant. A human being is growing inside of me right this very second.

I mean, I guess I already knew. But there is something so final about this, so completely irrevocable that I can feel it down to my bones. Deep down into the marrow.

"Right." I nod and try for the love of all things holy to get some moisture to my mouth. "Of course. Thanks."

I'm still nodding. I can't stop nodding.

"Robyn," Dr. Lassiter says gently, placing a hand gingerly on my knee. "Breathe."

"Yeah. Breathing's good. I like breathing."

She's trying not to smile despite the concerned look in her gaze.

"I know this is big news, and perhaps news you didn't necessarily want."

"I don't—um, I just don't know that I—"

"Relax. No explanations needed here. Just a few more procedures, then you can go home and process in peace."

"More procedures?" My voice cracks like I'm a fourteen-year-old boy instead of a twenty-three, soon to be twenty-four-year-old woman.

Dr. Lassiter nods and returns her attention to my chart briefly. "We're going to do a quick ultrasound and see if we can get some solid confirmation on how far along you are. You'll also get to hear the baby's heartbeat."

My mouth drops open and she speaks again before I can.

"Unless you wanted to wait on that. Some moms like for the dad to be present for the first time. And some don't want to hear or see anything until they're sure they aren't going to terminate or give the baby up for adoption. My guess is your baby is about the size of a peanut, so we might not be able to see much anyway at this point."

The mental image of someone crushing a peanut makes my stomach lurch.

"No, I'm definitely not t-terminating or, um, giving him or her up for adoption. And the dad's not exactly . . . he probably won't be coming to any of my appointments." The tension in my chest squeezes hard once before a new and overwhelming sensation takes over.

This is my baby.

Mine.

Innocent, helpless, and growing inside of me.

Inside of *me*.

Because it's mine.

Nothing will ever hurt this child. If anyone or anything tried, I would destroy them. Annihilate them. Erase their family tree from existence and burn their entire universe to the ground.

*Whoa. Where did that come from?*

A few deep breaths later, I rein in this fiercely protective side I didn't even know I possessed and smile at Dr. Lassiter. Maybe it's all the adrenaline, or just finally knowing the truth for sure, but a tranquil calm settles over me.

"I would love to see my baby. And I'm ready to hear the heartbeat, too. The sooner the better."

She looks as relieved as I feel. "Perfect. Be right back."

# 32 | Robyn

I AM PREGNANT.

And from the looks of the ultrasound screen, I am carrying an immensely adorable gummy bear in my belly. One that apparently hates Italian food, loves Chinese, and will violently reject any red meat or chocolate I try to consume.

*Chocolate, kid? Seriously?* Perhaps I'm carrying the spawn of Satan.

But I know I'm not because nothing that cute could be evil.

I stared at the blurry black-and-white image on the screen as Dr. Lassiter informed me I was nearly seven weeks along. Seven.

I knew exactly when and where my little gummy bear had been conceived.

"Denver," I whispered to myself as a steady pounding rhythmic sound filled the room while tears swam in my eyes.

I left the doctor's office with a serious hankering for pancakes.

Less than an hour later, in the middle of my second stack, I work through possible scenarios in my head. Most of them end with

Dallas glaring at me with horrified hatred in his eyes and telling me that I ruined his life.

So I'm not all that eager to update him.

"Sorry, hon. The waitress for this section was a no-show," a wrinkled woman with blue hair tells me as she refills my long-empty cup of apple juice. "Can I get you some coffee?"

"No, thank you. I'm good."

Once she moves on to the table behind me, I pull up the tour schedule on my phone, making every attempt not to get sticky syrup on it but failing.

After wiping it with a damp napkin, I click a few times and see that only four shows are left. Noting the dates, I realize it's only three weeks until it ends.

Nothing major is going to happen in three weeks. I'm not going to blow up like I swallowed a basketball or give birth, so we're good. Once the tour is over, I'll invite Dallas over for dinner and tell him in a warm and friendly environment that I'm pregnant and that he can be as involved or as uninvolved as he likes.

"We've got this," I say patting my full belly confidently.

But then a waitress about my age with hair in a falling-down ponytail and looking tear-stained and world-weary runs into the diner, apologizing profusely to the blue-haired woman who's now glaring at her from behind the counter.

"I'm sorry. I'm so sorry I'm late. The babysitter didn't show so I had to call my mom for help and she gave me this huge lecture about responsibility and then my car wouldn't start and I got stuck behind a garbage truck. I'm so, *so* sorry."

"You can be sorry all you want. Your pay is being docked. And you have two tables over there that probably won't tip you for shit."

I wince at her harsh words.

Is this my future? Have I been put here in this very place at this exact time to see what my life is going to be like?

"I need this job, Irene. You know I do. Randy still hasn't paid any child support and I'm doing the best I can. I have to get a new fuel pump on my car but I won't be late again, I swear."

"That's what you said last week," Irene of the blue hair says before disappearing into the kitchen.

The distraught waitress makes her way to me and offers me coffee, which I turn down but do so while smiling.

"You okay, hon?"

She gives me a weak smile. "This wasn't supposed to be my life," she says quietly. Her name tag has Lexi printed on it. "I wanted to be a nurse when I grew up. But what can you do, right? We don't get to choose the hand we're dealt, I guess."

Her eyes are watery and I suddenly feel every bite of pancake I've taken like a lead weight.

She's gone, having stepped over to the next table and moved on with her life, before I can say anything. Not that anything I could've said would've made her life any better. She wasn't confiding in me in hopes of garnering advice, I don't think. It was more like she had to say that out loud to someone and I happened to be here.

Knowing I should probably start being more frugal since I'm about to have another mouth to feed, but unable to just do nothing, I grab my wallet and a pen from my purse.

"It's never too late," I scrawl on a napkin. I pull out all the cash I have on me and lay it down. It's nearly three hundred dollars. I have no idea what a fuel pump costs, but I hope that it helps. Sometimes just a little kindness makes a big difference.

*It's never too late,* I think to myself as I leave. I believe that. Truly.

Maybe I'm wrong about Dallas. Maybe he doesn't just care about his music and his career. Maybe he cares about me, too.

But if he doesn't, if he wants absolutely nothing to do with me or my little gummy bear, then so be it.

This wasn't supposed to be my life, either; unwed mother at almost twenty-four isn't exactly my childhood dream come true, but it is my life now. And I'm going to live it the best way that I possibly can. My child will know love and kindness and if Dallas doesn't want him or her, I will want him or her enough for the both of us. And then some.

# 33 | Dallas

"BABE, I'M NOT TRYING TO HATE ON YOUR COOKING OR ANYTHING, but I legit have no fucking clue what these are."

Robyn's smiling at my ignorance when she comes back into the room with a tray of what I hope is recognizable food.

The tour just wrapped up last week and I have a few days before I leave for Mexico. Robyn blew me off for a while, saying she didn't want me to catch what she had. As much as I didn't want to sound like a lovesick idiot, I was twenty-five kinds of relieved when she finally called and invited me over for dinner.

"They're kale chips, silly. Try one."

"They're green and it looks like a plate full of the garnish I usually ignore when it's sitting next to my steak."

"How very observant of you. Just eat one. They taste like potato chips. I promise."

Reluctantly, I lift one to my mouth. "Here goes."

Robyn watches me, an amused grin playing at her lips.

"Stop smirking at me," I say once I've swallowed. "They're all right, I guess. Though you do know we have plenty of potatoes here in the great state of Texas, right?"

"Potatoes are full of starch, which turns to sugar."

I pop another freaky green baked leaf into my mouth. Now that I know when Robyn got so nutritionally conscious, I try to just go with it.

"So what other surprises have you got over there?"

"None. I made the Greek chicken that you like and sautéed some vegetables. Ones you'll recognize." She slides the tray of food closer to me. "There's flour tortillas if you want to make a fajita."

"Sounds good to me." I work on assembling my fajita while Robyn grabs me a beer. When she returns I see that she's drinking plain water.

"No wine tonight? Or good old Midnight Bay bourbon?"

I expect her to toss a throw pillow at me but she just sits down. Across from me instead of next to me, which is just plain disappointing. I'm pretty sure I was invited here for a specific reason, more than just to try kale chips. I have a bad feeling it's not a reason I'm going to like.

"Nope. Plain old water tonight. I'd never drink bourbon with dinner anyway. It's more of a dessert drink."

"Too bad. I'd hoped there'd be a bottle lying around somewhere. I wanted to celebrate."

Robyn's eyes widen. "Celebrate?"

"My big news. About the tour. I kind of hoped that's why you invited me over."

Part of me thinks she's messing around and that any minute she's going to bust out a bottle of champagne. Either she's developed some hard-core acting skills or she truly has no clue what the hell I'm talking about.

"Your big news," she says slowly. "News that I should've heard about by now."

"The international leg of the tour." I press my gaze deeper into hers, trying to figure out if she's playing dumb or if she really has no idea I'm about to be out of the country for nearly three months.

"The tour," she repeats, her intonation at the end making it sound like a question.

"The international dates have been confirmed. Mexico, Brazil, Canada, London, and maybe even Australia and Tokyo. We leave Monday morning. Did no one at work mention this to you? It's huge for my career and for Midnight Bay. So basically it's huge for both of us. I was kind of hoping you might be coming along." I take a bite of my fajita, and the slightly spicy chicken with the hint of lemon is the best thing I've eaten in forever. My girl is a fantastic cook, even if she does substitute garnish for potato chips. "This chicken is amazing, by the way. It's still my favorite."

Robyn is staring dazedly at me so I set my dinner on my plate and push it to the side.

"Robyn?"

Suddenly she shakes her head as if shaking herself out of a daydream. "Yeah, um, I mean no. No, I'm not coming on the international leg of the tour. But wow. That's . . . big news. Congratulations."

"I can't believe no one told you." This doesn't make sense. I heard Mandy and a few others talking about it. They mentioned Midnight Bay partnering with similar companies overseas. How do I know this and she doesn't?

"I knew Jase's tour contract was extended," she says slowly. "I was out sick for a bit and must've missed the announcement that they'd added you on to that leg of the tour as well."

"I would've asked how you've been feeling, but you look like you feel one hundred percent better." Or she did at least, until I mentioned the international tour dates. Now she's kind of pale and looking like she might be sick again. "You've been with the tour this long, I can't imagine they'd want to send anyone else."

I should just say it. I should just come right out and tell her the truth. I don't want to go to all of these new places where I'm going to be a fish out of water without her. The memory of the night in New Orleans is burned into my memory—and not just because of the sex—though, good Lord, I think records were broken and laws of gravity were defied. But the city came alive for me because of her. I want her with me. Always.

The startling realization leaves me sitting there stunned.

"We have marketing associates who specialize in those areas—speak the languages and know the trends—much better than I ever could. I could ask, but they wouldn't send me. If they did, I'd just be in the way."

"You're never in the way, babe." I try to catch her gaze, but it's focused on some point past my left shoulder. I glance in that direction but all I see is her spare bedroom door and it's closed. "You all right?"

"Yeah, um, yes. I'm fine," she answers too quickly. But then she returns her attention to her food and we eat in awkward silence. Or I do at least. She barely touches her chicken.

"You all done?" she asks once I've cleaned my plate. "I'm kind of beat. Being sick took a lot out of me."

I nearly get whiplash from the sudden turn of events. "I thought you invited me over here to tell me something. If it wasn't congratulations on the extended tour, what was it?"

Robyn pulls back and glances at the door. She's either ready for me to vacate the premises or anticipating that I will bolt after she tells me whatever she needs to.

"Dallas," she says softly. "I do need to tell you something and you might not like it."

"Okay." I stand in case it is something that makes me want to leave, but now I feel like I'm looming over her, intimidating her. Being sick did take a lot out of her. Looking closer, I can see that she's lost at least five or ten pounds. Crouching into her personal space, I lower myself onto the wooden pallets she's refurbished into a coffee table and place my hands on her hips, pulling her to me. "What is it? Whatever it is, you can tell me."

Her body is rigid in my arms, which is so completely unusual it causes me to take my hands off her.

"It's this," Robyn says, gesturing between us. "I can't do this anymore. Not with you."

Before my brain catches up, I have a physical reaction that I have very little control over. My heart pounds harder, my hands tighten on her waist before I release her. My mouth is dry and my brain empties of all coherent thoughts.

"I don't know that I understand exactly."

But I can see it in her eyes. For some reason, unbeknownst to me, she's quitting on us. Quitting on me.

Again.

"Robyn?"

"I'm sorry," she says, turning her head a second too late. I already saw the tears. "It's not because I don't care about you, Dallas. You know that I do. It's just—"

"Is your mom all right? Don't mess with me, Robyn. Don't do this shit to us again. If she's sick, you can tell me."

She shakes her head quickly. "No. It's not my mom. She's fine. Promise."

Well, that's a relief. But there's still something.

"Is there someone else?" Maybe I shouldn't ask, because truth be told, I really don't want to hear the fucking answer. But at the same time, I need to. She and Wade have been awful cozy at the past few shows and at the party in Nashville. If she's decided to take the clean slate over the guy she has history with, I have some news for her about the cleanliness of that particular slate.

"No. Not exactly. There's just—" Robyn stops midsentence, her eyes widening, and I'd give my favorite guitar to know what's going on in her beautiful head. "You're right. There is someone else. Someone whose needs I have to put before my own. I'm sorry."

Fuck his fucking needs is what I want to say. But I don't. Because what the hell can I say? Hey, Robyn, could you do me a favor and hold off on moving on until this tour is over so we can keep fucking? You're my muse. How about you let me squeeze a few more songs out of this?

I stand up because her apartment suddenly feels tiny even though it isn't. I need some distance. With her intoxicating floral and honey scent infiltrating my brain, I want to beg. My primal urges tell me to fight for her, to make promises I can't keep. But I won't do that to her.

"Dallas," she begins but I can't listen to her tell me about her new guy. How he's great and he wants the same things she does and didn't we say this was casual anyway?

"It's fine. Thanks for letting me know. I was supposed to check in with Mandy about some possible shows I might be doing on my own in smaller venues after this tour ends and I completely forgot to touch base with her. I'll call you later."

Robyn follows me to her door. I want to scream at her, ask her why she looks so damn sad if this is what she wants? She found someone else and no longer has to settle for the pathetic parts of a relationship I'm able to give. She should be happy.

"Wait, please," she says, her green eyes filling with tears. "At least let me—"

"There's no need." I give her the best smile I can manage. "Come on, babe. We both knew this was coming sooner or later. This was casual, right? Temporary. I'm glad you found someone willing to be a permanent part of your life. I'm sorry I couldn't be."

Her mouth drops open and pain ripples across her pretty face, a quick flash that hit just when I said the word *temporary*. It thunders into my chest at the same time, the jagged knife of the lie I tell in my tone. Like I don't care. Like it's not killing me where I stand to think of another man—any other man—touching her. Holding her. Calling her his.

*"No matter how many guitars you own, you'll always have a favorite,"* my granddad used to say. *"It probably won't be the most expensive one, or the one with the richest sound. Likely it'll be the one with all the scratches and the nicks in the wood. It'll be the one that's been with you the longest, the one you know inside and out because you've put it through the most hell."*

He was right, and not just about guitars.

I have to get out of here before I hit something and Robyn owns a lot of fancy breakable shit. Most of which I suspect she created herself.

Because she is amazing like that. And I am losing her. Again.

No. I'm letting her go. Because it's the right thing to do and because I'm leaving the country. I'm not exactly ideal boyfriend material.

"Goodbye, Robyn," I tell her, placing a chaste kiss on her cheek even though my body begs for more.

I don't look into her eyes as I leave. I can't. Seeing even the tiniest hint of regret in them would break me. I'd lift her sexy ass off the ground and carry her back to her bedroom like a caveman. What I'd do to her body would make it impossible for her to even think of another man touching it ever again.

My fists are clenched so hard I'm losing feeling in my hands so I decide to walk around for a while before going back to my cold, empty hotel room.

I want to fight.

I want to fuck.

And most of all, I want someone else to hurt as badly as I do.

My phone rings and it feels like the universe has sent me an answer.

"Hey, Mandy. I was just about to call you."

Mandy's room is only a few down from mine. I pace the hallway twice before knocking on her door.

This is stupid.

She's my manager.

But she has made it abundantly clear what she wants so maybe I should give it to her. This is all I'm ever going to get, right? Meaningless fucks and empty orgasms. Plus, at least I know she won't go to the media. My career is just as important to her as her own.

Once I've made my mind up and worked myself up good by imagining bending her tight, bare ass over her bed and fucking her hard and fast, I rap hard on her door.

"It's me," I say.

"Well, hello there, me," a man's voice says when the door opens. Jase Wade smirks at me. He's naked except a pair of black boxer shorts.

The image of him with Robyn in Nashville, side by side, heads bent together in intimate conversation, fills my mind until I see bright blinding red.

He's got to be the someone else. He's the only other man I've ever seen her so much as speak to. I've seen him whispering things to her that made her blush. And here he is fucking my manager on the side.

I swing before deciding to, connecting with the left side of his face, and he staggers back before coming at me full force.

He can bring it. I'm ready for the impact. Hell, I'm craving it.

The crack of his fist into my jaw is welcome relief from the pain I'd felt when Robyn told me she had someone else. I shove hard in hopes of backing him up enough to give me room to swing, but the motherfucker wraps me in a bear hug and slams me against the wall.

He hits me again and I laugh when I taste the blood.

"The fuck is wrong with you, man?"

He's looking at me like I've lost my mind. Maybe I have.

"Dallas? Jesus Christ!" Mandy calls out, stepping out of her room in a black silk negligée that barely covers anything. "What in the world are you doing?"

"You're a fucking piece of shit," I say to Jase Wade. "Do you just fuck everyone in your damn path?" I shake my head in disgust, which makes me feel slightly dizzy.

"I never knew you cared so much," Mandy says, stepping around him.

I spit out a mouthful of blood, causing her to jump back. "I don't."

"You need to get out of here. There's paparazzi up my ass everywhere I go," Wade tells me. The concern in his voice is genuine. And confusing. "Go get cleaned up and meet me down in the bar in ten."

"Go to hell."

"You need to chill the fuck out, man. And we need to get some shit straight before I end up dumping your body in a deserted alley in another country. Bar. Meet me. Ten minutes." He points a finger at me before going back into Mandy's room.

I right myself against the wall and ride out a wave of debilitating nausea. I'll give him this much, dude hits like a fucking freight train.

"I really hope this isn't about the scrawny redhead," Mandy sneers at me. "Seriously, Dallas. I thought you were smarter than this."

"She's twice the woman you are. And probably a hell of a better lay. Maybe we should ask Wade."

The slap comes, sending my ears ringing so hard I don't hear her comeback.

"Let's go, Casanova," Wade says, charging out of the room and dragging me down the hall by my shoulders.

"Get your damn hands off me." I shrug out of his grasp and he glares at me.

"You can wear my fist print on your face every day of this tour for all I fucking care. But we're going downstairs and you're going to hear me out. Like it or not."

I get more than a few strange looks when we exit the elevator. I'm bruised, battered and bloody, but I don't care.

"Bourbon neat," I say to a pretty curly-haired bartender who smiles at me when we reach the bar. I'd smile back but I've lost most of the feeling in my face.

"You got it. Maybe I'll make it a double for that shiner you got there. On the house."

I nod and Wade chuckles from beside me. Bastard.

"Water for me, darlin'."

"Pussy," I mutter under my breath.

He arches a brow, turning on the stool to face me.

"Let's get a few things straight, kid. You don't know much about

me, and what I know about you couldn't fill a shot glass. So I'm going
to lay some knowledge on you."

I just stare hard. I don't want to know anything about him except
why he's leading Robyn on and fucking Mandy.

The blonde delivers our drinks and he clutches his glass for dear
life. "It takes everything I have not to sit here and get shitfaced night
after night. I've been where you are and I've fallen down rabbit holes
a hell of a lot darker than anyplace you've ever been. I've been in
rehab more times than you've had your dick sucked. I have a little girl
who deserves better, so damn it, I try to be better. But some days . . ."

He shakes his head and stares into his glass of water.

"You want a gold star? One of those sobriety badges they
hand out?"

So it's a low blow, but the bourbon hasn't burned off my residual
anger and hurt on Robyn's behalf.

"Naw. What I want is to know where you got that chip on your
shoulder from and why it led you to Mandy's room tonight. More
importantly, I want to know why you're decking me for fucking Lantram when I'm damn near certain she's not the one who's had your
attention during this tour."

"You know why."

He smirks at me. "That supposed to be a joke?"

I stand up, but his hand lands heavy on my shoulder, shoving me
back down.

"Relax. Let's take it one thing at a time. You have something going
with your manager? 'Cause I gotta tell you, you're not the only—"

"No." I take a deep breath. "I mean, she's said shit. I just hadn't
actually considered it until tonight."

"Because . . ."

"Because of you. Because Robyn ended it because of 'someone

else.'" I narrow my eyes at him, knowing we're going to come to blows again, but unable to care.

"Whoa there, Hoss." He tosses his hands up. "Ain't me she's cutting you loose for if that's what you mean."

I want to believe him, so help me I do. But I saw the tender look of affection on her face when they were talking in Nashville. So maybe he doesn't feel the same way, but in Robyn's eyes he obviously comes first.

"Maybe you don't give a shit about her, but she—"

"She confronted me. Went pretty ballistic actually, thinking I'd requested her for this tour because I wanted to get in her panties." He levels me with his hand again when I rile up at his mentioning her panties. "I told her the same thing I'm about to tell you."

My fists are clenched waiting for his explanation.

"Take a drink, kid. Take a few. Then I'll explain."

I down my shot and slide it aside. "There. Let's hear it."

"Robyn Breeland is amazing. She's one of those women, the good ones. The genuine article. The kind you fall in love with. The kind you love more every day, appreciating each line, each wrinkle, and each gray hair because it only makes her more beautiful. She's a biscuits and gravy on Saturday morning girl."

Shows what he knows. Robyn won't touch gravy. But for the rest of it, he's pretty much dead on.

"So then why—"

"But," he says harshly, cutting me off. "I requested her on this tour for entirely different reasons." He takes a long drink of his water while side-eyeing a lanky brunette with silicone breasts passing by. "Honorable ones, if you can believe it."

"I'm not sure I can," I tell him honestly.

"Well, try." He shrugs. "She's young and she made a presentation that impressed me. She mentioned integrating social media into the tour promo and I'm not stupid. I know the guy with the Instagram and the Tweeter and all that shit is the one getting the most attention."

I'm pretty sure it's Twitter, but I'm with him there. Robyn handled that shit for the band when we first started out, then Dixie took over. I hate doing it now. I suck at it, too, which Mandy constantly reminds me. If it weren't for her nagging, I'd skip it altogether.

"So then nothing happened with you and Robyn? Ever?"

He finishes his water and shakes his head. "Other than her raking my ass over the coals because she thought I'd hired her for her body? Nope. And like I told her, I wouldn't kick her out of bed. But that wasn't my intention and it never made it there." There's a slight twinge of disappointment in his voice that makes me want to take another shot at him. "Funny thing," he says, gesturing to the bartender to refill my shot glass. "Once you showed up, she hardly noticed me anymore. And no offense, kid, but I'm a hell of a lot better looking than you."

I almost laugh. Almost.

"Yeah, well, she obviously got over it. Tonight she said we couldn't do this anymore and that there was someone else."

"Maybe she was lying."

I don't even pause to consider that. "Robyn doesn't lie. She's the most honest person I know."

"Did you ask who it was?"

"I kind of bailed before we made it that far. Or before I broke every stick of furniture in her apartment in a blind rage."

Wade rubs his jaw, then stares at me so hard I almost ask if he's trying to get my number. But then he leans back and winks at the brunette watching him from across the room. "Well, maybe she wasn't lying then. Maybe you just didn't give her a chance to tell you the entire truth."

"I don't know if it even matters. What matters is that she ended it."

Right? Fuck. Now I'm confused.

"Look." Wade clears his throat and turns to nod at the brunette. "I've got another situation to handle, so I'm going to make this quick. Listen close."

I take my second shot of bourbon and nod.

"When I was seventeen, I was nobody. A farmer's kid being groomed to take over a farm that had been in my family for decades. I went to a bonfire after graduation, thinking I'd get drunk and blow off some steam. Drink to the privileged motherfuckers going off to college while I shoveled cow shit."

Well, this is an unexpected trip down memory lane. I signal for another shot, twirling my finger so the bartender will keep them coming. Once Wade leaves with his barfly, I'll be drinking alone and it will be twice as pathetic.

"But you didn't, obviously."

"No, I did. But at that bonfire, I played a few songs on my guitar just for the hell of it. Then I went to put it back in my truck and caught some rich preppy asshole assaulting the prom queen."

Jesus.

"So I bashed the asshole over the head with my guitar and knocked his sorry ass out cold."

"Nice." I nod in appreciation. Sounded about like what I would've done.

"Yeah, well. Turns out Aubrey Evers—she was the prom queen— had left the party because she'd heard a song I'd sung and it had made her feel something. Something that made her want to get out of our small town and see the world. My song, some words I strung together out of nowhere, you know? Fuck, that messed me up good, knowing I'd affected her like that. I didn't think she'd even known I'd existed in high school."

"I'm guessing her boyfriend didn't appreciate the profound effect your music had on her?"

"Not so much." Jase's eyes drift and I see the longing in his face. I recognize it because I feel it every time I see Robyn's face. "He probably didn't appreciate me marrying her six months later or getting her pregnant the following year, either. But to hell with him. I should've killed that fucker. I loved that damn guitar and it was destroyed."

"So what happened?"

If Wade is still married, and he's still screwing everything with legs, I might have to coldcock him again regardless.

"She filed for divorce not long after I got my first record deal. She was tired of waiting for me to make her a priority and she met someone else. Someone who could be there every night instead of out chasing a dream that can't really be caught. She got remarried the day we celebrated the album going platinum in Nashville. That's why Robyn was being so nice to me. Not because she wants me, but because she felt sorry for my sad-sack ass."

"Damn."

"Well, I mean, she *might* want me. Most women do."

I roll my eyes. Then nod at the brunette stealing obvious glances our way. "I guess I can see that."

"Naw, man. They don't give a fuck about me. They don't even know me. They see the fame and the publicity and a chance to rub up against me in hopes some of that will rub off onto them."

He stands, jerks his chin in a clear signal to his new friend to leave the group she's with and head our way. She does, as if he's yanked an invisible string.

"Then why do you do it?"

He scoffs like it's a dumb question. Maybe it is. But then he shrugs and something about his expression is hollow and makes me feel almost sorry for him. Strange, since the brunette is bringing a friend over and I know he already got laid once tonight.

"When you lose the only person who actually matters, you realize the rest of it is just physical gratification. Life is short. You have to find what happiness you can while you can. Otherwise you're just existing instead of living. And who wants to sit around with old-man balls knowing he sat out his chance to live?" He dips his head toward my shot glass. "You've got your way of numbing the pain, I've got mine."

He offers his arms to the two women and they take them with matching smiles. The black-haired one with blond shot through like streaks of lightning turns to me. "You coming too, handsome?"

Before I can answer, Jase shakes his head. "Nah. He's nursing some serious heartbreak tonight and he's six sheets in the wind. He probably wouldn't be able to get it up anyway."

I kick out a leg but catch his stool with my boot instead of him.

"Too bad," she says as Jase leads them away.

I turn around on my stool and stare at my newly refilled shot glass, placing one of my hands over the other and resting my chin on them.

Touring with Jase Wade is like getting a glimpse into my future. Where all that awaits me is arenas full of screaming fans and nights filled with meaningless sex.

It used to sound pretty damn appealing, once upon at time. It might still if I hadn't gone on another tour just before this.

Touring with Afton Tate on the unsigned artists tour, I saw him

turn down women, record labels, managers, and even big-name producers that most guys would have given their left nut to work with.
On one of the nights when I joined him for a beer at a dive we'd
played at I asked him why he kept shutting everyone down.

"I shut the women down because they aren't interested in me, not
really. They're interested in what I can do for them, what my reputation and my name will mean when they can attach it to the story of
hooking up with me. It isn't real, and I don't have time or energy for
shit that isn't real."

It made sense. I'd nodded along. "Yeah, okay. So what about the
managers and the producers? They just want to fuck you, too?"

He looked at me like I'd said something amusing. "Pretty much.
They want me to leave my band, tell guys who've sacrificed just as
much as I have and who are just as talented and driven if not more so,
to take a hike so I can be the star of their bullshit show. I'd be a hell
of a lot easier to manipulate on my own, without these guys having
my back."

His words had struck a chord in me, one that had been exposed
since I'd left Dixie and Gavin behind to pursue this alone.

"You're a more honorable man than I," I told him. "Most people
wouldn't care so long as it meant they got what they wanted."

"Most people include you?"

I'd shrugged like it wasn't twisting my guts to hell and back to talk
about. "I'd rather have my sister and my drummer with me, yeah.
But it just wasn't the way it worked out."

Afton had stared off into the distance for a long time, watching
some girl duo perform onstage before he spoke. "Maybe that's why
I'm struggling to accept anyone else's input on my career. I'm too
much of a control freak to let it just work itself out. I'm willing to
work for it until I get it right."

That brief exchange was still jammed in my subconscious. Maybe I'd fucked up. Maybe I shouldn't have taken the first offer I'd gotten. I could've waited. Could've told Mandy I'd get in touch once Gavin had his probation worked out and Dixie was in a place where she could move past her grief. But I'd forced Dixie to suck it up and move on when our parents died; I thought I was doing what was best for her. I wouldn't do that again. This time I backed off and let her wallow if that's what she needed. Apparently a road trip had helped but by the time she was done traveling, I was already on Wade's tour and magically transformed into Dallas Walker, solo act.

There are two men inside of me: one I know well and one I am still getting acquainted with.

One of them tells me that Wade's life isn't so bad. Besides, I won't be stupid enough to get married and have to deal with that brand of hurt. But the other man in me, the one my dad raised to look out for his sister, the one my grandparents taught to believe in the integrity of music and of myself, he's still stuck on Afton's declaration. And not just where music is concerned.

Maybe I let Robyn go too easily. Maybe I should've fought for her, tried to make it work in a way that we both could handle and be happy with instead of just stepping aside to clear the way for the next guy. I walked away once before and I haven't stopped regretting it.

Robyn made a comment once, about how it was hard to tell if we were getting a second chance or making the same mistake twice. I voted second chance. She looked dubious. I don't know how I'm going to keep from making the same mistake twice, but somehow I have to try. One thing is for sure. I owe her an apology for not hearing her out. Not tonight, because I look and feel like shit, but I have to figure out a way to throw my hat in the ring before I leave the damn country.

# 34 | Robyn

WHEN THE KNOCK COMES, MY HEART NEARLY LEAPS OUT OF MY chest. Climbing out of the nest I've made myself on my couch, I try to work out in my head the words I'm going to say. They're like a puzzle with a bunch of pieces that don't fit. There has to be some way to tell him what I need to in a way that will soften the blow.

*"Remember how you mentioned being afraid a groupie would get knocked up on purpose just to trap you and tie herself to you for life? No need to worry about that anymore. I got it covered,"* just doesn't come off as gently as I would like for it to.

But when I open my door, it isn't Dallas standing there. It's his manager.

"Miss Lantram," I say in greeting. "What can I do for you?"

She gives me a smile that's more of a smirk and breezes past me into my apartment. The scent of expensive perfume, the kind that smells amazing but if you inhale too hard you choke half to death, wafts in the air behind her. I feel like Ms. Potato Head in her presence. Me with my gray sweatpants from the Pink store and a stained T-shirt from Midnight Bay next to her in black leggings and a leather jacket. Her stilettos are sharp enough to use as a weapon. Judging from the hostility in her stare that might be her intention.

"You could, oh, I don't know, do your job. That'd be a nice change."

I narrow my eyes because there are *a lot* of things I've done wrong, but my job is not one of them. "I can assure you, I have done my job and will continue to do it to the best of my ability. Maybe if you'd care to elaborate on exactly which aspect of Midnight Bay's involvement in the tour you're displeased with then I could—"

"It's not Midnight Bay's *involvement* I take issue with. It's yours. Specifically."

*Hence why she's in your apartment, Breeland.*

Watching her standing there glaring at me, I recall what Dixie said about her. How she's the one who told Dallas's sister to sit out the encore at the showcase that landed Dallas his career in a roundabout way. I can't help but wonder how differently things might have turned out if she hadn't made her particular suggestions.

"I see," I say evenly. "Well, I knew Dallas long before you did. So while I can tell that fact is upsetting to you, unfortunately I have yet to discover the formula for time travel. Guess there's not much we can do about it."

"Do you know what he did tonight? Where he is right now?"

"I don't know where he is now, but he came by earlier."

"And then he came to my room."

My stomach turns a full somersault at her announcement. "Congratulations. So you got what you wanted then." *Now kindly get the fuck out.* I hold the door open for her but she ignores my nonverbal parting gesture.

"Not hardly. Jase did get a fist to the face, though. Which he returned. Any ideas as to why Dallas felt the need to attack the head-liner of the tour he's on?"

I'm growing exceptionally tired of her guessing games.

"Much like time travel, mind reading isn't my forte. How about you just put your big-girl panties on and say whatever it is you came here to say?"

I lean against my door and wait for her to unleash her wrath on me.

"Fine." She breathes hard through her nose and pins me in place with a glare. "Whatever is going on with you and Dallas and/or you and Jase Wade needs to stop. Effective immediately. This is Dallas's big shot and the last thing he needs is some high school homecoming queen mucking up his life."

I arch an eyebrow. Not bad on the guessing. I was homecoming queen, mostly because I campaigned my ass off.

"More importantly," I begin, meeting the challenge in her eyes with a hard glint of my own, "you want me to get out of your way so you can get in Dallas's pants the same way you snaked your way into Jase's. Right?"

Her mouth gapes open and I take a step forward.

"See, I know about you. I know how you pushed Dixie Lark to not play at that showcase so you could get her out of the way and have Dallas all to yourself. I see you so clearly, it's almost scary. You push other women away because you feel threatened by them. You're de-pending on your looks and your sex appeal to make your career suc-cessful and so far that's worked for you. The guys have the talent and you have a client list full of moneymaking, ass-shaking superstars you get to bed down whenever you feel like it. I have to say, kudos to you. As one of very few women in the bourbon business, I can understand using what you felt you had to in order to get where you wanted to be. But as a woman with some integrity and self-respect, I can't say I would've gone the same route."

"You have no idea what you're talking about." Mandy Lantram gives new meaning to the worth *seething*. If I keep talking, I can probably make steam shoot straight out of her ears.

"Don't I? Then tell me, what was Jase Wade doing in your room tonight? And why was Dallas heading there?"

"Wouldn't you like to know? Speaking of which, I'm sure your boss would *love* to know how his company is being represented right now. Or the trouble his associate is causing between two of the hottest acts in country music and the tour that is very likely putting his company on the map."

She has me there. I don't know who she reports to or if they'd even care if she sleeps with her clients. But Midnight Bay is a family company with family values, one of the most heavily emphasized ones being that you don't put your own hedonistic desires above the company's bottom line.

"So what are you saying? You want me to quit the tour? Isn't it pretty much over anyway?"

"Not the international leg. Which is why I'm here. I want you to sit this one out, no matter what Dallas or your boss or anyone else says."

"Done," I say, because I already wasn't planning to go.

"In addition to that," she continues, "until this tour is completely over, I want you to leave Dallas alone. He risked his career tonight. One word and Jase can replace him as his opening act for the international leg of the tour in a heartbeat. Is that what you want? To keep him here and cost him his dream? Because I can assure you, if that happens, he will resent you for the rest of his life."

I'd already thought of that so her threat is empty. I can only imagine how insanely freaked-out she'd be if she knew I was pregnant. But I'm ready for her to leave so I nod as if we're in agreement. "Got it. If that's all, have a good night, Miss Lantram." I wave my arm toward my still-open door.

"Glad we could handle this like adults," she says with a self-congratulatory smile that makes me want to slap her. "I'd say see you around, but I'm sincerely hoping I won't."

The feeling is completely mutual.

"Don't let the door hit you where the good Lord split you, Lantram." Those are my final muttered words before I slam the door behind her.

Once she's gone and my apartment is free of her cloying scent and negative energy, I grab my cell phone off the charger on the kitchen counter and take it to the couch.

There's a missed call and a text from Dallas.

*Call me, please.*

I stare at it for several minutes before making up my mind. Once I've located the number I was looking for, I press call and hold the phone to my ear.

"Hey, you."

"Hey," I say on a sigh, thankful for the familiar voice. "Can you meet me? Say lunch tomorrow?"

"Thanks for coming, Dixie," I say when I sit down across the table from the lunch date.

"I love this place," she says, eyeing the Mediterranean restaurant appreciatively. "They have the best hummus dip."

I glance at the menu when our waiter arrives. He's cute. Tall, dark, and giving my Dixie some serious sex eyes.

"I'll have the grilled chicken wrap and a side of pasta salad," I say, practically nudging him with my menu. "And an ice water with lemon, please."

"Same," Dixie says, oblivious to the drool forming as he checks out the intricate tattoo that swirls around her delicate wrist. "Plus a side of hummus dip and pita chips, please."

"Of course. I'll get that right out to you. Nice ink," he says, nodding at her before he leaves.

"Um, thanks." Dixie meets my amused gaze with a perplexed one in her eyes.

"I bet if you leave your number our meal will be free," I tell her. "Dude was smitten."

She laughs like I'm joking. "Yeah, right."

"Uh, hello. Pretty sure he almost asked for your hand in marriage instead of what you wanted to eat."

She shakes her head, and then widens her eyes at me in a shut-up signal when he returns with our waters. He winks when he sets hers down and I have to stifle a giggle.

Once he's gone, I burst out laughing at her stiff posture.

"For goodness sakes, Lark. Do you imitate a corpse every time a guy flirts with you?"

She shrugs and sips her water. "He's not my type."

I glance over my shoulder and give him another once-over as he waits on a table a few rows over. The ladies at that table are clearly appreciating his obvious assets more than my lunch date is. "Ah, yes. Tall, broad-shouldered, square jaw, crystal-clear smoke-colored eyes and a chin dimple. It's like *GQ* custom ordered him. I can see how you'd struggle to find him attractive."

Dixie's cheeks redden and I feel bad about teasing her.

"I didn't say I didn't find him attractive. He just isn't my type, that's all."

I snort out loud because he's exactly her type—he's everyone with ovaries' type for that matter—minus the fact that he isn't Gavin Garrison.

"Speaking of Gavin," I begin, but Dixie cuts me off.

"We weren't. Speaking of him, I mean."

"Well, we should be. I've been a crappy friend lately due to my job and everything with Dallas. So give me the scoop. What the heck happened?"

"Did you invite me to lunch just to gossip?"

I nod. "Mostly. I have some news, too, but once I tell you mine everything else will pale in comparison, so let's talk about you first."

Dixie makes a face that can only be described as a grimace. Her features are so pretty, though, she's still attractive even with her face all twisted up.

"Jesus. That bad? What did he do? Rob a bank? Kick a puppy? Kill some nuns?"

"He didn't call me."

Okay, that was anticlimactic.

"He didn't call you? Like after sex you mean?"

She sighs and leans forward, her bracelets jangling against the table. Even her jewelry is musical. "No. I mean yeah. Sort of. He just didn't contact me. Like at all."

I nod encouragingly, hoping she'll explain further.

"His last words to me were 'Wait for me.'" She huffs out a breath as if becoming increasingly angry. "Wait for me, he said. So I did. For the most part. I mean, I drove my grandparents' RV around the country for a few weeks, but it wasn't like I was picking up guys or anything. Dallas didn't tell me that Gavin didn't go on the unsigned artists tour, and when I called him out on it, he seemed to be under the impression that Gavin would've already told me himself."

"But he hadn't?"

"Nope. Not a word."

Gavin always kept to himself, but in my years of dating his best friend and handling the social media outreach for Leaving Amarillo, I did learn that his mom is a drug-addicted townie who had no business being a mother, from what I saw and what Dallas told me over the years.

"And you still haven't heard from him?" Dixie's face pales and I feel bad for pressing. "I'm sorry. I shouldn't pry. You don't have to tell me if you don't—"

"Oh, I heard from him eventually. Not because he called or even texted to say he was alive. I ran into him by accident, actually. And he wasn't happy to see me. *At all.*"

Tiny fissures form in my heart as she continues. I knew the first time Dallas introduced me to his sister and his best friend that there was something between them. It was obvious, even if Dallas chose to remain oblivious; anyone with eyes could see how much they cared about one another. Sparks practically flew in the air between them every time their eyes met.

"Maybe you just caught him by surprise or something," I offer, knowing my words probably don't help.

"I caught him by surprise all right. He was with someone."

The fissures widen into full-blown cracks.

"Oh no. I'm so sorry, hon. Are you sure? Maybe it was something else?"

Not that I have any alternate suggestions.

"I'm sure."

I watch as she takes a deep breath before gathering the strength to continue.

"He works at the Tavern now. So he was literally fifteen minutes down the road and he couldn't even pick up the phone or stop by. I've been giving piano and violin lessons to some local kids whose parents can't really afford much. One of the moms was turning twenty-one; yes, she's twenty-one with a five-year-old, don't judge."

I put my hand up because I am the last person to be judging anyone right now. "No judging. Got it."

"And a group of them convinced me to go out for a night on the town. We got there and they all shoved me toward the piano. I figured what the hell, you know?"

God. I can see it. I can totally see Dixie playing the piano in this smoky bar and Gavin being drawn to the music and seeing her, and my stupid pregnant hormones are making this too much to handle. Dixie blurs before me as she continues.

"So I'm playing and I feel someone watching me and there he is."

A startled cry escapes me even though I saw it coming.

Dixie shrugs. "And he was with this . . . *woman*. She was blond and beautiful in a sophisticated street-savvy sort of way. And older than me. Probably late twenties or early thirties. They were talking all night, every time he took a break from bartending, and they were like forehead to forehead. She kept touching him and it was just . . ." Dixie shudders and so do I.

"He didn't even speak to you?" Now my hormones are vacating oversentimental land and heading toward blind rageville.

"Oh he did. He basically told me to go back to Houston because I'd be better off."

"I will kill him. He's a dead man."

She laughs a little, but then she looks at me and her eyes go wide. "Robyn? You okay? I promise, it's all right. I'm okay. Don't cry."

"Fuck. Am I crying?"

I wipe my eyes and sure enough, they're damp. Well, hell.

"How could he? I mean, it's so obvious that you two—"

She waves her hand. "I don't know. All I know is, whatever was going on, he didn't want me there to see it. He basically told me to leave and not come back. So yeah. I'm thinking of getting the first of many cats because I'm obviously destined to be a lonely old cat lady."

"Like hell you are. I will get this waiter's number right now and you will—"

I'm interrupted by the waiter in question. He sets our food down and grins sheepishly. So he heard me then. Good.

"Anything else I can get you, ladies?"

"You bet your sweet—"

"We're fine," Dixie says loudly. "Thanks."

He leaves us with another lingering grin.

"See?" I say, gesturing wildly toward his retreating figure and nearly knocking my water over. "There are other fish in the sea. Smoking-hot fish, mind you. Gavin Garrison can suck it."

Dixie takes a bite of her wrap, eyeing me speculatively while she chews. "You're really worked up today. What's going on with you?"

Crap. We've reached the portion of the lunch date that's about me.

"Eat a little more. Then I'll tell you."

"Robyn Breeland," she begins, setting her wrap down harshly. "If you invited me here to tell me you have a deadly disease or something awful and are just stalling for time by messing around about the waiter then I—"

"No, it's nothing awful." I sigh. "Well . . . I don't think it's awful anyway. Your brother might feel differently."

"My brother?"

I push my spirally pasta salad noodles around with my fork. "He and I have kind of been seeing each other casually during the tour. Since we were together so much anyway, it just sort of . . . happened."

"Feel free to spare me the details."

"No problem."

"Thank you."

"You're welcome."

"So . . ." Dixie prompts. "Now you realize you're in love and you want to tell him that he's the one and you plan to spend the rest of your life with him making lots of pretty babies for me to spoil?"

Score one for her. "Um, well . . . you got one part right."

"You're in love?"

I shrug. Yeah, I am. I always have been. But I don't think that necessitates a formal announcement.

She tries again. "You plan to tell him he's the one? Because you know how he is. Just because he might not say it doesn't mean he doesn't feel the same way."

"That's not it. Not exactly."

"So then . . . babies?" Her eyes light up and her mouth drops open.

"Just the one, I hope. At least, there was only one on the ultrasound, thank goodness."

Dixie makes an "ahh" sound that causes several people nearby to turn and look at us.

"Shh. Keep it down. I didn't plan to tell the whole restaurant."

"Oh my God." Dixie clasps a hand over her mouth. Another "Oh my God" still escapes, though it's muffled. Tears shine in her eyes.

"You're going to make me cry again," I say, because she is.

"Oh my God, Robyn. I'm so happy for you. For both of you." She reaches across the table and squeezes my hand, which causes my tears to fall because I've been so worried I forgot to be happy. Seeing her be happy makes me realize that Dallas be damned, I can be happy, too. "What did Dallas say?"

Well . . . I was happy for a second at least.

"He doesn't exactly *know* yet."

Dixie releases my hand. "Holy shit. I know before he does? Nice. But uh, you should probably tell him. Like sooner rather than later. He leaves for Mexico on Monday I think."

I nod. "Mexico. Then Canada. Then Brazil, I think. I'm going to. I just . . ."

"You're scared. I can understand that. But you still have to tell him."

"What if he hates me, Dix? You know him. You know he won't want this. He's living his dream right now. How am I supposed to tell him I'm about to turn it into a nightmare?"

"You stop right there, lady. No one calls my niece or nephew a nightmare. And as far as my brother goes . . . you might be surprised. Dallas is a lot of things. Driven. Stubborn. Sometimes downright obnoxiously overprotective. But he's a good man. And family matters to him. Maybe more so since we hardly have any left."

"I know that. I do." I take a few steadying breaths. "That's my other fear. That his values will cause him to leave his dreams behind to be with us. Then what? What happens two or three years from now when he resents us for costing him his dream? Can you imagine Dallas without music? Working some nine-to-five dead-end job he hates? Because I can and it isn't pretty. I won't do that to him."

Dixie looks so deep into my eyes I fear she can see my soul.

"Robyn," she says slowly. "You didn't see his face when he learned about your mom's cancer. It broke him, knowing you didn't trust him enough to tell him the truth that summer."

I might not have seen his face that night, but I saw it a few days later and I remember how furious he was.

Dixie continues before I can say anything. "And for the record, he wasn't the only one who was hurt by that."

The pain is evident on her face and my shoulders sag beneath the weight of it.

"I'm sorry. I should've told you, both of you. He was just so excited about that summer and I didn't want to take that away from him." The same way I didn't want to put a damper on the international leg of his tour now.

Remembering what he told me, about how he bombed his few performances that summer because of me, I feel myself sinking into the hopeless pit of despair. If I don't tell Dallas he'll be hurt later and if I do tell him now he'll be distracted on the road. Either way, I'm repeating mistakes I don't know how to avoid.

I haven't called or texted him because I just can't find the words. Now I know what he meant about the mind-numbing frustration of writer's block.

Dixie nods. "You're forgiven. I know you were trying to handle it on your own and your intention wasn't to hurt anyone. But I've learned a lot these past few months. I learned that I can live all on my own without my brother or anyone else dictating my life or my schedule. I've learned exactly how important music is to me and how much it means for me to be able to share it with other people. I've realized, in hindsight, that I should've told Mandy Lantram to go straight to hell when she suggested I sit out of my own band. And I've learned that some things are simply worth fighting for. So you might have to bail me out of jail when I back over Gavin's new lady friend with Dallas's truck. But of all that, the most important thing I've realized is that I should never, ever, underestimate myself. So I want you to take a long, hard look at yourself."

I glance down at my beige sweater and jeans. Nothing too impressive to see here.

Dixie disagrees, apparently. "You are independent and strong and amazing. You are one of the hardest-working people I know. And to top it off, you're a truly good person. You're funny and gorgeous, and mine and Dallas's lives are better because you're in them."

"Why must you insist on making the pregnant lady cry?"

She smiles at me and gives me the universal head tilt of sympathy. "Whatever his reaction is, you can handle it. I know you can. You put up with him for far longer than anyone else ever could."

"Maybe I could just wait until he gets back. That way he can focus while he's overseas and—"

"And he can come home to you and your baby bump knowing something very important was kept from him. Again. How well do you think that will go over?"

I place my elbows on the table and rest my face in my hands. I know she's right. It's probably why I told her before him, because I needed confirmation that telling him now was the right thing.

"Mandy told me to stay away from him," I mumble in a last-ditch effort to delay the inevitable.

"I will happily deal with Mandy Lantram if she gives you any grief," Dixie says, a level of ferocity in her voice I've never heard before. "You don't even think about her. Just tell him. Tell him about the baby and tell him what's in your heart. I know you, Robyn. And I know you want to give him the easy way out. The I'm-Robyn-Breeland-I-got-this-no-worries-I-don't-need-you speech."

I smile because she does know me. Every time I've rehearsed telling him in my head, there's an out clause.

She reaches across the table and takes one of my hands in hers. "Tell him how you feel. All of it. Even if he makes the wrong choice, at least he won't be able to say you didn't give him one."

# 35 | Dallas

I SPENT THE WEEKEND LYING LOW BUT WHEN I WAKE UP MONDAY morning, my vision is still blurry and my head has a heartbeat of its very own. Hangovers don't typically linger for more than a day. But then, I'm not usually beat to hell and back from duking it out with Jase Wade, either.

She hasn't called. Or texted. Or sent smoke signals. Nothing.

I've called and left voice mails and texted to the point that she could probably file a valid harassment suit against me.

I take my daily dose of extra-strength Tylenol, then some migraine medicine for good measure, and stumble to the bathroom. After a long, hot shower I feel marginally better. Still sore and tired, but human at least. Today I leave for Mexico and I still haven't talked to Robyn. I owe her an apology and I've decided that even if I have to swallow a year's worth of pride to do it, I am going to tell her that I'm happy for her. Deep down I am. Deep, *deep* down.

Telling her goodbye is going to suck. Telling her goodbye and knowing I'm leaving the girl I've thought of as mine on some level for the past seven years to some other bastard is going to suck hairy gorilla nuts. But it's the least I can do.

Getting dressed I think about the night she slapped me at the diner in Denver and the amazing sex that followed. If not for her and that night, I wouldn't have written "Tough All Over," it wouldn't be the headlining track on my upcoming album, and I probably wouldn't be going on this tour.

Memories of our amazing night in New Orleans and her celebrating my single's success with me fill my head as I pack the rest of my belongings into my bag.

This is my life, I might as well get used to it. Strangely enough, it isn't the shows I keep remembering from each city. It's the time I spent with her. The shows she didn't attend are hardly even memorable. I played, I grabbed some food and beer, and crashed alone. Without Robyn in my life, it's black-and-white. All work and no play. Which is odd since technically I "play" for a living. But when she's there, my world is in brilliant color.

Fuck.

I knew in New Orleans, and maybe I knew even before that. But damn it to hell, I love her. Not like I love my fans or my sister or my job or my music. I am crazy head over ass in fucking obsessive love with her. And there's not a damn thing I do about it. I'm leaving the country, for fuck's sakes. I can't exactly ask her to wait a decade or so while I make music until people get tired of me. She deserves better than that and it sounds like she found it.

I want to see her, to go to her place and apologize and lay my heart on the line. But now that it's time, I'm chickening out for fear of two possible outcomes. One, her new man is there and I kill him and go to jail instead of on tour. Two, she feels the same way and dumps her new man and spends her life sitting around waiting on me to finish living my dream.

Neither of those feels right.

Not really.

So I pull out my phone and take the mangina way out. Texting. Which was probably invented by a coward who'd acted like a jackass and needed to apologize to some girl but didn't have the balls to do it on the phone or in person. Cowards unite, Dude.

*I'm sorry for being such an ass. I understand why you haven't called me back. I'm happy for you and I should've said that instead of storming out. Tell your new guy he's lucky I'm leaving the country and that he better treat you right.*

When she doesn't reply, I send one more—one that says three words I should have told her in person—and then I shut my phone off because I've become too much of a pussy to even handle her goodbye.

"I'm so glad the label decided to add Rio to the tour. The food is amazing, the people are beautiful, and wait until you see the water. It's this incredible shade of aquamarine and so clear you wouldn't believe it."

Mandy prattles on in the back of the town car that's taking us to the airport. I couldn't give two fucks about leaving the country right now. Or what color the water is anywhere. The only color I care about right now is emerald. The color of Robyn's eyes. They darken to jade when I piss her off. And they're lighter, peridot maybe, when they're filled with tears.

Propping my elbow on the ledge of the tinted window, I stare out at Texas as it passes.

When we pull up to the Dallas–Fort Worth airport, the driver gets out and handles checking our luggage. I don't have much. A guitar. Two suitcases full of clothes. Everything else will be handled by crew members.

"Come on, Superstar," Mandy says, linking her arm with mine. The contact pisses me off.

"Enough with the superstar shit," I say, ignoring the years of manners that have been ingrained in me.

Mandy jerks her arm loose and glares at me.

"Excuse me? Do you have a problem we need to handle, Dallas? Because right now, on the way to the biggest opportunity of your life, I can't even imagine what could be putting you in such a bad mood."

"Guess you aren't very creative then," I grumble, following the entourage with us toward a private security entrance we've been cleared for. Behind me I can already hear people losing their shit over Wade. Camera phones are flashing everywhere. I keep my sunglasses on and my head down.

"Hey," she says, practically stomping her designer stiletto on the floor. "Talk to me. What's the problem here?"

I don't exactly have the words and if I did, she'd be the last person I'd share them with.

"I'm tired is all," I say. "Sorry."

"If you need to blow off some steam, it's a long flight. Our seats are together. We could—"

"No," I say too quickly. "No thanks, I mean." Pass, Mandy. Hard fucking pass.

"You should know something, Dallas," she murmurs low as she takes my arm again without my having offered it. "I always—and I mean *always*—get what I want."

"Must be nice," I say drily.

She huffs out a breath and whips her hair behind her. Within seconds she has her trusty cell phone out and is steadily ignoring my temperamental ass.

I'm lost in thought, when I hear someone calling my name. We're almost to the security checkpoint so I ignore it, assuming it's an over-zealous fan who won't be able to get through without a ticket. Our protective detail pulls in tighter so I can't see who it is anyway.

But then I hear it again and I recognize the voice.

"Back up, fellas," Wade tells the bodyguards from behind me. "He'll want to see this one."

I stop, causing several guys to bump into me. Mandy hisses something hateful under her breath but I don't care.

Robyn is here. And she's jumping up and down and calling my name and hand to God, she's the best sight I've ever seen. Even if it's just to say goodbye or piss off, I'll take it.

"Hang on, baby," I call out. "I'm coming."

I make my way through the crowd over to the window wall she's standing beside.

"Sorry," she says when I finally reach her. "I didn't mean to make a scene. I was afraid I wouldn't catch you before you hit security and I wouldn't be able to get through."

"It's fine. You okay?"

Her hair is in a messy ponytail, like she ran here from her apartment. Her face is flushed and her eyes are wide with panic.

"I will be. I just, I got your message and . . . maybe we should sit down." She gestures to a round cushion thing next to a plant.

"Uh, babe? I don't exactly have a lot of time." I glance over to the small group that has remained behind to wait for me. Mandy and a few security guys.

"Yeah. Of course. Right." She looks nervous, terrified actually, but I can't imagine why.

"Are you coming with us to Mexico?" Because that would be fan-fucking-tastic if she were.

"No," she says softly. "I came here to see you before you left because I have to tell you something. Something that couldn't wait three more months until you got back."

"Okay. I'm all ears, darlin'."

*Say there isn't really someone else. Say you ended that because you don't love him like you love me. Say you'll come with me on tour.*

Her chest rises and falls with deep breaths. I reach out and take her hands.

"Robyn, whatever it is, it's okay. Just tell me."

*Unless you're getting married. Then don't tell me. Just shove me out this plate glass wall instead.*

She sucks in one more breath and presses her gaze into mine. "Did you mean it? The text?"

I nod. "I'm sorry I waited so long to tell you. I'm a fucking idiot." I run a hand over my head. "I told myself if I ever got another chance I'd fight for you, no matter what. The way I should have that summer. If I hadn't walked away, if I'd—"

"I love you, too, Dallas Walker Lark," she announces. "I love you and because I love you, your dreams are as important to me as my own. And that's why I didn't tell you about my mom. That's why I ended things that summer—because I couldn't stand the thought of being the reason you missed out on something you wanted, something you'd dreamed of and worked so hard for. But looking back, I could've handled it better. I should've told you the truth. I'm not a scared kid anymore and I'm not going to make that same mistake again." She pauses to pull in more air and either I'm imagining it or she's trembling before me. "I'm pregnant, Dallas. That's the someone else. We're having a baby and I was terrified to tell you because I didn't want to mess up your life right in the middle of all of your dreams coming true."

She lost me at pregnant.

I should say something. But I can't find any words.

I'm just standing here, staring blankly. You know that feeling, when a limb falls asleep from lack of blood flow and the numbness is like a thousand pinpricks? That's how my face feels right now. It's like when I had writer's block. Like staring at a blank page and knowing there should be lyrics on it but having lost all ability to combine letters to make words.

"So . . ." she says, biting her lower lip. "There's that."

I can barely hear her over the white noise in my head.

"I . . . you're . . . we're . . ."

Yep. That's what I came up with.

"Pregnant," she says slowly. "And I promised your sister I wouldn't do this, but you look like you're about to pass out, so I'm going to anyway."

"My sister?" I choke out.

"Yeah. I told her first to see if she thought I should tell you now or wait."

My face is numb. A thousand invisible needles are pricking the hell out of it. "Okay."

"Maybe I should've waited," she says softly. "But, Dallas, I don't want to be the reason you punch out Jase Wade. Or the reason you miss out on this tour. This is huge. Your career is growing astronomically at a rate most people can only dream of. I am so proud of you. So believe me when I say, I didn't come here to tell you this so that you'd stay behind or whatever. Go. Live your dream and show those people how we do music in Texas. I will be here when you get home and we can talk. But know that if you decide you don't want this, me or the baby—both or either—that's okay. I'm okay. I can do this on my own. You can be as involved or as uninvolved as you like.

That's what I invited you over to dinner to tell you. Then you told me about the tour and you were so excited and I didn't want to piss on your parade, so to speak. But I won't make the same mistake I made when I didn't tell you about my mom."

"So there isn't someone else?"

There you are, words! Finally.

Robyn shakes her head slowly. "Well, technically there is, but he isn't born yet."

"He?" Christ, I hear my own voice crack.

"I don't really know for sure," she tells me. "But it feels like a he to me. I'll find out in about six to eight weeks. I'll text you. I can even send the ultrasound picture. If you want me to, that is."

"Denver," I say, finally putting the pieces together as my brain catches up. We weren't careful. Several times.

"Yeah. Denver. And I take full responsibility because I missed two birth control pills that week. I didn't even realize it until later. So this is on me. I am not upset. If anyone was going to knock me up, I'm glad it's you. I am just so sorry that I have to put this on you when so many amazing things are happening in your life."

"Don't do that. I was there, too. Don't be fucking sorry." The command comes out harsher than I mean for it to and Robyn flinches.

"Dallas," Mandy calls out from behind me. "We need to get moving."

"You should go," Robyn tells me. "Don't want to miss your flight."

I drive my hands into my hair and leave them on top of my head. My head is shaking back and forth. Go? I can't go. I can't leave her. I won't. What the fucking fuck is happening to my life right now?

"I just . . . I thought you'd met someone. I thought you and Wade—"

"No," Robyn says, the corners of her mouth lifting slightly. "There's never really been anyone else for me, Dallas. I kind of thought you knew that by now."

That feels so damn good to hear, I feel like I could sprint to Mexico.

"Dallas!" Mandy barks again. "Time to go!"

"Wait," I say more to Robyn than Mandy. "Then how'd you know I punched him? Wade tell you?"

"She mentioned it," Robyn informs me, nodding at my manager, who's growing more impatient by the second. "When she dropped by my place to tell me to stay away from you."

The fuck?

"She what?"

"She's also the one who told Dixie to sit out the encore at the showcase in Nashville. Said she was holding you back. You might want to discuss that with her."

My blood pressure rises so high I can feel it. Dixie's hang-up about holding me back makes so much more sense now.

"Dixie tell you this?"

Robyn nods. "I'm happy for you, Dallas. I am. And I meant what I said about being here when you get home. Regardless of what you decide. But one thing is for damn sure. You need a new manager. Like yesterday."

She glances around me to glare at Mandy.

"You can say that again."

"Okay, I will." Robyn leans up and brushes her sweet little pouty lips past mine on her way to my ear. "You. Need. A. New. Manager."

God her voice does it for me. I let my hands fall to her hips. "Message received, sweetheart." I wink while simultaneously lowering my head to give her a kiss.

She pulls back before I make contact. I squeeze her hips firmly in protest.

"Let's not do this here right now. Just take some time and think about what you want, okay? I love you, you know I do. But things are different now. We can't do the casual hook-ups anymore. We're going to be parents."

"I'd argue we can hook up all the time since technically you can't get any *more* pregnant." I grin and she slaps me playfully on the chest.

"I'm being serious, Dallas. I mean it. I don't want you in our lives because you feel obligated or something. I want you to think long and hard about what you want. Okay? Promise me?"

"I promise. But I want you, baby. I've always wanted you and I will always want you. I already know that. I've known that for a long time now."

Robyn makes a sound like I've kicked her and there are tears forming in her eyes.

"It's not just me anymore, okay? And it's one thing to say that and another to mean it."

I can already picture her growing round with my baby in her belly and fucking hell, I've never really had a hard-on for pregnant women, but this one, this one being round with *my* baby is about to push me over the edge in a crowded airport.

"I love you, Robyn Breeland. And I'll come home as soon as I can so that I can show you just how much I want you and all that comes with you. Or . . . tell me to stay. You need me to stay, pretty girl? Say the word and I'll tell them to go on without me."

And now she's crying.

"Dallas!" Mandy has lost her patience and marched over into our moment. "We have to go right now."

"No, Dallas. I couldn't live with myself if this held you back from your dream. Go. I'm fine," Robyn says through her tears. I wipe them with my thumbs and kiss her gently.

"There. She said go. Let's go," Mandy demands.

"I'm on my way." I turn my attention back to my girl. "You'll text me every update?"

"I will. Promise."

I steal one last kiss. And then another. And then one more, until Robyn pushes me toward the escalator.

The numbness wears off and reality settles in as I make my way through security check.

I'm having a baby.

With Robyn.

I'm going to be a dad.

I couldn't be more ill-equipped if the pilot announced we had to jump from the plane.

# 36 | Dallas

"WHAT IN THE EVER-LOVING HELL IS YOUR PROBLEM, DALLAS?"
Mandy's shrill voice greets me as soon as I step foot offstage. I've
barely pulled my in-ears out when she starts in on me. "You've been
avoiding me since this leg of the tour began and now you're performing like a brain-dead zombie out there. Care to tell me what exactly
is going on with you?"

I rub my throbbing head for a solid minute while she waits for my
response. What exactly is going on with me, she wants to know. I can
only imagine her face if I gave her an honest answer.

"Not particularly," I tell her while pulling out my phone to see if
Robyn's sent any more updates. Nothing since last night. I frown at
the screen.

"So help me, God, I will have your phone cut the fuck off if you
don't put that away and give me a straight damn answer."

"Easy, Lantram. Damn," Jase Wade calls out from behind her as
he approaches. "This is a chill zone and I need to get in the right head
space before going onstage. Give the kid a break, will you?"

She glares at the both of us before pointing a finger at me. "Get your shit together, Dallas Walker. I mean it. You are replaceable. Keep that in mind."

I stare blankly after her as she storms off and I slide my phone into my back pocket.

She's right. Dallas Walker is replaceable. Hell, Dallas Walker doesn't even really exist.

I glance at the leather pants I hate, the boots I never would've bought myself, and the torn T-shirt she said "enhanced my edge"—whatever the fuck that is.

I don't even know who Dallas Walker is. And I don't think I even like his ass.

"You all right, kid?" Jase Wade kicks my boot, startling me out of my stupor. " 'Cause Lantram wasn't entirely out of line for once. You have seemed pretty fucking out of it since we left the States."

"Yeah. I'm great. Jet lag," I lie. Mexico was a blur. Canada was a blink. I just played my first show in Rio and I can't remember a single second of it.

"Nothing to do with a certain redhead we both know?"

His mention of Robyn surprises me and brings out a primal surge of protectiveness. "I know her a hell of a lot better than you do."

Wade laughs at my outburst. "Easy, killer. I know you do. That wasn't my name she was shouting across the airport. I gotta say, after a scene like that, I'm kind of surprised you made it here."

"Why wouldn't I be here?"

"Honestly? Girl looked like she was about to propose to you. I figured you'd be on your honeymoon by now."

I snort, but there's a part of me that wishes he were right. Brazil is beautiful. Colorful and vibrant like Mandy promised. But all I can think about is the way Robyn came alive in New Orleans. How she'd dance in the streets here, too, and moan about the food in a way that would have me hauling her back to our hotel room at lightning speed.

If I don't tell someone, I'm going to explode before sound check.

"She's pregnant," I say quietly so none of the road crew members hear. "With my baby."

"Ah. Congratulations." Wade claps my shoulder hard and shakes my hand. I feel the maniacal grin spreading across my face.

"We'll find out the sex of the baby this weekend. She's going to text me the ultrasound photo."

At that, he frowns. "Text, huh?"

I nod. It sucks but what else can we do?

"You know, I got a lot of updates about my daughter via text message, too." He rubs his chin thoughtfully. "That she was taking ballet. When my wife found out she was allergic to strawberries. Several years' worth of school pictures. Dance recital videos."

He lets out a low sound, laughter devoid of humor, as if he's forgotten I'm even in the room.

"Hell, I even got the 'Jase, I want a divorce and full custody' update via text message. Gotta love technology, right?"

I don't miss his hidden meaning. "You trying to tell me something, Wade?"

"Not at all." He shakes his head like he feels sorry for me. "I'm too busy trying to figure out what the hell you're still doing here."

"She told me to come. She said not to put my dreams on hold for this and that she's fine. She can do this part without me."

Again he gives me this look, like I'm a complete and total dumbass.

"I got news for you, kid. She can do *all of it* without you. The part you were needed for has already come and gone, so to speak." He claps me on the shoulder again and turns to leave. "Have a good show. And when you get that text message telling you that she's moved on, found someone who'll hold her hand during the ultrasound and be there when she hears the baby's heartbeat for the first time, call me and I'll buy you a beer."

"That won't happen to us. She understands. We got this."

"Then do something for me. Picture her sitting all alone in the waiting room watching all those moms-to-be with their husbands next to them. Imagine what that must feel like for her. Picture her going into labor while you're onstage somewhere and no one can get in touch with you to tell you until after your show. Picture your kid's first birthday party and imagine attending it via FaceTime on your phone because you're in some godforsaken city three thousand miles away."

Christ. I can picture all of that. His words come to life behind my eyes and there's a pang deep in my chest.

"Now picture her face. Picture her raising your child by herself while you live your dream. Picture her seeing thousands of fans commenting online about how badly they want you and posting pictures of you with them in bars and buses and at parties. Tell me that girl understands. She's a tough chick. Maybe she does understand. But just because she understands doesn't mean she can live that life. It's lonely and most women don't do lonely well. For that matter, who does?"

"I have been picturing that," I practically yell at him. "Every second of the damn day and night. It's why I look like a member of the living dead onstage. But what am I supposed to do? Just walk away from everything I worked for? Give up my dreams to sit in waiting rooms and at birthday parties? Because I'm thinking I could give my kid a hell of a lot better life on this income than if I go home to Amarillo and work in construction. I don't see you running home to the missus."

Shit. That was low. The guy told me about his divorce and his ex-wife getting remarried recently. But I can't help it. I'm in an impossible situation and I know it.

Wade leans down, putting his face level with mine. "If I had it to do over again, I would run home before you could say my name three times fast. But you're right. These are the decisions you have to make. Sacrifices. No one said it would be easy." He straightens, nodding at someone who's entered the backstage area to announce that it's time for him to go on. "Good luck to you, kid."

I hear the unmistakable click of heels coming toward my room, then a knock rattles my door. I highly doubt I have groupies in Rio de Janeiro, so that only leaves one person.

"There you are," Mandy says, sliding open my door and slapping me with a hate-filled glare. I switched seats with my drummer on the plane so I didn't have to deal with her. She wasn't too thrilled about it.

"Here I am," I say evenly.

"So I heard you have big news. I'd say congratulations, but I figured we'd find another way to celebrate."

She pulls a bottle of champagne from behind her back and it's like a twisted scenario of when Robyn helped me celebrate "Better to Burn" going gold.

"Celebrate whatever it is for me. I'm pretty beat. Jet lag. You understand."

Her eyes narrow on me and she stalks over to my bed. I wasn't ready to discuss Robyn and the pregnancy so I've been avoiding my manager mostly. And I was angry about how she treated Dixie and afraid I'd lose my temper. But it looks like she's going to force a confrontation so it must be time to get it all out in the open.

"Dallas, I'm going to try my best to make something very clear to you." She sits down and I fight the impulse to shove her into the floor. "I have a very special relationship with my clients. One that allows me to become as close to them as I possibly can. It makes for a much more symbiotic relationship, in my opinion."

"Meaning you fuck all of them, right?" Afton Tate mentioned this to me on the unsigned artists tour. He turned her down so she wouldn't sign him.

"Meaning we don't keep secrets from each other. Meaning I know everything about their lives so that if they knock up some random hanger-on from their hometown I can do what needs to be done before it affects their career. Do you understand?"

"Wade talk to you?"

She nods. "He was my client once. He knows how important it is to me to know what's going on with my clients."

"For you to know about it, Mandy? Or for you to try and control it? Because the way I see it, you told my sister to sit out in Nashville, then you told my pregnant girlfriend to stay away from me. What I can't figure out is why you think either of those women is any of your business."

"*You* are my business, Dallas. So anything or anyone that affects you is my business. If I hadn't told your sister to sit out that number, you wouldn't be here right now. And if your *girlfriend,* or whatever she is, hadn't gotten knocked up and trapped you in a relationship, I wouldn't be having to try and contact every one I know who can help us frame this in a more positive light."

"Don't bother. Far as I'm concerned, you're fired anyway." I stand and walk over to the door. "Here. Let me walk you out."

Mandy stands, staring at me like I've said I want to rap folk music with a gospel choir. "Are you insane? Do you really want to throw all of this away? After how hard we've worked for this? You signed a contract. I can sue you."

"How hard *I've* worked, you mean? And no, I don't plan to throw everything away. Just you. Sue away, sweetheart."

I don't bother waiting for her witty comeback. I just guide her gently out of my room and close the door behind her.

# 37 | Robyn

SEVERAL WEEKS AFTER DALLAS LEAVES, MY BOSS MAKES A BIG AN-
nouncement. The Martin family has decided to expand into more
than just bourbon. They've partnered with a midsize rum distribu-
tor they'll be renaming Sunset Bay. Next up is a moonshine manu-
facturer they plan to call Moonlight Bay.

Everyone is ecstatic, hugging and cheering, and already chatter
about who might head up the teams for the new companies is flood-
ing through the conference room.

"You're the front-runner for the PR campaign on the expansion,"
Katie tells me as the conversations around us die down. "Drew said
he overheard Mr. Martin talking about it this morning when he was
taking some photos for the press release."

"Thanks for the heads-up." I should be thrilled. This is huge,
even bigger than the promotion I've been vying for. Instead I just
feel . . . overwhelmed. I still haven't told my boss I'm pregnant and
I'll need to schedule my maternity leave. If I do that now, it's likely I
won't get to head up this campaign or even be involved with it at all.

As the meeting comes to a close, I hear Mr. Martin call my name.

I wait for the room to clear before making my way to where he stands. Thankfully, Katie hangs back with me.

"Good news," he announces with his booming voice as I approach. "The board voted and we want you to head up the campaign to promote the expansion. We need new logos, new label mock-ups, new banners on all the social media pages, and something huge to celebrate. I'm thinking a gala downtown. I'd like to see a list of ideas in my email inbox by tomorrow. And reach out to local vendors and see who might want to host exclusive previews of the bottles once we've updated the labels."

"Yes, sir. I'm on it." A cold, clammy sheen of sweat rolls down my neck to the middle of my back. "Thank you for the opportunity, sir." I smile at the executives standing beside him.

"Oh, and I'll need you to stay late this evening and then again tomorrow. We're doing a tasting of the new products after work."

"The new products?" I can literally see my worlds colliding. I've tried to keep them separate. In one I'm a successful marketing assistant and promotions specialist and in the other I'm an expectant mother. Now I have to figure out how to be both at the same time.

"The rum today and the moonshine tomorrow," he clarifies. "Call a local sandwich shop, that one we get those Italian subs from, and have them bring several platters over. We'll need something to soak up the liquor."

"Yes, sir." I'm frozen, stuck in place and unable to figure out what to say to avoid this impossible situation.

"Actually, Robyn, didn't you say you had that thing after work today? That new, um, class? The one you can't miss?"

"Right," I say with a sigh of relief. "Wow. I totally forgot about that."

Mr. Martin looks skeptically at the both of us. "Class?"

"Um, Spanish. I'm taking a Spanish class at the university. I was hoping to branch out so I could be more of an asset for our international clients." The lies are just spilling out of my mouth at this point.

"I can handle the tastings. And the sandwich order," Katie offers "I'll fill Robyn in once she gets home from class."

I want to tackle-hug her right this second. Or collapse on her when the tightly wound strings of tension holding me together unravel.

Mr. Martin frowns. "Okay. I guess that will work. In the future, please let me know if you're taking any classes that might interfere with your work schedule."

I nod quickly. "Yes, sir. I definitely will."

Like when I have to take that Lamaze class. I am so screwed.

"Thank you," I whisper to Katie on our way out. "I owe you one. More than one."

"You're welcome. You know you're going to have to tell him eventually."

I swallow the lump in my throat. "I know. I will. I just . . . I need to tell my mom first. I keep thinking I can wait until Dallas gets home but they just added more dates to the tour and—"

My voice cracks as I try to choke out the words.

"Hey," Katie says softly as we reach my desk. "Just because your situation is unconventional doesn't make it impossible. My brother was serving overseas when both of his kids were born. He loves them, they love him. He and his wife are happy. People can make these types of situations work. They do it all the time. If anyone can handle unconventional it's you."

I try to smile but my mouth has other plans. "You're right." I pull it together the best I can. It's time to be a big girl and face facts.

"But I need to tell my mom and Mr. Martin sooner rather than later. Dallas or no Dallas."

This is my life now and a baby isn't an accessory I can just add on. Everything in my life is going to change. It has to.

Lying in bed at midnight, knowing it's somewhere around four in the morning where Dallas is, I scroll through the few messages I have from him.

He didn't call tonight and I'm trying not to dwell on how few times we've actually spoken since he's been gone.

I don't know when I became this person—this woman who stays up late on a work night waiting for her boyfriend to call. I wasn't even this girl in high school. But then, he called when he was supposed to back then.

And he was five minutes down the road instead of on the other side of the world.

Katie's moving in with Drew and I'm turning her room into a guest room and what was once the home office into a nursery. I tried to put the crib together today and ended up crying in the middle of the floor surrounded by wooden pieces I wanted to light on fire.

My chest tightens as I realize this is my life now. Dallas's life isn't going to be conventional and neither is our relationship. That was the word Katie used earlier. She'd told me that if anyone could handle an "unconventional" relationship it was me.

I hope she's right.

I should be okay with this. Part of my job was to set up opportunities for him to get his picture taken with women who wanted to get close to him.

I try not to imagine Brazilian models fawning all over him but the image comes anyway.

Screw it.

I try to call him.

No answer.

I drift in and out of consciousness for a while until my phone buzzes in my hand.

Dallas finally texted.

*Call you tomorrow. Show ran late. Love you.*

Once my eyes have adjusted I text him back that it's okay and I love him, too. But I miss him, so I pull my laptop from my nightstand and pull up his fan page.

New pictures have already been added. He looks so handsome up onstage. The way the light shines behind him makes him glow like an otherworldly being.

My larger-than-life Dallas Lark. I can feel my heart swelling with pride.

Below the official ones are some fan-posted ones.

Girls are draped all over him, hugging him, taking selfies with him, kissing him on the cheek.

I can handle this. I can. I have to.

But Lord help me, some of these women are insanely gorgeous. Very soon I am going to look like I swallowed a basketball. I already have a bump, one I can't hide much longer. And Dallas is going to be surrounded by perfection.

I need to hear his voice. Need to hear him tell me good night. I pull up his name on my phone and listen to the ringing.

When his voice mail picks up, I open my mouth but nothing comes out.

I won't do this. I won't be the pathetic girlfriend at home making him feel guilty because she misses him. Besides, it's not just about me anymore. I can't keep doing this. The last thing I want my kiddo to see is Mommy sitting around pining for Daddy.

"Sweet dreams, baby," I say into the phone as new pictures pop onto his page.

I hope he does have sweet dreams. But I have a feeling I'll be having nightmares.

I curl up to my pillow, trying not to dwell on the fact that even though I'm technically already one myself, I need my mommy.

# 38 | Dallas

TIMING WAS THE THIRD MOST IMPORTANT THING I LEARNED about playing music. Nana would reiterate its importance to Dixie and me over and over during our piano lessons.

Papa taught me about patience and persistence, but Nana taught me about timing.

"It's not enough to just play the right notes," she'd say. "You have to play them at the right time, play them when you feel them and not a second sooner."

Timing.

It could be a bitch sometimes.

Robyn and I keep missing each other.

We've both called. Left messages. Texted.

But every time I have a free minute, she's in a meeting or in bed. The times she's tried to call I've either been tied up in interviews or sound checks or trying to catch what little sleep I can between shows.

Now I was up in bed failing at sleeping again, knowing I'd have to be at the airport heading to London in a few hours, but unable to really rest until I heard her voice.

I listen to the last voice mail she left until I fall asleep. "Sweet dreams, baby," her sultry voice says over and over. I'd get a hard dick if I weren't so wiped out.

Fucking timing.

W e're heading to a private airstrip in Brazil to catch the flight to London when I'm checking my phone messages. I keep expecting some major backlash from firing Mandy, but so far no one has said a word. I suspect she hasn't told anyone yet and I don't even want to think about what she might have planned to try to convince me to change my mind. I'm cringing at the vast possibilities when I see that I have a voice mail from Robyn.

I've been aching to hear her voice since she left me a very sexy erection-inducing "sweet dreams" voice mail that I played repeatedly last night. But when I press play this time the sound that fills my ears tears at my chest instead of my dick.

*"Hey, babe. It's me."* My girl sounds tired. More than tired. Drained. Weary and exhausted. *"I just wanted to let you know that the ultrasound is tomorrow and the doctor said if the baby is turned the right way we'll be able to tell if we're having a boy or a girl."* She pauses before continuing. *"I'll try to call you when I find out. The appointment is at three in the afternoon so I'm going to leave work a little early. I can't remember which time zone you'll be in by then but I guess if I can't reach you I'll text. Oh, and I told my mom and she's very happy for us. I hope everything is going well in Brazil. I love you."*

I love you.

She loves me.

Loves me enough to raise our child on her own, to sit through appointments and ultrasounds by herself while I go out and live my dream, or some distorted version of it anyway.

My strong independent girl . . . is going to *text me* the sex of our baby.

She sounded so damn tired. Like she needed me there to rub her feet and hold her in my arms and tell her to take it easy since I know she won't unless I'm there but I'm not there. Because I'm here.

I can hardly keep track of where "here" is anymore.

I have to make my own choices, just like my granddad said. More important, I have to stand behind them, live with them. I keep thinking about what she said in the airport, about not making the same mistake she made all those years ago. Every choice has a consequence and my brave girl risked it all to tell me the truth.

Now it's my turn. I'm going to fight for her, for us. I'm going to be there, with her, where I belong.

I can't get on another plane and leave my entire world behind. I did that once before and it was a colossal fucking mistake. I'll be damned if I make the same one again.

I tap on the back of the seat in front of me. "Sir. Could you turn the car around, please? I need to go to the actual airport instead of the private one."

I try to search international flights to see how soon I can get home, if there's any chance in hell I can make that appointment tomorrow.

"Sir," I practically yell at the driver, a nervous-seeming gray-haired man who doesn't speak English. "Can you take me to the International Airport of Brasilia instead?" I'm reading the flight schedule on my phone as I make my request.

He turns to look at me, and I glance up. I see it before he does. The truck in front of us is stopped already for whatever reason. And we're going to plow directly into it.

The last thought that flits through my brain before everything goes black is that I'm going to die without ever seeing my kid.

I'm going to die when I've only just realized I've been living my life all wrong.

The fucking irony.

# 39 | Robyn

"HEY," KATIE SAYS, POPPING HER HEAD INTO MY OFFICE. "I'M heading out and grabbing some dinner with Drew. I'll probably stay at his place tonight but do you want me to go to your appointment with you tomorrow?"

I close out my email because my eyes are crossing. It's finally here. Or it will be tomorrow anyway. The day I learn the sex of my baby. "Nah. I was going to ask Dallas's sister to come. Or maybe my mom. She took the news better than I expected. But it's like you said. This isn't a conventional situation so I might as well get used to doing things on my own, right?"

"Robyn," Katie says softly, stepping all the way into the room. "I didn't mean it as a bad thing. I just meant—"

"It's not a bad thing. It's just . . . different."

Katie gives me a weak smile. "I can only imagine just how different it is. But I'm also here for you, if you need anything. And just because he isn't here doesn't mean you have to do everything alone. You have me, and Dallas's sister from the sound of it. And your mom, of course."

My mom was beside herself ecstatic about becoming a grandma. I was expecting a lecture, or at least a strict talking to about responsibility. All I got were happy tears and hugs and promises that she is going to be here for me every step of the way.

I nod. "Thanks. I appreciate that."

"I stocked the freezer full of ice cream last night, by the way. Help yourself," she says as she stands to leave. "Promise you'll tell me if there's anything I can do. I was my sister-in-law's Lamaze coach when my brother was serving overseas. I have excellent recommendations on my labor-assisting skills."

I smile. "Thanks, roomie. I'll keep that in mind."

A pang of loneliness hits me unexpectedly. Katie won't be my roomie much longer. She shouldn't have to be woken up all hours of the night by a screaming baby. She's not the one who got knocked up.

After shutting down my computer for the day, I grab my purse and head downstairs. Voices clamor up to me and I see a small crowd gathered around the front desk.

Alex and Bennett Martin are both standing with two police officers and a few girls from reception.

" . . . serious injuries," a voice from the speakerphone on the front desk says. "But we're trying to find out about Renee now."

"What's going on?" I approach the group carefully. I can't justify how I know that whatever's going on somehow affects me, but I do. I can feel it.

Alex Martin turns to me, but it's Katie's face I see. She's behind the group, standing with Drew, and she's pale, looking at me like she's afraid I might have yet another emotional meltdown.

"There was an accident on the BR-101. The convoy taking Jase

Wade and his crew was involved. Renee Vasquez was among the injured, but she's getting medical attention and should be fine."

Renee is an international consultant for Midnight Bay. I've met her a few times but I don't know her well.

"And the others?" My voice is leaving me as I yank my phone out of my purse.

My clumsy fingers drop my phone and Katie steps around and hands it to me. "Robyn . . . I have to tell you something. It's about Dallas."

No. *No no no.*

This isn't happening. My Dallas, my sweet backward-ball-cap-wearing boyfriend from high school, the handsome man who exuded so much raw masculinity I was liquid in his hands every time he touched me, the famous musician who charmed a diner full of little girls, the father of my baby, he has to be okay.

*He has to be.*

"Breathe, Robyn," Katie says, wrapping an arm around me. "They didn't say he was hurt or anything. It's just that he isn't accounted for."

"What does that even mean?"

I'm losing my shit in front of both of my bosses, but they're still busy with the man on the speakerphone.

"It could mean anything. Maybe he's fine and didn't need medical attention."

*Or maybe he's dead.*

No, he can't be. I would be able to feel that, wouldn't I?

My hands are shaking, or maybe that's my knees. All I know is that the world is moving too fast and I want to get off this ride right this second.

"Let's get you home, okay?" Katie's eyes are wide with concern and I watch helplessly as she motions Drew over.

"No," I practically yell. "I'm staying right here by this phone until they say he's okay."

"We'll keep you posted, Robyn," Drew promises. "Go home and try to rest and I swear, the second we hear anything, you'll be the first person I get in touch with. Cross my heart." He makes a motion over his heart.

"He has to be okay," I tell Katie as she practically drags me out of the building and to her car. "He has to be."

# 40 | Dallas

THE FIRST THING I'M AWARE OF IS THE BLOOD. IT'S WARM, TRICK-ling red trails down my arm.

I can't feel my fingers.

This is not good.

The driver is unconscious with his head on the steering wheel. There's blood seeping into his hairline from a gash in his forehead.

"Hey!" I shout, because I'm afraid to move for fear I'll do myself worse damage. "Hey, we're in here!"

In my head all I can think is *We're not dead* over and over. And I can see it, what I walked away from, what I'm risking losing forever flashing behind my eyes.

It wasn't my life that flashed before my eyes, not the one I've been living.

It's the one I'd miss if I died, or if I let my career come first.

"Everyone okay in there?"

The voice comes from the sunroof. A golden-haired guy has his face shoved into it. "Help is on the way. Just sit tight."

"What happened?"

"There was a car accident up ahead," golden-haired guy from the sunroof informs us. "You all ended up in the pileup."

"Sir, sir? Can you hear me?" I reach forward to nudge the driver but I catch sight of the gaping laceration that has practically ripped my Lark tattoo in half and I almost lose consciousness.

I'm sitting there, stunned, and staring at my torn tattoo for what feels like eternity as the rest of the world falls away.

Lark.

It's my last name.

My family name.

The one my kid will have if Robyn will allow it.

The one *she'll* have if she'll have me.

My head is spinning but even though my vision is blurred, everything else is in high definition.

My parents died, my grandparents even passed away, but I still have family and that's what matters.

Dixie. Robyn. Gavin.

My unborn peanut.

They're my family.

And I've walked away from them for what? To nearly die in a car accident in a foreign country? To be onstage night after night alone, wishing my band were there? Wishing my girl was in the audience? To sit in bars and diners by myself thinking of a woman who'd make me order something healthier because she wants me to live longer?

No. Fuck this.

Dallas Walker died in that car, but Dallas Lark is alive and well.

I've been settling for some half-ass version of my dream, a pathetic piece of it instead of the real deal.

I want to make music and record an album, but I want to do it with my band. And more than any of that, whatever I do with my life, I want Robyn Breeland beside me. I want us to raise our kid together. I want to be the kind of dad my father was, and his father before him. I want to be at the birth and all the birthday parties after that.

I can't do that from a different country.

Paramedics are surrounding us and only some of them speak English.

They climb in to help us out. The driver is disoriented so they put him on a stretcher.

A blond girl who looks barely old enough to drive a car places butterfly stitches down my arm in the back of a funky-looking ambulance.

"There. That'll hold until we get to the hospital." She looks into my eyes. "Sir? I need to ask you a few questions. Do you know what day it is?"

"Um, Thursday?"

She gives me a smile and a nod. "And do you know your name?"

I glance down at my new stitches as she wraps my arm in gauze. Something Afton Tate says comes back to me. He said if I let Mandy and the industry change me, then I didn't really make it big— someone else did. He was right.

"Lark," I tell her. "My name is Dallas Lark."

And I'm not going to the hospital like she thinks. I'm getting the hell out of here. I will be damned if my girl is going to *text me* the sex of our baby. I will be at that appointment tomorrow come hell or high water.

# 41 | Robyn

"SWEETIE, COME ON NOW. YOU HAVE TO EAT SOMETHING. YOUR mom is worried sick and frankly so am I." Katie is holding a bowl of soup but I can't even imagine putting the broth in my mouth. "Whether you're hungry or not, the baby needs nourishment."

"I have to call his sister. She needs to know. It will be on the news soon and what if she—"

"One of Jase's PR people already called her, Robyn. I talked to her last night. She's worried, too, but she's okay. Relax. They are doing everything they can to find Dallas. We can go to Amarillo and see her after your appointment. But first, eat."

I stare at the fleshy noodles swimming in the soup. There is a human being growing inside me and no matter how I feel, it's not okay to let my baby go hungry.

I close my eyes and gag on several bites. "That's the best I can do for now," I tell my roommate. "I'm sorry."

"It's fine. You did your best. Let's get some clothes on so you can get to your appointment."

I shake my head. "I can't go. I was supposed to text him a picture."

I look at my phone. Nothing. I've texted, I've left a dozen messages telling him to call me, that I love him and need to know that he's okay.

No response.

Now I know how he felt when I blew him off before. The only difference is, he knew I was alive.

After Katie helps me get dressed and puts me in the car, the tremors come back. Instead of crying, my body has decided to do this weird seizing that scares Katie half to death.

"Even if you don't want them to tell you if you're carrying a boy or a girl today, it's good to check on the baby. And I'd like to see if they can give you something mild to calm your nerves while we wait for news."

Her knuckles are white on the steering wheel. I'm stressing her out and I feel bad but I can't hide this. I've always been so good at hiding my emotions, keeping up the tough-chick exterior, but I can't anymore.

"Did I ever tell you why we broke up?" My throat is raw and my words are raspy.

Katie glances over at me. "No. I don't think so."

I lean my head against the window, agitated that the sun has the audacity to shine today. It's cold out, but the damn sky couldn't even cooperate with my gloomy mood.

"I was supposed to go on a six-week summer tour with his band, help with their outreach and social media and such." I close my eyes. I can still remember it so clearly. I was so excited about the road trip. We'd both been so busy—me with school and him with odd jobs and the band—we were looking forward to the time together. "I had a music mix made and everything. A lifetime supply of beef jerky. All the road trip must-haves. That was supposed to be an epic summer."

"Sounds fun."

I swallow hard while trying not to lose myself in the memories. "It should've been. But then my mom got sick. She had stage two breast cancer. The lumpectomy wasn't enough. She spent the summer in chemo treatments."

"I'm so sorry, Robyn. I didn't know."

"She's doing really great now and she's big on looking forward, so I try not to dwell."

"Sounds smart," Katie says, side-eying me as she drives. "But surely Dallas understood. I mean it wasn't like you just blew him off for no reason. It was your mom."

"I didn't tell him. I just bailed on the trip and told him I thought we needed some space. I can't even remember exactly what I said. But it hurt him. It hurt us. When he came back at the end of the summer things were different. Over."

I don't tell her how many nights I lay awake wondering how things might have been different if I'd just told him the truth.

"Wow. Well . . . You were young, Robyn. People make mistakes. I'm sure Dallas has made plenty. He's probably forgotten all about it by now."

"He hasn't. He mentioned it in Nashville, when I tried to blow him off the night I got sick. And we talked about it a little in the airport before he left." Tears stream down my face as I continue. "I almost did the same thing with the pregnancy. I just didn't want to stand in the way of his dreams, you know? Just like I didn't want this baby to derail his success like I ended up doing that summer even though it was the last thing I wanted. But now I have this piece of him forever and I can't even be grateful for that. I keep thinking, what if this is all that's left? What if I never get to see him or hold him or kiss him again?"

"Don't think like that. Let's just focus on today, okay?"

Katie does her best to console me, but I'm gone, over the edge of sanity and dissolving into a puddle of misery. I can't wipe my tears away fast enough.

Everything that happens after that is fuzzy. We go into the sterile gray offices and wait until they call my name. The technician does the ultrasound, placing it in an envelope and telling me the baby's sex is printed on there for when I'm ready to look.

Katie, God love her, murmurs softly to the doctor about what's going on with the father, but she doesn't name him, which I am grateful for. I hear them talking about bed rest and keeping my stress level and blood pressure down.

I leave with my envelope in hand feeling grateful for Katie but knowing I'm going to have to start handling these things on my own. Just like I will have to face the rest of my life on my own.

Katie squeezes my hand as we leave the office and step out into the sunshine. I stare at the sidewalk. The not knowing is awful, but I think it might be better than confirmation that he's gone.

"Robyn," Katie gasps, squeezing my free hand. "Look up, sweetie."

I rub my eyes behind my sunglasses. They're still sore from crying. "Why? Can't you be my Seeing-Eye friend? My head is killing me."

"Because you need to see for yourself. Dallas is fine. He's okay."

"What? How do you know that?" My heart races nearly out of my chest as I look around for a newsstand or television screen or something announcing this.

She laughs, grips me by my shoulders, and turns me to face the opposite direction. "Because he's standing right there."

# 42 | Dallas

ROBYN COMES OUT OF THE BUILDING JUST AS I'M CROSSING THE street and I finally feel like I've found my center of gravity.

Two hitched rides, a flight with a layover that involved a dead sprint across an airport, and one smelly cab ride later, I made it. Judging from the envelope in her hand, I missed her appointment, but I promise myself that it's the last one I'll miss.

"There's my girl," I say as she bolts across the street and into my arms. "Hey, baby."

She's a wreck, crying and sobbing and saying incoherent words I can't make a single bit of sense of. I look over her head at her assistant.

"Did I miss the appointment? Is the baby okay?"

In the second Katie hesitates, my confidence falters.

"You did but the baby's fine," Katie tells me, ending the agony. "Everything is fine. I'll let you two talk. My car's on level D," she tells us, nodding to the parking garage across the street. "I'll wait as long as you need me to until y'all are ready to go. It's good to see you, Dallas."

"Oh, thank God. You, too. We'll be up in a minute." I hold Robyn tightly until she pulls back to look at my face. I grin when she touches it like she can't believe I'm here. "I'm sorry I missed the ultrasound. I got here as soon as I could. Are you going to tell me if we're having a girl or a boy or leave me hanging in suspense?"

Robyn looks at me like I'm speaking Greek.

Then she squeezes me hard enough to hurt just before whacking me hard in the chest and starting to cry all over again.

"I thought you were dead, Dallas Lark. What the hell happened down there? They said you were unaccounted for after the accident." Noticing my arm for the first time, she pales. The butterfly stitches are caked in dried blood. "Oh my God."

"We were in an accident and I decided to come home instead of checking into a hospital in Rio. My phone was destroyed but my arm will be okay. It's fine. I'll be playing guitar in no time."

Maybe. Truth is, I haven't even stopped to think about that yet.

Right now the most important thing isn't my arm, it's *in* my arms. Both of the most important things.

"Dallas . . ." Those shining exotic-jewel eyes I love so much stare up at me.

"Yeah, baby?"

"I'm so sorry. For everything. For not telling you when my mom got sick and for getting pregnant when—"

I cut her off with a kiss, pressing my lips harder against hers until the fight goes out of her body.

"Do not apologize for giving me the greatest gift in the entire world. We're in this together, Robyn. For always, okay?"

She nods against my chest. "For always."

Her body trembles in my arms and I know it's already a huge moment, but there's more I have to say and I have to say it now.

Pulling back, I look into her beautiful face. "My luggage was already gone, except for one thing. I keep it on me almost all the time.

It was in a carry-on bag that was salvaged from the car and I need to give it to you."

I pull the ring out of my pocket, wishing I'd had time to find a nice velvet box to place it in. But it was given to me in a plastic bag with Mom's belongings after she and my father were killed. If Dixie had wanted it, I would've let her have it, but some part of me wanted desperately to give it to someone someday. I just didn't realize how soon that someday would come. But I think I knew this girl was my someone the day she yanked me up by the arm and made me listen to her favorite song in the back of a pickup truck.

"This was my mom's, but before I ask you to accept it, I need to tell you something. Several somethings."

Robyn swallows hard and nods eagerly for me to continue.

"I know how this looks. How it must seem and maybe even how it will be portrayed in the media. But I don't care about that. I care about us. Because the most important thing here is us."

She sniffles, which I take as agreement.

"And I don't want you to say yes because you're pregnant. I don't want you to say yes because I was in an accident and you were worried. I don't even want you to say yes out of pity for the poor sucker who walked away from his entire career to come ask you this very question. You with me so far?"

She nods. "Um, I-I think so."

I pull in as much oxygen as my lungs can hold and drop to one knee. "Robyn Breeland, I love you. I have always loved you and I will always love you. I want you to marry me because I can't lose you. Not for music, not because of crazy managers, or cocky country music singers who charm their way into your life—present company excluded—and definitely not because of my own fear of not being able to give you everything you deserve. I will do whatever it takes to make you happy because if I lost you, I'd have lost my best friend, my heart and soul, my muse, my everything."

A small cry breaks free and Robyn gapes down at me with watery eyes.

"I want to be successful. I want to make music. I love being onstage—creating that experience for the audience—and I'll never pretend otherwise. That is my dream. But nothing, and I mean nothing, is worth losing you. I will not walk away from my family ever again. And if you say no today, then I will keep asking. Because you are my family, baby. You're my family forever."

Fuck. Now I can't keep my shit together, either.

"Dallas," she says, surprisingly calmly. "Just give me a second."

That wasn't a yes. I am not moving from this spot until she says yes.

"Stand up."

I shake my head. "Not until you say yes."

"Please. I need you up here with me. We need to talk."

"We will talk. After you say yes."

She huffs out a breath. "I just spent twenty-four hours thinking you were dead. You have no idea what I've been through. And now there's this. Stand up right now, Dallas Walker Lark, or I'm bringing my pregnant self down there."

I do as I'm told.

"I love you," she says, clutching my hands tightly. "And I want you. Only you. I want us. Always. But I don't want to be the reason you miss out on your dreams, Dallas. I don't want you to look at me and our child in a few years—or even sooner—and wish you weren't stuck with us and that you'd stayed on that tour. I love you enough not to cost you your dream. So I will say yes, on one condition."

"Name it." I want to tell her I will never feel that way, that I know this because I had the fame and when I had it without her it didn't matter. But right now I just want to get this ring on her damn finger so I can breathe again.

"Promise me you will not give up on your dreams. Promise me you won't pass up opportunities to succeed even if it means upsetting me. Promise on everything that you will be honest with me always. None of that sissy sparing each other's feelings stuff for us, okay?"

I nod. Then I reach for her hand.

"Now you promise me something."

Robyn smiles. "Yes, the baby is yours."

I bump my forehead to hers. "Damn straight it is." She kisses me softly, but I won't be distracted so easily. "Promise me you won't give up on your dreams, either. You are damn good at your job and you don't have to give that up unless you want to."

She nods. "I'm going to talk to my boss about less travel and more behind-the-scenes event coordination. It will all work out however it's meant to. Katie has volunteered to step in when needed."

"So are we good now?" I ask, holding the ring at her fingertip before slipping it all the way on.

Robyn pulls back once more. "You sure this is what you want? It's not just the concussion talking?"

I laugh low against her lips. "Do you want to know what I saw when we were about to hit that truck? What flashed before my eyes?"

She nods and her body trembles against mine at the mention of the accident.

"I saw you. I saw us. I didn't see my life as it was because there wasn't much to see. Hotel rooms, tour buses, and audiences full of strangers—none of that came to mind. I saw the life I wouldn't get to have if I died, or if I lived and walked away from you. I saw you holding our child in your arms and smiling up at me with those beautiful eyes of yours. I saw birthday cakes and toy guitars and God help us, the drum set Gavin will buy this child to bang on all hours of the day. I saw you in a white dress becoming my wife. I saw my family." I hold her close and kiss her hair. "Be my family, baby."

"Yes, Dallas," she says through her tears. "A million times yes."

Once we both pull it together and my ring is on her finger, where it will damn well stay, I nod to the envelope she's still holding.

"Are you going to do the honors?"

She hands it to me. "I think you should. I mean, you came all this way."

As we make our way across the street I slide my finger into the seam. A small black-and-white square sits inside. Taking it out gently once we've reached the parking garage, I stare at it, feeling the sunshine on my face and wondering if my parents and grandparents are smiling down on me.

There's a song here somewhere, but I'll write it later.

"Congratulations, Daddy," Robyn says softly, taking the picture from my fingers. "It's a boy."

"You have a name picked out yet?" If I know Robyn, she has an entire list.

She leans against my arm. "I was thinking . . . Denver."

I can't help it. I laugh. I want to pick her up and spin her around and shout from the top of the parking garage that I am officially the luckiest man in the universe.

"So what now?"

My girl always has a plan.

"Now we go get you some real stitches in that arm. Then we go get some pancakes because I am seriously starving."

"Sounds good. Then what? We just wing it?"

Robyn scoffs at me. My girl doesn't wing it.

"Then we live happily ever after."

# Epilogue | Robyn

"DIXIE SAID YOU'D BETTER CALL HER YOURSELF SO SHE CAN HEAR your voice. I think there was one heck of a vigil going on over there. Sounded like she had a house full," I tell my fiancé as he pulls me onto his lap. "Did you talk to Gavin?"

Dallas kisses me on the tip of my nose and places his palm on my protruding belly. "I will. And yeah, I did. He had some news, too, actually."

"He finally talked to Dixie and they're getting married, too?"

"Uh, no. Why? What did she say to you about him?"

"Not much. Just that she saw him with some chick she plans to back over with your truck and that he acted like an asshole."

Dallas makes a growly noise of discontent in the back of his throat. "Remind me to hide my truck keys when we go to Amarillo."

I rest my head on his shoulder and close my eyes, savoring the clean wood-infused scent of him. "Okay."

"Speaking of Amarillo," Dallas says, shifting me so that I lift my head. "We need to finalize the wedding plans because I have another proposal for you, but I don't want to add any additional stress on the mother of my baby."

I roll my eyes. I basically thrive on stress and Dallas knows this. "Tell me what's going on, Lark."

"Gavin works at that huge new bar downtown—the Tavern."

I vaguely remember Dixie mentioning that that's where she saw him. "Okay," I say slowly. "And . . ."

"And Rock the Republic Records is hosting a Battle of the Bands there in a few weeks. First prize is twenty-five thousand dollars and a one-year recording contract."

I sit up so fast I nearly head-butt him. "Are you serious?"

Dallas grins and nods. "Yeah. Since Capitol is probably already drawing up the paperwork to drop me like a bad habit, I'm thinking it's time for the band to get back together and give it another shot."

I can't even contain my squeal of joy. "I can get y'all a fan site set up right now. We can do a Facebook promo to get people to come out and—"

"Babe, slow down." Dallas tightens his grip before I can jump up out of his lap. "I was hoping you'd help out with that stuff. But there's plenty of time for that. First I have to make sure Dixie is on board and that those two can put their drama aside to do this. Then maybe Leaving Amarillo will get a second chance. Think we can convince my sister to give Gavin one?"

"Well . . . you know how I feel about second chances." I place kisses along the edge of his jawline when he reaches over to place a protective hand on my slightly protruding belly bump—something he does often and I'm not even sure he's conscious of.

He rests his forehead on mine and I am swept away by the overwhelming love and adoration in his gaze.

"That I do, sweetheart. That I do."

# Loving Dallas Playlist

"Crazy Town," Jason Aldean
"Ho Hey," Lumineers
"Smoke," A Thousand Horses
"This Town," Clare Bowen and Charles Esten
"Even if It Breaks Your Heart," Eli Young Band
"I See You," Luke Bryan
"Texas Was You," Jason Aldean
"Springsteen," Eric Church
"Distance," Christina Perri featuring Jason Mraz
"Dancing Away with My Heart," Lady Antebellum
"Hope You Get Lonely," Cole Swindell
"Wheels Rollin'," Jason Aldean
"Easy," Rascal Flatts featuring Natasha Bedingfield
"Make You Miss Me," Sam Hunt
"Come Over," Kenny Chesney
"Love You Like That" Canaan Smith
"It Goes Like This," Thomas Rhett
"I Walk the Line," Johnny Cash
"Save Your Breath" Josh Dorr
"Let Her Go," Passenger

"Mine Would Be You," Blake Shelton
"More than Miles," Brantley Gilbert
"Run Away with You," Michael Ray
"Crash My Party," Luke Bryan
"I Won't Give Up," Jana Kramer
"Simple Man," Lynyrd Skynyrd
"Say You Do" Dierks Bentley
"Play It Again," Luke Bryan

# Acknowledgments

FIRST OF ALL, I OWE A HUGE THANK-YOU TO ANYONE WHO READS this book. Readers make my world go 'round and have given me the amazing gift of allowing me to live my dream. There literally are not words in existence to fully express my gratitude. Thank you for investing in the Neon Dreams series and for continuing on the band's journey with me! Thank you for putting your faith, trust, and hard earned dollars into this series. I pray I don't let you down. Thank you for taking a chance on me and my books! I know many of you are planning to throw your books and e-readers at me because you are ready for Gavin's story. It's coming, I promise!

To my friends and family, I am so thankful for each and every one of you. I am eternally grateful and indebted to you for the love, support, guidance, and listening ears you have been. Thank you for tolerating and embracing my brand of crazy. I am so grateful for each one of you. It means the world to me to have such amazing people in my corner.

Speaking of my corner, I have so much gratitude and appreciation for my editor, Amanda Bergeron, who is so very patient and understanding. She pushes me to be a better writer and she makes my characters better versions of themselves. Without my awesome agent, Kevan Lyon, this book wouldn't be in your hands, so big hugs of love and thanks to her as well! Thank you, Dianna Garcia and Onalee Smith at HarperCollins for all that you do. Patricia Nelson and Gabrielle Keck, you both do fantastic jobs at keeping the ships running smoothly and your e-mails make me smile. To the cover design team that works on this series, thank you for being so patient with me and for all of your hard work making these books so pretty.

The ladies on my social media support team, CQ's Road Crew, have been instrumental not only in helping to spread the word about this series but in making it better by giving me their honest feedback along the way. Thank you so much, ladies! The Backwoods Belles are also a fantastic group that works hard to share the book love and I am eternally grateful for everything that they do!

Thank you to those of you who buy books, leave reviews, love on authors, and make recommendations to your friends. I can't even tell you how much I appreciate your love and support. You make my dreams come true—literally! Big tackle hugs of love to everyone who came out to Austin Book Fest and helped make *Leaving Amarillo* such a hit!

To anyone with a dream, keeping chasing it. If you catch it, chase another. And another. Unlike most things, dreams are free and un-limited. I'm a firm believer that you can never have too many.

Last but certainly not least, thank you to my fellow authors and colleagues who take time out of their own busy careers to read, cri-tique, blurb, and promote each other's work. I am so fortunate to have found such a great group of ladies to hold my hand along the way. If this writing thing doesn't work out, maybe we can start a band.

## *MISSING DIXIE* COMING OCTOBER 2015

*Fighting for redemption . . .*

I've lived most of my life in darkness, beneath the shadows of secrets and addictions. The last thing I ever wanted to do was hurt the only girl I'd ever loved—the one who brought me into the light. In my entire life I'd made one promise—a promise I'd intended to keep. I've broken that promise and now I have to live with the fallout. Dixie Lark hates me, and I have to tell her that I love her. I also have to tell her a truth that might destroy us forever.

Can she love me even if she can't forgive me?

*Learning to move on . . .*

Gavin Garrison broke his promise to my brother and he broke my heart in the process. I may never love anyone the way I've loved him, but at least I won't spend my life wondering what if. We had our one night and he walked away. I'm finally beginning to move on when my brother's wedding and a battle of the bands brings us back together.

Our band is getting a second chance, but I don't know if I can give him one. How do you hand your heart back to the person who set it on fire once already?

*"You know you really love someone when you can't even hate them for breaking your heart."*
—*Unknown*

# Prologue | Gavin

"I NEED A MICHELOB LIGHT, TWO JACK AND COKES, A BOURBON on the rocks, and a Sex on the Beach," a waitress named Kimberly calls to me over the crowded bar.

"Yes, ma'am," I shout over the din while filling the order quickly, tossing an umbrella into the fruity drink and briefly wondering what the hell kind of group orders such random drinks. It's an odd number, so probably not a double date.

Once Kim's tray is full, she takes off into the crowd and I take a few more orders from patrons sitting at the bar. The house band announces that they're taking a break and I'm grateful that the bar is full enough to keep it from being quiet.

Silence has always been my enemy. Hence why I play the drums, the loudest most deafening musical instrument in existence. They're the only thing that drown out the sounds in my head. Once my customers and waitresses have been taken care of, I do a quick wipe down of the bar and restock the highball glasses.

It's in the brief moment when the pool balls knocking together and the raucous chatter dies down that I hear it.

Someone is playing the piano, the old Wurlitzer that sits abandoned in the back corner of the Tavern. It's not the music itself that stops me where I stand. It's the way it's being played. A combination of effortless and meticulous that I've only known one musician in my entire life to be capable of.

Glancing in the direction where the melody is drifting from I notice I'm not the only one mesmerized by the sound. Half the bar has made their way to the back corner to get a closer listen. My boss, a perpetually red-faced man named Cal, is going to kill me, but I have to see. I have to know if it's her. My body propels itself around the bar just as a voice from my right calls my name, startling me out of my trance.

Turning, I look directly into a pair of gleaming green eyes beneath a perfectly even bob of blond hair.

Ashley Weisman stands across from me in her pencil skirt and oxford dress shirt with two too-many buttons undone to be here for professional reasons.

"You've been avoiding my phone calls," she says evenly.

"Been busy." Huffing out a breath, I place my hand gently on her elbow and attempt to steer her toward the exit.

Stilettos planted firmly on the liquor-sticky floor, she purses her full mouth at me and glares into my eyes. "You can't ignore me forever. I'm your attorney. Besides, what's the rush, Gavin? Not even going to offer me a drink? What kind of bartender are you?"

"One who doesn't have time for this right now. I'll call you tomorrow."

I can't explain it, but deep in my soul—if I have one that is—I know exactly who's playing the piano behind me. I don't know why she's here, I don't know if she knows I work here, and I sure as hell don't know if she'll want to see me. What I do know is that she and

Ashley cannot cross paths right now. Not yet. Not before I've told her everything.

"I think I'll take the drink now, thank you very much." Twisting out of my reach, she hops up onto a barstool and steadily ignores the scowl on my face.

The music continues swirling around us and all I know is right now, I need to know who is playing that damn piano.

Clenching my fists, I walk around behind the bar and wait for her to tell me what she wants.

"I'll have a screaming orgasm, please." Her eyes gleam and I meet her interested gaze with a dispassionate one. "Multiples, actually."

I barely suppress a loud sigh and grab the Bailey's and a top shelf bottle of vodka. Once her drink is mixed I set it down in front of her.

"On the house. Feel free to take it and go."

A frown mars her attractive face. "I don't think I've ever seen you in such a hurry to get rid of me. You have a hot date later?"

I can't help it, I glance over toward the piano. The music speeds up and so does my heart rate. The notes call to me like a siren song and I know I won't be able to keep myself from barreling over there for much longer.

"The piano player? I saw her when I came in. She's pretty."

"You done?" I nod to a newbie barback named Jake to come get her empty glass and he does.

"Oh, I see," she says evenly, watching me carefully. "It's her, isn't it? The one you're so eager to get your shit together for, huh?"

"I need to get my shit together regardless, Ashley. You know that. How about helping me do that instead of causing more trouble?"

Her lower lips thrusts out in a pout that irritates me. "But trouble is so much more fun."

Closing my eyes, I inhale through my nose and exhale out my mouth like the meetings have taught me. "Then go find some."

Cal walks by and I call out that I'm taking my break. Without waiting for his response or approval, I move out from behind the bar and make my way through the sea of bodies separating me from the girl behind the piano. Once I've navigated the treacherous waters, I see her. It's smoky in here tonight and several women I'm not familiar with are surrounding her but I see her sitting there playing her heart out and all I can do is watch. She doesn't make music, or create it. She is music. It flows through her as she plays and it's an incredible sight to behold.

There she is. My beautiful bluebird.

My stomach tenses and my throat constricts.

She shouldn't be here.

I shouldn't be here.

Seeing me here will hurt her and there is nothing I wouldn't give to prevent that.

Before I can even begin to formulate the words in my mind that I should say to make this okay, to make it somehow hurt her less, the music stops and she turns as if she can feel me standing there. Applause breaks out around us but it fades into background noise.

There isn't a name for the emotion that crosses her face, darkening her eyes and causing the fire in them to flare at me. It's part shock, part betrayal, and complete pain.

My jaw clenches and I force my eyes to remain on hers even though they'd prefer to close and block out the sight of her wounds deepening.

"Taking requests?" Ashley's voice calls out from beside me as a hand snakes around my forearm.

Dixie Leigh Lark arches an eyebrow at her and then shoots me a scowl of pure disgust before answering with a short, "Not at the moment."

"Too bad," Ashley says, tracing my serpent tattoo with a sharp fingernail.

Jerking my arm out of her grasp, I step closer to Dixie just as she shoves the piano bench backward, scarping it across the hardwood floor. Before I can blink, we're face to face and if looks could kill, someone would be performing CPR on me in a matter of seconds.

"Dixie, I—"

"Go to hell, Gavin," is all that escapes her beautiful mouth. Her rage hits me with the force of a plate glass window shattering over me.

I turn to watch her storm out, feeling the heat of several angry glares from other women around me.

Ashley smirks from behind her glass as she polishes off another drink I didn't realize she was holding. "Well that escalated quickly."

I am so fucked.

# About the Author

Lauren Perry, Perrywinkle Photography

CAISEY QUINN lives in Birmingham, Alabama. She is the bestselling author of the Kylie Ryans series as well as several new adult and contemporary romance novels featuring Southern girls finding love in unexpected places. You can find her online at www.caiseyquinn writes.com.

# GET BETWEEN THE COVERS WITH THE HOTTEST NEW ADULT BOOKS

## JENNIFER L. ARMENTROUT

**WITH YOU SAGA**
Wait for You
Trust in Me
Be with Me
Stay with Me
Fall With Me
Forever with You

## NOELLE AUGUST

**THE BOOMERANG SERIES**
Boomerang
Rebound
Bounce

## TESSA BAILEY

**BROKE AND BEAUTIFUL SERIES**
Chase Me
Need Me
Make Me

## CORA CARMACK

Losing It
Keeping Her: A Losing It Novella
Faking It
Finding It
Seeking Her: A Finding It Novella

**THE RUSK UNIVERSITY SERIES**
All Lined Up
All Broke Down
All Played Out

## JAY CROWNOVER

**THE MARKED MEN SERIES**
Rule       Jet
Rome     Nash
Rowdy    Asa

**WELCOME TO THE POINT SERIES**
Better When He's Bad
Better When He's Bold
Better When He's Brave

## RONNIE DOUGLAS

Undaunted

## SOPHIE JORDAN

**THE IVY CHRONICLES**
Foreplay
Tease
Wild

## MOLLY MCADAMS

From Ashes
Needing Her: A From Ashes Novella

**TAKING CHANCES SERIES**
Taking Chances
Stealing Harper: A Taking Chances Novella
Trusting Liam

**FORGIVING LIES SERIES**
Forgiving Lies
Deceiving Lies
Changing Everything

**SHARING YOU SERIES**
Capturing Peace
Sharing You

**THATCH SERIES**
Letting Go
To the Stars

## CAISEY QUINN

**THE NEON DREAMS SERIES**
Leaving Amarillo
Loving Dallas
Missing Dixie

## JAMIE SHAW

**MAYHEM SERIES**
Mayhem
Riot
Chaos